ALSO BY WILLIAM SHATNER

TEKWAR

TEKLAB

TEKLORDS

TEKVENGEANCE

TEKSECRET

TEKPOWER

TEKMONEY

MAN O' WAR

WILLIAM SHATNER

G.P. PUTNAM'S SONS

NEW YORK

G. P. Putnam's Sons
Publishers Since 1838
200 Madison Avenue
New York, NY 10016

Library of Congress Cataloging-in-Publication Data

Shatner, William.
Man o' war / William Shatner.
p.   cm.
ISBN 0-399-14131-6 (alk. paper)
I. Title.
PS3569.H347M36   1996   95-44921   CIP
813'.54—dc20

Printed in the United States of America
1   3   5   7   9   10   8   6   4   2

This book is printed on acid-free paper. ∞

Book design by Julie Duquet

Leslie, Lisabeth, and Melanie have been the joy of my life
and have also become my friends.
This book is dedicated to them and to our love for adventure.

I want to acknowledge Chris Henderson, who is a man of discipline and imagination and whose Chinese food I have yet to eat . . . but will very soon.

I want to note also that Carmen LaVia may be the greatest literary agent in the world.

And Susan Allison, with whom I have been associated now for several years and several books, is without peer.

"A diplomat is a man who always remembers a woman's birthday but never remembers her age."

ROBERT FROST

"If you are to stand up for your Government, you must be able to stand up to your Government."

SIR HAROLD, LATER LORD, CACCIA

"A man-of-war is the best ambassador."

OLIVER CROMWELL

MAN O' WAR

PROLOGUE

There were no directional markers in the dark hallway. It held no communications boxes, was not painted with any classification or designative stripes. It was one of the old passageways, dug out of the flesh of the ground by directed lava flow and human hand, so ancient its walls were made of nothing more than beams and soil. It was unlike the upper cavities, the sprawling network of factories and homes and all that went with them. Those had been laid out neatly, with a vigorously antiseptic sense of functionality, by the central planners, who had followed the first expedition of miners. The Above was solid and secure, with floors formed from strong ceramics, and walls and ceilings poured and sprayed and molded into place. Nothing from the outside world would intrude.

This tunnel was not neat, however, nor did it follow any kind of plan. It was an old explorer bore—one of the snaking, wildly arching deep-digs the Originals had chewed out back when the worth of the entire venture still needed to be proved. In its time it was not exactly sturdy, now it was a treacherous leftover, sealed off and labeled AVOID in black and yellow at every entrance.

Over the years the crumbling overhead had filled the corridor with a reddish yellow dust. It was a cold and desolate place, with neither heat nor lights. Air was still allowed to filter into it, only because sealing it off would have been prohibitively expensive. It was an old and profitless place, abandoned by the corporations because it had ceased to offer them any profit. Which is what had made it perfect for the Resolute.

A man and woman, both members of the secret group, walked through the old passageway. They kept to the left side, unsure whether to move quickly to stay warm, or slowly, to keep from being heard. Each was wrapped in several layers of clothing. For both, it was most of the clothing they owned. They had but a single light with which to find their way, an old recycled thing powered by an open-water battery.

Their breath came out in silver-gray gushes that evaporated behind them. They said nothing, their attention on the path both ahead and behind. They were certain they had not been followed. Why would they be? No one above the pit-and-bang level knew of the Resolute. It was off-shift time. There was no reason for anyone to look for them.

And yet . . . and yet . . .

People were reassigned, work groups were disbanded, shuffled—for no apparent reason. Some people disappeared. Security monitors were being installed in new places all the time, in spots where one would not think they would be needed—not unless someone was looking for something.

Concern over that fact prompted the man to whisper to his companion, "Sometimes I still wonder if management suspects."

"Gerald, you have to stop worrying so. There's no way for them to know of our existence," the woman assured him. "We've been too careful."

"Maybe, Marta," he answered. Their pale light illuminated the fine dust on the floor, showing them brief glimpses of the rolling clouds their feet were kicking up. "Maybe. But ever since Renker and Samuels stumbled over what's actually going on Above, nothing's been the same."

"Don't start," hissed the woman through clenched teeth. "This debate just never ends. We have been careful. As careful as we can be. We've left no trails, stolen nothing. All the proof we've gathered has been copied."

Marta stopped moving. In spite of the cold, she wanted to see her husband as she talked to him. As he turned to her, she looked into the deep lines carved around his face, at the gray of his skin and the concern etched into his eyes, and her heart ached for him.

He worked so hard. She did, too, but he was the one who never stopped—never stopped working, never stopped worrying, never stopped pushing himself and all around him.

"Listen to me," she said, putting a finger to his lips, trying to find the energy to smile. "The Resolute is unknown. We are safe. We haven't even done anything wrong."

"Neither did any of the people who have disappeared since all this started."

"They gave up, they went to the Earth," she reminded him, straining to keep from her voice the exasperation and fear she was feeling. "We saw the passage bookings."

"Yes, we did," he admitted. "But that's all we saw. One minute we had friends, the next their quarters are empty and they are supposedly on their way to Earth."

Gerald had to stop talking for a moment, had to set his fragile lamp down and back away from his wife so he could clap his freezing hands together. Marta, as chilled as her husband, crossed her arms and beat her shoulders, trying to drive away the cold.

Then they started walking again. As always, they avoided the right-hand side of the tunnel, but abandoned caution when listening for anyone who might be following. Time was too precious.

It meant the possibility of extra shifts and perhaps even rest. It meant moments with children. Free time even allowed the liberty of thought. They did not have the right to waste any more of it. Not theirs, and certainly not that of the rest of the group.

"I don't want to sound the same old horn," Gerald whispered as they walked. "But you know none of them had the units to pay for passage. No one's ever earned enough to get back to the Skyhook, let alone all the way down to Earth. Not working in the mines. Not in the factories. Not anywhere on the whole stinking planet."

"Please," asked Marta. "Let's leave it for now, all right?" She was just as wearied by the conversation as her husband. And just as frightened.

Rounding the last corner of their route in silence, they came to an old pressure doorway. The door itself had been removed long before. Metal was too precious to waste. But the frame had been built into the walls. To dig it out might have caused a cave-in, and so it had been stripped to its barest and left behind. In the larger hollow on the other side, the pair reached their goal.

"Finally," came one voice from the small crowd within. "We thought you'd decided to work another shift."

A number of those gathered chuckled. Gerald entered nodding his head in agreement. He switched his poor lamp off. There was already one light burning in the room. And it was turned up too bright. Wasteful.

"I had thought about it," Gerald answered, somehow finding the energy to generate a weak smile. "After all, who wants to sit around in an old, cold tunnel when he can keep warm in a nice, steamy bore tube, eh?"

"Making lots of money," shouted Samuels. "Right?"

More voices joined in the bitter laughter. Gerald moved his head, locking eyes with a number of people around the room as he said, "Right you are. There's money to be made anywhere here."

"Why, it's practically growing on trees."

"I'm sure if we had trees," added Renker in mock seriousness, "it would be."

"Who needs money trees?" asked a woman standing against the back wall. "Not me. Not when there are so many units to be had watching the pressure in the sponge/mush vats, or running checks on a stapling unit, or stacking bar metal, or reeling conduit wiring, or . . ."

One of the men in the rear raised his left arm. He kept his right at its regular station, resting on the heavy black lever built into the back wall. He was laughing as hard as anyone else, but he waved his arm frantically, crying out over the voices of the others, "Enough. We can't risk the time. We've got to get on with things and get out of here."

"Fennel is right. What's the word? Do we have everything we need, or don't we?"

"It's all right here," answered Gerald. Pulling an old message tube from beneath his innermost layer of clothing, he held it up for everyone to see—proof they were not risking their own and their children's lives for nothing.

"Every encodement we have copied, every file we have accessed, every single scrap of information we have been able to gather to show what they are doing to us—what we know they will continue to do to us, and to our children and our grandchildren. . . ."

Tears suddenly pooled in Gerald's eyes. He was surprised, not that he could grow so emotional, but that his body could spare the water. And then, before he could continue, someone in the crowd asked, "What was that?"

Everyone went still. Their single light was clicked off. As they strained to listen, all present heard the same noise: a steady, heavy tread out in the hall. Panic filled the room. Some grabbed for their lights. Others stumbled toward any of the three exits, groping their way through the thick darkness. Several pulled out the feeble weapons they had brought: clubs or homemade knives.

Gerald simply sat down amid the flailing commotion, waiting for the inevitability he had been dreading. Marta joined him, somehow knowing what he was doing. They held each other tight, not trying to talk over the screams and cries all around them.

"It's security!" someone shouted through the darkness.

Instantly Fennel depressed the heavy lever. Homemade shock mines embedded along the right side of the access tunnels blew outward. Tightly packed metal, glass, and rock scraps tore through the air with devastating force. Eight of the invading figures went down under the violent barrage, torn to shreds. Unfortunately, that was not enough.

The gunfire began immediately after. It came in wide, inescapable patterns, guided by harsh white light, cutting down everything in its path. Expanding sprays of bearing shot slammed through bodies, throwing them against the dusty walls and into each other.

Men and women ran forward with their clubs and blades, screaming their rage. Those closest to the exits took the full brunt of blasts and were cut in two. Blood arced wildly, spinning in the air as the bodies fell. Most of those behind were only wounded.

"Cease."

The single word rang electronically through the sealed helmets of the gunmen. Any other type of signal would have been impossible to hear over the firing. The echoes of their attack in the enclosed space had almost completely deafened those still alive.

Walking into the room, the apparent leader of the attack surveyed those who remained, using the harsh rifle lights that still panned across the chamber. He was satisfied. His people had efficiently expended as few shells as possible. Most of the laborers who had chosen the name the Resolute were dead, their movement crushed before it even began.

The only exceptions were the two sitting in the center of the room. Ironically, by accepting their fate, they had been spared—momentarily. The commander moved up to them, preparing to bring that moment to an end.

"Gerald Cobber . . . and wife."

The man's voice came out of his darkened helmet through an electronic filter. Obviously he knew the couple, but they did not recognize him. His helmet did enhance his voice just enough for them to hear over the ringing in their ears.

"I suppose I'm not surprised. You've always had a very loud voice—but not enough bank to back it up."

"My apologies."

"If only that were enough," came the staticky voice. "But . . . anyway, stand up, you two. Let's get done."

As the couple rose, Marta asked, "What will you do"—her hand swept the room—"to explain all this?"

"What? Why—we will tell everyone what happened." The man lifted a hand so he could count off his explanation on his fingers. "How, in your hopeless despair, you all banded together in a suicide pact . . . assigned all your assets in a standard pooling packet to your surviving children, registered your remains to be nutri-vatted so that the early-retirement benefit could pass into the pool as well."

The black helmet swung back and forth sadly.

"Such a waste. If only you had had a stronger sense of vision, instead of filling your heads with nothing but resentment and defiance."

Turning his head away from his wife for a moment, Gerald stared at the unknown commander. Pulling forth all the juice he had within, cursing his weakness for having wasted any on tears, he said, "You want an act of defiance? I'll give you one."

He spat forth his last free drops. As they splattered against the black helmet, he shouted, "There. Recycle that."

Then he turned to his wife and kissed her. Their arms tightened around each other, their eyes closed, and they drew on each other's strength one last time before two shotguns erupted, knocking them back and down.

In his last seconds, Gerald heard the commander chastising his people for having wasted shells when he and his wife could just as easily have been clubbed to death. He wanted to laugh, but too much of his body had been destroyed. Although his brain had given the order, it was no longer connected to anything.

His eyes blinking, he saw a recycler moving a canister hose forward to suck the thin sliver of spittle from the commander's helmet. Then, as other recyclers moved into the room, Gerald finally died, at least spared from having to watch that final indignity.

1

Lightning split the sky immediately below the military jet. Almost
unaware of the growing storm, Benton Hawkes scanned the diplomatic corps' reports in his hands once more, hoping something
would catch his eye that he might use in his own defense. Nothing
in particular rose up to volunteer.

"Let's face it, Benton," he said, throwing the wad of printouts
and notes onto the small user table the flight steward had installed
next to his chair, "you've cooked yourself royally this time."

"Don't say that yet, Chief."

The voice came from a tired-looking younger man sitting at
another of the small tables across the way. Rubbing at his eyes, he
put down his own stack of papers.

"You'll see," he continued. "There's a way out of this. We just
haven't dug down deep enough."

"No, no, I . . ."

"I'm serious. We just get the right spin . . ."

"No," said Hawkes. He spoke the word quietly, but his aide
understood the finality intended. "It's over. I did what I did and
that's all there is to it."

Hawkes picked up his drink and took a sip. It was a mixture of

Amaretto, Kahlua, Jack Daniel's, and milk, a concoction he and some camping buddies had created more years in the past than he cared to remember. They had named their creation "Happy Times," and the taste of one always reminded him of such. At the age of fifty-six, it was one of the few true pleasures he still enjoyed. He set the glass back on the table and folded his hands in his lap.

His aide said nothing, hoping that all the ambassador needed was a moment's rest. The younger man was visibly nervous. They would have to get back to work soon if they were going to piece together a political defense for his final actions during the Pacific Rim Unity Conference.

"Go get some sleep, Danny."

"I'm no more tired than you are, sir," answered the aide, choking back a yawn.

"Well, I'm damn tired, so go get some sleep so I can get some— all right?"

"But, sir—with all respect—if we don't come up with an ample American interest to justify what you did . . . I mean, sir, your career . . ."

"Has lasted ten years too long already." Hawkes pushed against the base of his spine, kneading his fingers into the ball of pain that had gathered there. "Now go on. There's only a couple of hours left before we land in Washington. Get some rest. You'll need it to look for a new job."

Daniel Stine, twenty-eight, top aide to his nation's foremost career diplomat, gathered up his papers again and made a step toward the door. Deep down he knew Hawkes was right. There was no political defense for what his boss had done. The ambassador had thrown his career away over a moral issue. Still shaking his head over the insanity of it, he put his hand to the door release, indexing the green panel.

"We'll find something, sir. We'll survive."

As the door sealed shut behind him, Hawkes shook his head, muttering, "Survive? I'll be happy if I can just get this crick out of my back."

Too much sitting, he thought as he continued to work the aching spot. Too much time spent looking through books and poring over regulations and working out arguments to keep this or that greedy bastard from legally stealing his enemies and his neighbors and his own citizens blind.

Suddenly his fingers moved just the right way and the pressure point in his back relaxed. Hawkes stretched his arms out to his sides and sighed in relief.

"Well, that's one pain in the butt taken care of."

The ambassador debated whether he should do any more work. He stared at the two different stacks on his table. One was made up of the corps reports he had filed during the Rim conference. If he really wanted to save his career, combing through those was the key. The other stack made him wonder if he really wanted to. The second consisted of information on the bid by Clean Mountain Enterprises to annex a large section of the Absaroka Range in Wyoming. In many ways, helping block that takeover meant more to Hawkes than preserving his career.

At that moment, however, he could not look at either. Turning his back on both, he walked across the cabin, drawing back the sliding shutter from one of the windows on the left-hand side. Darkness filled his view. The vast cloud cover just below the plane was still too dense to allow even a glimpse of the ground. Not that he would have been likely to know where they were at this altitude, even if the sky was clear.

As another lightning bolt crashed down, flashing the clouds with a moment of brightness, he sighed and turned away, leaving the shutter open. Walking down the length of his on-board quarters to the mirror over his private vanity, he ran his hand along the sink counter, admitting to himself, Nice perks in this work. I almost hate to give it all up.

The ambassador stared into the mirror, searching for something in his reflection. All he saw was the same solidly chiseled face, strong, thick-boned shoulders, and slightly graying hair he had grown used to over the decades. There was weariness around his blue-gray eyes, though, that had not been there years ago—a sad, tiring weight that had been dragging at him for far too long.

Reaching across the counter, he touched his forefinger to the water control, automatically indexing the flow rate and temperature level he desired without having to think about it. Reaching under the spout, he cupped his palms until they were full and then splashed his face with the tepid water—once, twice. Indexing for it to halt, he took down a towel and dried his face and hands, and then went back to his seat, pausing only to turn down the lights along the way.

He sat back firmly in his chair so as to lever out its hidden hassock. Then, with his feet up and his eyes closed, Hawkes reached out unerringly and snagged his drink. Taking another sip, he nestled the glass on his chest and reviewed the choices he had remaining, wondering if he had any.

Well, a voice sounded in the back of his mind, you could always get a job rigging on the Skyhook.

"Not in a million years," he muttered, wondering how even his most cynical self could come up with such a thought. Always the diplomat, however, he admitted, "And that's not my own personal distaste for them coming through. It's a new world out there, Bennie. And nobody in it needs the likes of a Benton Hawkes anymore.

The ambassador rubbed at his tired eyes, wondering if he was actually right. He could remember his father talking about how so much had changed during his lifetime. He wondered what the gruff old rancher would have thought if he had lived long enough to see the changes in his son's.

Benton Hawkes had been born in 2013, the same year the world pooled its resources to begin the Great Diversion. At least the old man had seen that much, the ambassador thought, and sighed—eight nations pulling together to send a single ship to the asteroid belt. Before he was gone, they had even intercepted their target—a miles-wide hunk of ore the scientists had said held the key to the future—attached their explosives in the right places, and blown it

out of orbit and onto a trajectory that would bring it within a radi-
cally close half million miles of the Earth.

He had not lived to see the erection of Lunar City, though, or the
expedition of its fleet to intercept the meteor. None of the discover-
ies that the countless tons of ore brought his world helped him—
neither the universal conductor, nor the permanent filament. These
new materials built the Skyhook, took mankind to Mars, allowed
the red planet to be colonized and worked—allowed the asteroids
to be mined.

One move by bold men and women that had changed the destiny
of the Earth forever. Absolutely forever.

Yeah—it's just a great big new world out there, his cynical side
reminded him. So forgive and forget. Get a job on the Skyhook.
Space—that's the career for you.

"Never," he said quietly. He took a sip from his drink, and
placed the tumbler back on his chest, though the sweet taste on his
lips was not enough to cover the rising bile in his throat. He opened
his eyes but could still see the picture he wished to avoid—could
still remember every detail of his father's death more than forty
years earlier. He could see the burning wreckage of the ore lifter,
remembered his screams, old Ed keeping him back from the
flames—back from his father . . .

"No," the ambassador said with finality. "No, I don't think so."

Clean Mountain had been a much younger company then. When
they had been granted the government contract to gather ore for use
in building Lunar City, they had been little more than wildcatters.
The deal they made with Hawkes's father had been for mining
rights throughout much of his property. Then, before all the proper
documents could be completed, the ambitious young company had
sent one of their processors out to the Hawkes ranch to get a head
start.

An eager executive, a rash pilot, an old ship that had been jury-
rigged and patched too many times, and suddenly an eleven-year-
old Benton was an orphan. His father's foreman stayed on, ran the

farm in his friend's name, raised his son. The contract with Clean Mountain was never completed. Old Ed and young Benton were so adamant, they were never even allowed back on the property to clear the crash site. And now, because of that ancient wreckage and paperwork left unfinished nearly a half century, CM Enterprises' lawyers thought they had a legitimate claim to not only the ranch, but to almost two hundred square miles around it.

"You know, Dad," he said quietly to the air, "this is not the way things were supposed to work out."

Hawkes had entered the military at eighteen, a compensatory donation of time to the government to repay their "beneficence" in allowing him to keep his own property after his father's death. At the age of twenty-two, he had gone directly into the diplomatic corps, encouraged by Val Hensen, his commanding officer, to make the move straight out of his military tour.

He scored a number of remarkable coups in his time, most of them in his youth. Sent from one violent field post to another, he had crafted honest, carefully deliberated judgments between warring factions, carving out a name for himself as a trustworthy man of high morals.

Right, his cynical side chided. And you've spent the rest of your life since then trying to live up to it.

You know the only reason they kept sending you from one trouble spot to another, came another level of his brain. They just kept hoping you'd get yourself killed.

Holding his drink on high, his tone filled with bitterness, Hawkes growled, "Well, here's to me. I sure showed *them*, didn't I?"

After a while, the people above the ambassador finally learned their lesson. Seeing he was too stubborn to be cowed or bribed or in any other way turned to playing their game, they put him outside of it. He had gained too much notoriety to be simply dismissed, so from then on, Hawkes was posted only in tranquil positions, ones where he could not harm the ambitions of those above him.

In 2067, however, circumstances forced a dispute between the governments of Australia and Deutcher Chocolate, International, formerly known as the country of New Zealand. Back in the early forties, Deutcher had gone through all the proper legal negotiations to buy out the at-the-time struggling country's controlling interests in itself. Its citizens were offered jobs, certain health and security benefits, etc., and after the United Nations had handed in its usual rubber-stamped approval, Deutcher went from being simply an international corporate power to being one with its own post office, treasury bonds, and yearly military-buildup allotment.

That was all well and good. But twenty-five years later, Deutcher ran out of arable land of its own to turn over to cocoa farming. They offered to buy or lease vast tracts of Australia, but their offers were all rejected. Then an invasion was hinted at, and the two countries' shared coasts found themselves hosts to massing troops and their equipment.

After that, a clever legal attaché somewhere in the bowels of the Deutcher chain of command came across a near-century-old economic agreement. It was a showpiece kind of thing, one made between New Zealand and Australia for the benefit of an American president with foreign aid to grant, and who needed political points in return. Everyone knew it was a worthless document, meant only as a justifier and nothing more.

"What is it everyone knows and no one can prove?" Hawkes asked the air in a quiet whisper. "Oh, I remember now, that would be . . . the truth."

The lawyers who got their hands on the old agreement decided it gave them every right to seize lands in Australia, and presented it to the Americans for their opinion. Or, more specifically, to the majority leader of the United States Senate, one Michael Carri. Carri was a twenty-three-year man whose war trunk contained hefty contributions from scores of buyers seeking to own their part of the American government.

"And," Hawkes muttered to himself, "Deutcher's helped buy all your elections since the beginning—right, Mick? And so you made the offer to send down an American mediator. One who would come with express instructions to make sure the tide turned in favor of your boys. Whether they had the slightest right to what they wanted or not."

When the situation had first grown explosive, Senator Carri had stepped forward and offered to send an American to be the case's supreme arbitrator. The U.N. backed the idea at once. Deutcher had agreed instantly.

The Australians, seeing everyone lining up against them, sensed their disadvantage. They refused the offer, then threatened to boycott the conference and prepare only for war. When the U.N. asked what it would take to get them to the conference table, they had demanded the right to name the appointee.

Everyone agreed. Hawkes was the one chosen to accept the appointment. It was not what anyone else involved wanted, but they had no choice other than to accept. Deutcher sputtered, but they could offer no reasonable objection to Hawkes. Realizing they could not block the ambassador's appointment simply because he was honest, the corporation put on its most pleasant face and agreed.

Hawkes had been pulled from his assignment at the time—a post he actually had learned to enjoy, one for which he had worked long and hard—and was sent to the highly touted peace conference to evaluate the situation.

Yes, he thought cynically, draining his tumbler, as always—go in, calm everyone down, see what's going on, hear all the demands, look everything over, judge all the evidence impartially and fairly, and then render the verdict you were told to in the first place.

Finishing his drink, he banged his glass back on the tabletop. As he did there was another lightning flash at the shutter, one that coincided with a cannonade of thunder. The plane rocked violently. Hawkes's papers and his tumbler were all thrown to the floor. Sighing, he pushed himself up out of his chair to attend to the mess.

At the same time, a knock came at his door. His call for whoever it was to enter brought him one of the plane's air force crew. She was an attractive officer, with intelligent eyes and a pleasing smile. Highly trained, she was capable of flying fighters or commanding deep-space missions. Yet because of her looks, she had been given the title of security chief and slotted for high-level transport missions, serving more as eye candy for VIPs than anything else.

Apologetically, as if she had some power to change things, the woman told him, "Sorry, Ambassador. The word is it's going to be a rough trip the rest of the way in."

"That's all right, Major," he assured her.

As he fumbled with his scattered papers, she went down on one knee to pick up his tumbler, which had rolled almost all the way to the door. She stretched out and snagged it from under the table, then crossed the room again to return it. As Hawkes accepted it, she asked, "I know it's late, Ambassador . . . but if I could just say one thing?"

With over thirty years of training there to keep him from showing how he truly felt, he answered, "Of course . . . ," looking as charming as always, as if he had just awakened from a full night's rest and could not think of anything he wanted more than to hear what she had to tell him.

"Sir, there're a lot of people who were awfully surprised at how the conference went."

"Yes," he said, keeping all but a hint of irony out of his smile. "I imagine there were."

"I mean, most people really thought the country was going to sack the Aussies. The press, the White House, everything you saw on the vid or in the nets—private ones, public . . . it didn't matter—it just looked as if everyone was on the side of the damn chocolate Nazis . . ."

"Chocolate Nazis?" Hawkes interjected with amusement.

"Oh, I'm sorry."

"Don't apologize," he told her honestly. "If I don't hear what people really think, then . . . well, then I don't know what they're really thinking, do I?"

"No, sir." The major, feeling as if she had overstepped her bounds, took several backward steps toward the door. As her hand hovered above the green release panel, she found the courage to intrude upon the great man for a moment longer and said, "It's just . . . I wanted to say how grateful so many people are that you didn't just play the game down there."

And then, before he could comment, she had indexed the panel and slipped out the door. It slid shut as soon as she was through, sealing itself quietly. Hawkes set the papers back down on the table. Then he returned to his vanity with the tumbler in hand.

As he rinsed it out, he looked up at a photo he had wedged in place in the upper corner of the mirror. It was a picture of his dog, Disraeli, a large, black Labrador he had not seen in almost eight months.

"You know, Dizzy," he said to the picture, and his own reflection, "ten years ago, an attractive blond telling me my honesty was necessary to the world might have been enough to get me to change my mind."

The thunder came again. It banged against the outer walls of the jet in a blasting series of explosions that promised more would be following. Hawkes washed away the residue of his drink, dumped the cloudy water, then rinsed his glass again, saying, "Hell—five years ago. Five months ago, even. But, no . . . not now."

His mind reviewed the constant barrage of screaming communications between himself and Carri over the past eight months—the insulting orders, the veiled threats—all of it working to force him to side with Deutcher. Hitting the proper panel, he dropped the water's temperature down to near freezing. Then, filling his glass, he lifted it in a toast toward the picture of his dog and said, "Not now. I'm coming home, Disraeli, old boy. This time I'm coming home for good."

Nodding his head to the dog, he tilted it back and took a long drink, the intensely chilled water washing the taste of his last drink from his mouth.

Outside, lightning flew unabated, lighting the sky and blasting the land below. At the same time, the thunder lived up to its promise, violently rocking the jet as it blew the heavens apart.

2

"**H**e's in town? Here in twenty minutes?" the large man behind the desk confirmed what he had heard. "Thank you. No, no—no stalls—no. I'll be ready for him."

Damn, he thought. Who in hell shows up early for anything in this town? Let alone a ball-ripping ass-chewing?

Someone trying to catch you off guard, a separate voice in his head told him. Someone who isn't a part of this town's establishment.

Yes, he thought. And that would certainly describe Hawkes, all right.

He cradled the phone receiver, distracted for a moment by the information he had just received. Hoping to pull him back on track, one of the people waiting in his office asked, "Senator Carri, could we pick up where we left off this morning . . . your approach to the debate the opposition has scheduled for this afternoon? When the contents of the package bill are revealed to the public . . ."

"What?" asked Carri, slightly stunned. Caught off guard, he answered in a louder-than-normal voice, "The public? What's the public care about anything?"

The senator's voice was as large as his frame. When he wanted to use it to his own advantage, he could make grown men wince with its power.

"Sir, you're looking to have the Tenth Amendment to the Constitution repealed. That's sure to draw some attention."

"Peterson, get with the program. 'The people' didn't have anything but praise for us when we struck down the Second Amendment eight years ago. 'The people' are a passel of gutless cattle. As long as we keep enough of them on the federal payroll, they'll moo just the way we tell them to."

The younger man moved uneasily in his chair. He began moving his hand as a prelude to giving a verbal answer. Before he could, however, the senator leaned forward over his desk. Giving his chief of office operations a subtle signal only she would notice, he continued talking to the freshman congressman, telling him, "Don't worry, I know where you want to go next. You want to tell me that we're not going to be dealing with just the man in the street when we strike the Tenth. You're thinking that if we move to eliminate the blocks between federal and state power that we'll end up fighting our own kind. Right?"

"Ah, well . . ."

"Sure you are. The masses we can trick, but fellow politicians, they'll see what we're up to."

"It is possible . . . yes, Senator."

"Mayors and governors, all with their own police forces and militias. They might not stand for it. Might threaten to fight, or secede." Carri sat back in his chair, shaking his head sadly. "The Civil War was a long time ago, son. It's been two hundred years since anyone's thought about trying to leave the Union or use force on Washington."

"But, sir," countered the younger man, "I was thinking more that voter resistance might be their line of attack. Forcing out incumbents."

"A sensible thought, Peterson—worth the time you've taken. But we've been at this game a long time. Trust me, it's already covered.

Pomeroy's got the bill scheduled for committee now, which means we'll vote in less than six months. It'll all be in the bag long before anyone can even start trying to organize any of the voters, much less lever any of us out of office. I appreciate your watching out for the old man, son. . . ."

"As you've said yourself, sir, you are the meal ticket."

Waving his hand to encompass everyone in the room, Senator Carri turned his head as he moved, then added jokingly, "And don't any of you forget it."

As everyone chuckled appreciatively, the committee chairman brushed a wild strand of hair back off his forehead. A year earlier, as he approached sixty-five, he had asked his barber to do something to make people forget the fact. She had started cultivating a wild lock for him to give him a more boyish look. Over the year it had grown to where he could simply turn his head and flip it down into his eye. It would have looked affected for many other men his age, but so far Michael Carri had been able to maintain his weight and health and looks. To most people he looked no older than forty-five.

As the polite laughter died down, Carri waved his hand, calling for it to cease. Then, before anyone could bring up any other distracting matters, Gladys Beckett, his chief of office operations, moved forward and broke up the fun—playing the heavy and calling the meeting to a close—as she knew the senator wanted. After everyone filed out, he told her, "Gladys, we've got advance warning on Benton Hawkes—he should be here in about fifteen minutes."

"He's here today?" she said without shock, not thrown by the abrupt change in schedule.

"What can I tell you?" answered the senator, shrugging his shoulders. Turning up the wattage in his smile, he said, "I guess you give some guys a Nobel Prize and they figure the rules don't apply anymore." As his operations chief gave him an appropriate chuckle, Carri got serious, asking, "So, just what do we need to do?"

The senator had started his adult life on the football field, a top player for a major team, leading the way to several Super Bowl victories. It had been an important stepping-stone to a choice spot in the automotive industry. Showing he had brains to offer as well as fame, Carri had used his time there as an audition for a larger role in the world of communications financing. With his past fame, voter recognition, contacts in heavy industry, and access to both funding and the media, he had all he needed to reach the goal he had sought from the beginning—politics.

Quickly looking around the senator's inner office, the woman analyzed every aspect of its layout.

"Get your jacket off, Mick," she told him, bending over a panel on the far side of the room. "And loosen your tie." While the senator did as he was instructed, Beckett killed the air conditioning. Her fingers dancing across the control array, she pulled back the curtains covering the massive windows in Carri's office, then opened several panes at varying angles.

"Hawkes is an outdoorsman," the woman explained, lowering the overhead lights until they only complemented the natural light. "Lives on a ranch in the mountains when he's not posted out country. Best bet is to subtle him over."

"It's awful humid after last night's storm," the senator complained. Even a minute without climate control had started him sweating. He could feel drops forming along his hairline and beading at the back of his neck.

"That's why you should be unbuttoning your top button," Beckett told him. "You're a man of the people—you work hard. Get your nose in some papers and be ready to slip your jacket on when he gets here. Effect a surprised look."

"Can I roll up my sleeves?"

"Can you get them up past your elbows?" she asked, more interested in getting the paper stacks and books on Carri's sideboard in order. Her advance research had told her that Hawkes was an orderly man—impressed by straight lines, right angles.

Neatness counts, she told herself, squaring everything off.

"No," said the senator, trying to roll up his sleeves. "Must be European cut. There's not enough give."

"Then leave them down. But unbuttoned is okay."

Paying the senator no further heed, she buzzed Carri's makeup staff and then began to index through his paintings, looking for something suitable for the upcoming meeting. The office was equipped with five different acry-vid screens, framed monitors meant to appear as actual paintings. She knew that simply setting them all to outdoor scenes would not fool a man as seasoned in the game as Hawkes.

She left the second largest, the ornate multiple-imaged portrait of the senator at the various stages of his way-to-the-top journey alone. Most people knew it existed, and besides, she thought, the ambassador would expect at least that much arrogance from Michael Carri.

She almost replaced the senator's personal favorite, a long rectangular shot of a naval battle from the late 1800s. It was the largest and usually was the first to go in such situations. But the override files programmed into her wrist-link accessory reminded her that Hawkes was a former military man. That painting stayed.

Anything to create a bond, she thought, realizing in the back of her mind how difficult that task might be.

The computerized bracelet suddenly beeped—the five-minute warning.

Goddamnit, she thought. No time—hell, just let the machine do it.

Quickly, Beckett pulled out a connector line from her wrist-link. Plugging it into the control panel to Carri's office, she gave authorization to her main computer to finish tailoring the senator's office to his advantage. If the computer made some mistake or other, there was always the chance she could catch it.

She hoped so, anyway.

It was the best she could do. Time seemed to be against them, although she had no idea why. For some reason, they had to let Hawkes walk through the door on his own schedule, without hesitation.

As soon as the computer connection was made to the program the operations chief had prepared earlier that morning, the spectral fibers in the carpeting instantly shifted to a deep blue from Carri's preferred charcoal gray. The walls dropped a degree in vibrancy but stayed the same tone of white, as did the ceiling. The paintings remaining on the walls shifted. An old-fashioned gas-burning racer flickered out, replaced by a dark scene from a deep forest: dense, old-growth pines, the kind Beckett's research said Hawkes had on his own property.

Scanning the room, the operations chief zeroed in on several bird portraits that had been artistically enhanced and added to the program the last time the screen had been used, a retouch that had been added the year before, when Carri had entertained the Audubon Society. She had them zapped back to the clip file.

The other vids shifted, one after another. Before Beckett could give her approval, however, the makeup staff finally arrived. She grabbed her own hair specialist, along with his utility cart, before he could join the crowd around the senator, telling him, "I need a gel upsweep, no spray or pins. Old-fashioned, turn-of-the-century. Get to it—you have maybe five minutes. I need it in four."

The man set to work immediately, asking, "Gel? My God, you really do want turn-of-the-century. Who's coming to lunch? Your grandfather?"

"A man who loved his mother," the operations chief answered absently. She continued to turn in a slow circle, trying to take in all of the computer's decor decisions without moving too fast for the man rearranging her hair.

As soon as she was satisfied with the look of the room, she unplugged her wrist-link from the control panel, announcing at the same time, "I'm heading for the mahogany straight-back, Clifford."

"That's good news," answered the hairdresser. He moved as she

did, not watching where he was going, concentrating only on Beckett's head. "I actually do a much better job when my work isn't
spinning about."

As the woman sat down, she brought her link steadily up to eye
level and keyed in a variety of commands: everything from piping
in what she hoped would be the best background music for Carri's
upcoming confrontation to ordering him a take-out meal from the
congressional commissary—hand-held items, all easy to eat while
working—a sandwich, coffee, banana . . .

No, she thought, strike banana. Hawkes is from the Northwest—
make it an apple.

Turning slightly, not enough to throw off Clifford's ministrations,
but just enough to allow her to rest her eyes on the senator, she
thought, Ladies and gentlemen, and especially the mindless of all
voting ages, may I present to you that hardworking, self-effacing,
tireless, devoted man of the people, Senator Michael J. Carri. Snap-
shots will be five units. Please deposit your contribution in the
barrel at the tent flap exit.

Beckett's eyes narrowed. Benton Hawkes had recently cost her
boss plenty. The ambassador should have been returning to a class-
A, red-hot poker—one to be applied long, deep, and often. Instead
he was getting the kind of circus she usually put together for the
head lawyer from the petroleum lobby.

What's going on, Mick? she wondered. Just what the hell could
you possibly want from this guy bad enough to jump hoops when a
few days ago you wanted to be dancing on his grave?

Clifford finished his ministrations forty-eight seconds early.
Beckett checked herself out in his utility mirror while he packed
up his tools.

"I like the flat streak on the side," she told him honestly. "Like
I've been pushing at it all day."

"Designed to look as if you walked in with it this morning," he
answered, proud of the touch.

"You're an artist," she said, giving him a kiss on the cheek.
"Now get yourself and the rest of this bunch out of here."

"An artist," he answered, "nay, fair lady. I am but a humble workman, toiling in the fields. If thou art happy, then I am happy."

"Git, hair jockey," she said. Her tone was teasing, however, one that turned into a laugh as he clicked his heels and bowed with a flourish.

"And thus I take my leave."

Beckett smiled. She was lucky to have been able to pull together some of the people she had for Carri's staff. Looking over at him, she wondered again, What could he be up to? Benton Hawkes had cost the senator possible millions in future contributions, not only from Deutcher—which was not only a lost cause, but already sending checks to the opposition—but from countless others who may have had their faith shaken in Carri's ability to deliver.

And yet she watched him putting on his best poker face, preparing for . . . for . . .

What, you devious bastard? What in hell is going on here? So important you're willing to let Hawkes off the hook—so secret you don't trust me to know about it?

She examined the touch-up job the crew had done on Carri. The normally pale senator now had a nice, outdoorsy tan, perfect down to the bit of burn they had blushed into his bald spot. Staring at the thin patch, she thought, They can grow hair on a billiard ball these days, and yet you let yours thin because you don't want to be thought of as affected. Every move you make is politically motivated, Mick. I sure wish I knew what was motivating you this time.

Knowing how much their present act would gall Carri, how much it must be galling him already, Beckett thought, Hawkes, when I think about the kind of payback he must have in store for you, I could almost feel sorry for you.

Suddenly, her wrist-link beeped again—the thirty-second warning. As she shut down the electronics in the gold-and-jewel-encrusted accessory, she fingered the expensive gift and smiled to herself. Then she took a deep breath and whispered softly, "Almost."

3

Hawkes walked down the marble-and-wood-corridor, wondering if it were at all possible to catch someone off guard who was as savvy and enduring in the game as Michael Carri. The ambassador had no doubt the senator knew when his plane had arrived, when he had gotten up in the morning, when he had caught his cab . . . He certainly knows when I entered the building.

So, he asked himself, if he knows you're here, then why hasn't anyone stopped you from going in? You weren't supposed to be here until tomorrow. After what we cost him, you know he has to have some kind of special humiliation all choreographed for us. The good Senator Carri isn't the kind of man that lets revenge slip by that easily.

Who says he's letting it slip by? another voice in his head asked, one to which Hawkes usually listened.

"Well, yes," Hawkes whispered to himself, his smile growing grim, "there's a thought."

The ambassador kept his pace even. Not politic to let anyone see him moving too slow or too fast. It was an old trick—one learned in the military, and reinforced by the corps. Never dawdle, never run. Both looked bad, showing either a lack of preparation or nerve. Neither was good—for the careers of officers or diplomats.

Of course, there's not much career left to worry about now, Benton. You made sure of that.

Hawkes ordered his carping inner voice to be silent. He had done what he had done—what his conscience dictated *had* to be done—and that was it. There had been no other choice. He simply could not allow a corporation—not even a corporation with its own embassies—to steal millions of acres of private land.

Anyway, what did it matter? It was done. He had won the fight for the Australians. Now, ironically, he had to return home to fight the same kind of fight for himself.

Nothing ever changes, does it?

A great many things in the world were uncertain, but of that one small point, the ambassador had little doubt.

Arriving at the outer office to Senator Carri's chambers, Hawkes unconsciously straightened his tie and ran a hand through his hair, then opened the door and went inside. He found Carri's chief of operations giving orders to the aide presiding over the reception desk.

He noted her hairstyle, gently upswept, gelled in place. It took him back to the past for a moment—made him feel old, comfortable—and strengthened his resolve. Walking up behind her, he said,

"Hello, Gladys. I like your hair."

The woman turned around, feigning annoyance at the interruption until she could pretend to be surprised at who it was, and then feign covering up her initial pretense.

"Ambassador Hawkes . . . ah, my—you weren't scheduled to be here until tomorrow. I mean . . . oh, please, sir, don't take that the wrong way. I'm sure the senator will be pleased to see you, it's just . . ."

"Don't apologize," he told her. "You're not the one who stepped in anything. I got in early. Didn't see any reason not to let Mick have the fun of throwing me out and telling me to come back when I was supposed to."

"Ambassador . . . really . . ."

"Please, don't try to spare me," said Hawkes, a touch of humor smoothing his tone. "I'm a big boy. I like to at least *try* to be responsible for my actions. I'll take what I earned." The ambassador tilted his head and then, with a twinkle in his eye, added, "Unless, of course, he's planning to have me killed or something. You could spare me that."

Gladys Beckett's smile jumped nervously, her eyes blinking at the same time. Hawkes noticed, wondering exactly what the sudden agitation in her face boded. She instantly covered with a clever rejoinder, but at the same moment let Hawkes know that he was in for something. Deciding to do some fishing, he asked, "So, just how deep in did I step?"

"Ambassador, I'm just a poor working girl," answered Beckett, stepping back toward the senator's office. "He doesn't tell me anything except what he wants and when he wants it." With her hand to the senator's door, she indexed Carri's confidential lock code for access, adding, "Let me find out if he can see you now." Then she turned toward the opening door and moved inside, saying, "You'll never guess who's here."

Hawkes listened to the lilt in her voice. Something was wrong. It was a slight thing, but he had been in the game too long not to notice. The operations chief was good, he granted her that much. But he was being gamed, and he knew it. Benton Hawkes might not have liked Michael Carri, but he had enough respect for the senator to know that the man had not survived and prospered in Washington, D.C., for more than two decades by being lax or stupid.

You're being set up, his dark inner voice told him. Carri knows you're here. He *knows*. There's no way he doesn't. Watch your step—you're in someone's crosshairs.

The door opened again. The senator stepped through, shrugging his jacket on, extending his hand at the same time.

"Benton Hawkes! Just the man I've been waiting for."

The ambassador took the hand, almost caught off guard. He had expected Beckett to come back and usher him to a chair. He had expected Carri to be facing a wall, standing, so that he could turn and attack a sitting target. Hawkes took the senator's hand and shook it. He gave Carri a greeting as noncommittal as the senator's, then followed him into the office. Taking the seat offered, he waited while Carri hurried himself back behind his desk.

The senator rustled through his papers, clearing away what seemed to be a mountain of paperwork.

"Look at all this," he said absently as he worked at restoring the desktop to its former order. "I remember my grandfather telling me that people thought computers were going to do away with all this. 'The paperless society'—that's what they called it—what we were supposed to have." Carri sighed convincingly, then waved his hands about him, adding, "But look at all this."

"Well, no one's come up with anything cheaper," Hawkes offered, waiting for the bell so the first round could begin. Before Carri could answer him, Beckett buzzed, letting the senator know his lunch had arrived. She ushered in the staged "working-through" snack, setting it off on the sideboard.

"I apologize for this," said Carri, indicating the prop lunch. "No time to get out these days. Too much to do. Which makes me ask"—the senator notched a growl into his voice, moving into the character Hawkes had expected—"just exactly what are you doing here already? You weren't supposed to be here until tomorrow."

"Well, I . . ." The ambassador waved his hands. His mind was racing, trying to catch whatever angle was being thrown at him.

He recognized Carri's ploy . . . could see that everything about the man's attitude was being engineered to guide him somewhere into something. . . .

But where? And what? What's going on here? Hawkes wondered. Just what the hell am I missing?

Finally, deciding to risk simply going with the truth, he said, "I thought it was such a wonderful day . . . why not drop in on my old friend Mick Carri. We could catch up on old times. I could tell you why I threw a moat around Australia, you could tell me I was finished in government service . . . you know. Fun stuff."

"Ben. Ben." The senator reached down into his lower ranges for a suitably hurt tone. "What? You want to get right down to . . . all of that?"

"Unless you need that extra day to sharpen some kind of retributional tools . . ."

"Ben, for God's sake . . ." Carri did his best to appear flustered, even embarrassed, covering the raging anger that burned within him convincingly. "Is this your opinion of me? That the only thing that counts is some dollar-studded bottom line?" Putting up his hands in an attempt to look frustrated and possibly hurt, he said, "All right, you want to get into it—fine." The senator pushed himself back in his chair, giving himself more room. Rubbing at his face, he said, "Let's get down to business. Did you cost me something? Oh, yes, quite a lot. Deutcher's already backing my opponent in the next election. What a surprise, right?"

"I'm sorry about that, Mick."

"Of course you are," growled the senator. "You're comfortable Benton Hawkes. Snug and warm in your blanket of respectable ethics. Spitting your pious sentiments down into the grave as you shovel the dirt in on top of the rest of us."

Carri reached for the sandwich on his sideboard. As he turned away, he allowed his eyes to go hard, allowing Hawkes to see the move. The senator turned back and took a bite, then started talking again, putting on one of his nastier faces.

"It must be easy to be you. Everything for you is laid out in such lovely shades of black and white." Shaking his sandwich at Hawkes, Carri snarled, "You take a hard line and everyone just assumes that it was the right thing to do. You're the good guy, you're the goddamned cowboy with the goddamned white hat, and anyone that says nay to you is some moustache twirler in a black one."

The senator looked at the sandwich in his hand. Having purposely mashed it for effect, he threw it back on the plate, as if seeing what he had done to it had taken some of the fight out of him. Looking around him wearily, Carri continued, asking, "I mean, did you think I liked giving you the orders I did? We're the same kind of person, Ben." Waving his hand toward the pine forest vid with calculated casualness, he said, "We want the same things, love the same things. But you aren't willing to do your share so that America holds its place—so that we get to keep what we have."

Hawkes started to protest, but Carri put up his hand, blocking the ambassador's effort. Acting as if he had wearied of their conversation, the senator shifted gears and started in on another track, bringing their conversation back to its beginning point to keep Hawkes confused.

"And so you want to know if you cost me? Yeah, you cost me. You cost me big, you bastard. You backed me into a corner and cut my balls off. And you sit there wondering how I'm going to thank you for it." The senator paused for a breath, then asked in mock earnestness, "You tell me, Ben, what am I supposed to do, throw some kind of hissy fit and hand the media a field day? 'Carri Says: Fuck the People' . . . that would look good in ninety-six-point type, wouldn't it?"

"I had to do it, Mick," said Hawkes defensively. "They wanted to take people's land without the slightest right."

Carri sat back in his chair, not commenting. His face glazed over in a cold, hard set.

"It was a corpor/national wanting to start a war—itching to kill people in the name of securing a better third quarter. I couldn't let it happen."

The senator continued to sit back, doing nothing but staring forward. Frustrated, Hawkes added, "Damn it, Mick, I told you not to send me. I told you what would happen."

"Oh, now there's a good excuse. 'I didn't want to do my job the way I was supposed to. I told you I wouldn't.' What do you want from me, Ben?" asked Carri, taking another bite of his sandwich. Still chewing, he said, "The people said, 'Send Hawkes.' And they said it loud enough that for once we had to give them what they wanted. I'm not an idiot. I knew what you were going to do. But I didn't have a choice. So I sent you and then threatened and fought with you on a regular basis to try and keep you in line. When they come to grill my ass black and bleeding, you will attest to the fact that I did try, won't you?"

Hawkes thought back over the blistering arguments he and Carri had had during the conference. He had been kept under constant pressure, every day, and most nights, hounded by the senator and his people to relent and throw the game to Deutcher.

"Oh, yes, you tried."

"Yes. Tried and lost. For then. But this is now. I won't ask if you have anything you want to say in your own defense, because frankly, I don't give a damn."

All right, thought the ambassador, actually relaxing somewhat now that Carri was getting to whatever he had planned on getting to all along. Here it comes.

"Oh . . . yes?"

"And don't take that tone with me. Damn it, Ben, you like honesty, okay, fine . . . I'll give you honesty," the senator lied carefully. Letting his true anger come forth, he growled, "I swear to you right now, if I could afford to have you cut up into fish bait and dropped in the river, you'd be there before dinner." Carri used a free finger to press together crumbs that had fallen from his sandwich. Licking them off his finger, he said, "But, you miserable fuck—I can't."

Hawkes sat forward, his mind racing. What was his opponent playing at? So far the senator had been wearing the mask of a hurt friend. He had even bothered to drag in the truth. But the ambassador had been certain it was all just a buildup toward his dismissal.

What's going on? he wondered. What in God's name could you want from me now, Mick?

Without any further hesitation, the senator told him.

4

"We've got big troubles, Ben," Carri started. Sucking his anger back down, he laid out his problem to Hawkes.

"From what I've gathered so far, there's a potential for riots brewing, illegal strikes. I have rumors of people being killed, children pressed into forced labor, contracts broken. We're looking at threatened disruption of the world's food supplies—possible work stoppage on the processing of a hundred different alloys, rare earths, and the such that would cripple a thousand different industries."

"Wait a minute, Mick," said Hawkes, afraid of the direction he thought the senator was taking. "What are you talking about?"

"We need you to negotiate a settlement in a spot so hot that no one's even going to come to the table unless everybody thinks they've got someone in the middle they can trust."

"Who is this everybody?"

"The upper management, officers, staffers, and workers of Red Planet, Inc." As Benton Hawkes's eyes grew wide, Mick Carri reached for his apple.

"That's right," he said, holding the dark scarlet piece of fruit a few inches from his mouth. "We want you to assume the governorship of Mars."

"What?" Hawkes's voice sank to a whisper. He could not have been more surprised if the senator had suddenly melted down into a pool of jelly or sprouted flowers from the ends of his fingers. As the ambassador stared in dumbfounded amazement, Carri went on: "We need you to head out to Mars as soon as possible. We don't know what to expect for sure, but we know there's going to be trouble—probably bloodshed—if we don't move fast to cork it."

"Now wait a minute . . ."

"Don't worry," the senator growled. "You'll have complete autonomy. We've got no time to play politics with this one. It's too big."

"That's not what I meant," answered the ambassador. "I don't want to go to Mars."

"Who does?" countered Carri. "But that's not the point, is it? That's where you're needed, so that's where you're being sent."

"No, you don't understand," explained Hawkes, dancing his way through the minefield the senator was laying out. "I *refuse* to go. The grand race to get to the stars is what killed my father. I swore decades ago I'd never set foot off-planet."

Carri returned to the tactic of folding his arms across his chest and silently staring, forcing Hawkes to keep talking. The ambassador had no difficulty in continuing.

"Everyone in the corps knows that. *You* know that, Mick. You *know* it. You can punish me any way you like—go ahead. Go ahead. But I'm not going to Mars."

The senator maintained his silent stare. Hawkes kept on rolling.

"I'm not. Strip my power, take my job, take my pension, do whatever you want. I'm not going. And you don't have anything in your stockpile of fast answers that's going to change my mind."

"You don't mind if I try, do you, Ben?"

"Of course I do. I don't want to be convinced. You've got a thousand other people you could send to Mars."

"Not like you," answered Carri. His smile grew wide. "Not like Benton Hawkes, the man who turns against the wishes of his own government to side with the little guy . . . the man who always

tells it like it is . . . who averts world wars for breakfast." Carri
dropped his hands down to his desk as he continued.

"Your little escapade down in Australia sealed you into this one.
You're the diplomat's diplomat now. Whatever hell is brewing up
there, it's bigger than any of us. Everyone up there thinks he's in
the right, and won't settle for anyone less than . . ."—the senator
paused for dramatic effect, lifting his left hand slowly, finally pointing at Hawkes's forehead—"you."

"Well, I don't care. I'm not leaving. Let them solve their own
damn problems. I've got some of my own. CME is trying to annex
the whole Absaroka Range. My ranch is in there, Mick. The bastards that killed my father are now trying to take his home from me
as well."

"Damn you, Hawkes," roared Carri. He stood up from his chair,
pointing again. "Damn you. Just who in hell do you think you are?
We're not talking some fucking little border dispute now. This isn't
the fate of a few paltry millions now. This is the entire fate of
mankind."

"Overreaching hyperbole? This soon after lunch?"

"Don't patronize me," growled the senator. "You know as well as
anyone how important Mars is now. I would hope better. Mars and
the asteroids supply half our food and two-thirds of our raw materials. Riots, a civil war, what do you think that would do to this
country—to the whole planet, for Christ's sake?"

Carri pushed his chair back, stepping free into the large space
between his desk and the wall. Pacing about, keeping his eyes
glued to Hawkes, he snarled, "We're talking about the possibility of
mass starvation. If the situation were to deteriorate and fall into
even just a bargaining situation—one that only lasted as long as
your stay in Australia—we could have tens of millions dead worldwide."

Hawkes turned away from Carri's relentless glare. He knew
there was no disputing the senator. The Earth had gotten itself into
a precarious balance by allowing itself to become so overly depen-

dent on the outer colonies. He knew there was no exaggeration in Carri's facts. Before he could try, however, the senator was at him again.

"I'd give anything to crush you like the pompous, self-important shit you've turned out to be. And, God help me, you weasel your way out of this, and I will. But . . . I'm as close to begging you here as I have been to anything. For once, get beyond yourself and consider what we're talking about here."

Carri moved around his desk slowly. Stopping directly in front of Hawkes, he settled his weight onto the edge of his desk. Looking down at Hawkes, he said, "If Mars cuts off services—whether in some kind of united strike effort, or because they've been crippled by internal conflict—that'll be the end of us. You know warships will be sent in. You know it. But it'll be too late."

Reaching behind him, the senator grabbed up the papers he had set out previously. Pulling them around, he handed them to Hawkes, telling him, "Here are the projections the computers have given us. Figures on what we get if we let this situation degenerate. The worst-case scenario foresees a new dark age here on Earth, with all life outside our atmosphere coming to an end."

As he dropped the papers in Hawkes's lap, Carri continued, saying, "Now, you say to yourself, well, that's the worst case. But, what's the best? I'll tell you. The best we can hope for . . . if things only get to, say, a week or two of work stoppage due to riots or sabotage or whatever . . . system wide—two point eight billion dead."

Two point eight billion? The ambassador's brain reeled from the impossibility of the figure.

"We've overextended ourselves for too long in too many directions. Every country in the world is guilty of it. No question."

Two point eight billion?

"But that's besides the point now."

Carri struggled to keep a grin of triumph off his face. He knew exactly how much Benton Hawkes hated the idea of going off-world, of leaving behind his precious outdoors for vacuum hulls and air locks. He also knew exactly how much the ambassador wanted to stop CME from taking his home.

"The simple reality is that mankind bet its future on moving out into the solar system. Our chips are on red, Benton . . . and right now, you're the only person in the world that can keep the ball from falling into the black."

Two point eight *billion?*

Senator Carri watched as Hawkes's eyes closed. He could see the pain etched around them, could follow the agony inching through the ambassador's body. Not able to help himself that time, the politician smiled. He finally had Benton Hawkes where he wanted him.

And, no matter what happened next, he had to admit, it felt damn good.

5

"**D**izzy," Hawkes shouted, growing somewhat impatient with the barking dog, "for God's sake, will you shut up?"

The big retriever had been barking and running around the barn ever since they had come outside. Loping over to the ambassador's side, he playfully snapped at his master's left boot, then ran back to the other side of the truck, barking again. Deciding to give up on the dog for the moment, Hawkes grabbed up two pairs of work gloves from the utility table built into the wall.

"All right," he said, slipping on one pair, handing the other to Daniel Stine, "time for you to learn to work for a living."

"Really, sir," answered the ambassador's aide, holding the gloves away from his body as if they were some sort of dangerous insects, "this is not quite what I had in mind when I said I'd like to help you get your affairs in order."

"Well," said Hawkes, studying the engine before him, not looking at the younger man, "next time you'll know better."

As Disraeli continued to bark, the ambassador pulled a dog biscuit from his vest pocket and threw it as far as he could into the tall grass beside the barn. As the retriever took off after it, Hawkes said, "Damn dog's going to drive me crazy." Then, poking his head back under the hood of the truck, the ambassador asked the other man present, "So, what's the problem, Ed?"

"Caught me there," the much older man admitted. "Truth, just got to her today, so I don't rightly know yet."

"Well, I see you got the oil pan off. What's it look like in there?"

"Oh, that's fine. All clean wet. Little metal, sure, but just specks. Normal bushing and thrust-washer wear. You know. Nothing serious."

"You check all the other fluid levels? . . ."

"Oh, yeah, always do the easy stuff first. Everything's topped off, all the colors are good. None of the hoses are cracked, all the vacuum lines are connected."

Hawkes stood back from his old 4 × 4 and frowned. Several decades earlier, personal vehicles had begun to disappear in America. Using public transportation had become the government-mandated mark of a good citizen. Gasoline and diesel fuel had been taxed excessively to give the infant electric and hover transportation industries an advantage.

Both of the new technologies shared the problem of working efficiently only in massive constructs, though. So for the good of the environment, and the bank accounts of several well-placed individuals, private ownership of vehicles was labeled un-American, elitist, racist, wasteful, phallocentric, and just plain bad. The cities and suburbs of America were given over to selected monopolies to move people about as they saw fit.

The problem for Hawkes was twofold. First, none of the monopoly-run bus, floating platform, subway, or train lines came anywhere near his property. And secondly, even if he were to apply for a private hovercraft ownership permit, it would do him no good. Hover technology still had not conquered the upgrade barrier. Any elevated plane that rose quicker than twenty-nine degrees caused all hover engines to choke. It was due to their inability to break away from the Earth at certain speeds, all of it beyond the ambassador, and all of it useless to a man who lived in the mountains.

So Benton Hawkes had been forced to learn to care for his four-wheel-drive vehicles. Over the years he and his foreman, Ed Keller, had tracked down parts from around the world, learning to build the ones they could not buy or barter. It was either that, or sell off the ranch and move into a city, Ed had joked once.

"I'd rather switch to forty-four-caliber mouthwash," the ambassador had answered. Ed had nodded grimly, and they both laughed.

The memory of that day came back to Hawkes as the two stood staring at the engine in the cold morning air. However, the moment was suddenly shattered as Disraeli bolted back into the barn and began barking once more. Sighing, the ambassador smiled, then told his foreman, "Listen, maybe it's a fluctuation problem in the oil pressure. You've got Danny here. Why don't you two cycle the transmission, see if you can find any aeration."

"I don't know if I'll be much help, sir."

"Well, there's only one way to find out."

As Hawkes threw his gloves on the utility table, Ed asked, "Where'll you be, case I need to find you?"

"I'm going to walk the back divide, check the fence. Get used to things again."

"You think that's more important than getting this heap running?" the old man shouted over the Labrador's deep barking.

"I figured I'd take Dizzy with me."

"Deal," answered Ed, laughing. "No wonder they made you a negotiator."

"Well, it was easier than working for a living."

"They could still use you, sir," Stine threw in hurriedly. "Now more than ever."

"Danny . . ."

"You know they need you."

Hawkes turned with a cold look in his eye. In a quiet voice filled with steel, he said, "It's a long walk down the mountain, Stine. I'd think about helping to get the truck running."

And then he turned and walked away, Disraeli snapping at his heels. Silently, Hawkes disappeared into the livestock barn, the dog sitting down quietly at the front entrance to the larger building. Staring at the scene, Stine asked the foreman, "What's in there?"

"Horses," Ed answered, patting the 4 × 4's side. "No sense in wasting fuel when you got hay burners. 'Sides, he's going out to check the Scar. Ain't no roads back there."

"The Scar?" asked the ambassador's aide. Like any young man confronted with a job he did not wish to do, he badgered the foreman with distractions. "What's that?"

"It's where an ore ship fell out of the sky—killed the boss's daddy."

"But why did you call it the Scar?"

" 'Cause that's what it looked like. Damn thing tore up the ground, burned all the trees, poisoned everything for a long time. Ground cover just started coming back these last few years."

Ed turned at the sound of horse and rider erupting from the barn. Hawkes was giving the mare he had picked its head, letting it move as fast as it wanted. Disraeli bounded along behind them, snapping and barking. Watching them disappear around the edge of the main house, Ed said, "I know him. He ain't been out there since he got back. He's got to pay his respects."

"You seem to know the ambassador better than anyone I've ever met," said Stine. "I've never known him to get close to anyone before. Have you worked for him a while?"

Ed Keller took a long look at Stine. He had been foreman for Benton Hawkes's father—had raised him after his father's death. He knew other people never got the chance to know the real Ben Hawkes—the one he knew. Oftentimes he thought it was a shame. But he also knew the reason why the ambassador kept people at arm's distance. It was an old thing, a private thing, one he was sure Hawkes still meant to keep private for a long time.

Keller studied Stine for a moment. He knew the younger man wanted to get closer to the ambassador. He wondered briefly if perhaps it had been kept private for too long.

"Hand me that bit of hose, will ya?" was all he finally said to the younger man, however, deciding that the Ben Hawkes he knew was old enough to make his own friends and choose his own company.

The dappled mare bolted as soon as she reached the open path for the back forest. She and Hawkes left Disraeli far behind, leaving the poor retriever's piercing bark to fade quickly to nothingness. As he raced through the trees brushing close on either side, the ambassador momentarily forgot about CME, the continual pleas as well as the campaign to get him to go to Mars . . . forgot about everything except the reins in his hands and the breeze in his face.

It felt good to be back in the saddle, back in the mountains—his mountains. His throat went dry from the air rushing into his open mouth. He knew it was no way to ride, but it had been too long; the feel of the air—over his teeth, through his hair, on his head, over the back of his hands—it felt so . . . right.

The crushing pain of Washington, of Carri's demands—both in Australia and in Washington the week before—the brutal reality of Clean Mountain and their designs on his heritage . . . the weight of it all began to break up, to fold down into smaller, more manageable packages. On what seemed an hourly basis, the government was leaking stories that Hawkes would soon be leaving for Mars. Pressure had been brought from every direction to try to get him to change his mind.

So far he had refused. Send someone else, he had told Carri. Tell them I'm sick, tell them I'm dead, tell them I just don't care.

Benton Hawkes had selflessly given the world more than thirty years of his life. Now, in the end, he had little more than when he had started. His father's ranch was all he had ever wanted, and it was all he had. All his resources were tied up in keeping it going— in simply keeping it, period. He had gotten nothing out of his years of service except a handful of private gifts from grateful parties.

Yes, he thought, and a dozen powerful enemies for each piece of junk I bothered to keep.

Eventually the mare sensed her rider's growing calm and began to slow her pace. Hawkes paid scant attention. His conscious mind relaxed as he watched the birds and insects move in the forest, darting his eyes from one patch of breakthrough sunlight to another. Beneath the surface, however, he finally began to replay his meeting with Michael Carri, trying to determine what the senator really wanted.

Can it be as simple as he laid it out? Australia was no big deal . . . I'd like to kill you, but we need you on Mars, so all is forgiven . . . pack your bags—and that's it?

Hawkes wondered if it was possible he was overcomplicating things, suspecting Carri of duplicity not because he could actually see any, but because he did not like the man's style. The thought gave him pause to remember the words of Camillo di Cavour. Hawkes studied the nineteenth-century Italian statesman's work when he had first entered the corps. One quote had been burned into his mind when he first saw it, and it never left him: "I have discovered the art of fooling diplomats," the long dead politician had said. "I speak the truth and they never believe me."

Is that what I've done? Allowed Carri to chase me off with the truth? Is it possible he *doesn't* want me to go to Mars? Is he using my own vanity against me? . . .

Like you've done to so many others? his cynical side asked.

Yes, he admitted, just like that.

It would have been a subtle irony, one Hawkes had not thought the senator capable of. It made sense. So far, all of the ambassador's research had failed to find any lies in what Carri had told him. The situation on Mars did look bad. Desperately bad. News traveled so slowly between the two planets, especially real news. Voices and pictures could be beamed back and forth quickly, but solid, tangible evidence that could be turned over in one's hands, that still took weeks.

Still, he wished the government would stop issuing statements that they were in negotiations with Hawkes to send him to Mars. It had been more than a week. They ought to know he was not going to go.

Of course, he thought, that could be Carri's game, as well. Since he knew damn well I wouldn't want to go, maybe he's just priming the well. "We asked, but the bastard wouldn't do it." Bad Ben Hawkes, good Mick Carri.

Disraeli glided through the ground cover next to the ambassador's mount. An old and seasoned hunter, the retriever had approached in virtual silence. Hawkes had sensed his presence more through his kinship with the large black dog than through anything else.

Looking down and smiling at his only friend, he said, "What do you think, Dizzy? I mean, on the one hand, taking this governorship would have tremendous advantages. CME certainly couldn't annex the home of a territorial governor—especially the governor of a whole planet. And, I must admit, after all the years of guys like Carri and the rest of the Beltway Circus trying to lose me in one rummy assignment after another . . . putting the end note to my career by shaping the destiny of all humanity . . . well, it is an appealing thought."

But it's not an appealing world, asked a sour voice from the back of his brain, is it?

Hawkes's mare stopped at the edge of the Scar. The ambassador looked out over the burned and ruined gash in his mountains, and suddenly all he could see was the surface of Mars. It was a lifeless vision: one of blowing dust and ten-kilometer-wide craters; frozen ground covered with permafrost; a bitter, dead world, nothing more than a giant space factory with no residents other than the employees of Red Planet, Inc.

People didn't really live there, he reminded himself, they went there to work, period. Like the jobbers who flocked to the Moon and the Maldives when Lunar City and the Skyhook had to be built

. . . or to Alaska a century earlier, when the great pipeline was constructed . . . or to Panama before that, to dig the great canal . . . or the gold fields . . .

"Damn it—so they've got tough lives," he spat, looking out over the acres of poisoned land, at the enormous skeletal remains of the fallen aircraft at its center. "What does that have to do with me? Why does that mean I have to eat fungus and go live the rest of my life in a cave? Why me?"

No more steak, started a litany in his head. No more Happy Times—no more fresh water—no more horses—no more trees—no more sunlight—no more grass—no more calamari—no more beaches—no more birds—no more . . .

His eyes narrowed on the massive rusting framework of the fallen ship. Closing them, he could see the ore carrier in the sky once more. His mind took him back to that day completely.

He was eleven again. His father was there with him. They had ridden out to the touchdown site to watch the approaching freighter. They had taken a lunch with them and it had been a happy outing—for a while.

Young Benton had spotted the ship first. At least that was the way he had always remembered it. It had loomed up out of the clear sky, a pinpoint that grew into a larger and larger shape, dazzling in the reflected sunlight. It moved with a fascinating majesty—slowly, calmly, and orderly—until the moment when a thin line of fumes began to spray outward from between a set of strained connector plates. After that, it took only seconds for the ship to list badly. A moment after, it began to shake. Another moment saw it shudder as a massive jolt shook the entire vessel. And then, as an exhaust of white mist darkened to fumes of purple, the stricken ore ship began its final, sickeningly dizzy descent. Long before the younger Hawkes had realized what was happening, his father had understood.

"Get to your horse, son."

"Dad, what is it?"

"Move, Ben—now!"

Benton turned to do as he was told, but it was too late. A massive explosion tore the sky apart, blowing a hole in the clouds above the freighter. Benton was thrown to the ground. The sky filled with flames and a thick dark blanket of oily smoke. Benton's horse bolted, racing away in fear.

The senior Hawkes, still standing, his hands on his own horse's reins, looked up—saw what was coming toward them. Benton staggered to his feet, his arm bruised, face bleeding. Without a word, his father grabbed him from behind with one hand and then threw his son up into the saddle of his own horse.

"Ride, boy," was all he said to Benton before he ordered the stallion home, cracking its flank with a vicious slap.

Try as he might, the boy could not turn the horse back to the death his father had foreseen. The horse galloped madly, crashing through the brush in between trees. Benton hung on with all his strength, screaming for his father. Burning chunks of steel and plastic fell all around them, setting the forest on fire. The horse kept running, its fear giving it a speed it had never known before.

In the end, young Benton escaped the slamming, burning carnage by the merest of seconds. His father had been right: had they both attempted to escape on the same horse, they both would have been dead.

Hawkes opened his eyes with a shudder. Still gazing out over the edge, he watched a gigantic shadow move across the face of the Scar as a cloud drifted over the ruin. The massive dark oval blotted the dead zone, tricking the eye for a moment, making the land look the way it did when the ambassador had been a boy. He could feel his father at his side for an instant, looking out over the Scar with him. Pulling on his reins with force, he turned his mare away from the view, pointing her back toward the deep forest.

"They're not going to take the ranch, Dad," the ambassador promised. Then, glancing down to his side, he saw his faithful retriever staring up at him with a mournful look.

"And I'm not spending my last years on a frozen dustball, living in an elevator shaft. No way, Dizzy." He nudged his heels against the horse's sides, snapping the reins at the same time.

"I'm staying here," he told himself with almost vicious defiance as he rode away. "Right here."

Disraeli raced past the barn where Hawkes stopped, heading back to bark at the 4 × 4. As Hawkes handed his mare off to one of his ranch hands, he could hear Keller cursing the dog. The ambassador walked on, sighing. As he neared the barn, he called to the retriever, asking, "Dizzy, for God's sake, boy, what's got into you?"

The black Labrador kept barking, however, not coming out of the barn. Hawkes went in, wondering just what had caught the big dog's attention. Before he had gone riding he had simply thought the animal's carrying on had been enthusiasm.

As he stood next to the still-barking dog, the ambassador decided it had to be something else. "It's happened before, you know."

"You think maybe a chipmunk or something's climbed up inside the damn framework?" asked Keller.

"Maybe we should just let it get out on its own," offered Stine, seeming somewhat uncomfortable at the thought of confronting a wild animal.

"Oh, don't be such a baby," said Keller. He had grown a bit tired of the city-bred aide during their repair session. If there was an excuse to put down tools and keep away from grease, the old man was sure Stine knew it.

"Well, there's obviously something down there that's got his nose going," agreed Hawkes. Getting down on his hands and knees, the ambassador crawled forward, saying, "And if we want to shut him up, I guess I'm going to have to see what it is."

As soon as Hawkes began to move for the truck, Disraeli dropped down onto his belly and scrambled forward under the

4×4's front axle. The ambassador frowned, then shoved himself forward, pushing himself along the ground on his back. Disraeli stayed calm as his master approached. Out of the corner of his eye, Hawkes could see that the dog was staring upward, his muzzle pointed straight at the section of undercarriage beneath the driver's seat.

"You see anything?" called Keller.

"Yes," came Hawkes voice. "I certainly do."

The ambassador began wiggling his way back out from under the 4×4. Disraeli simply went forward, coming out from beneath the front bumper. Keller and Stine both met Hawkes on his side of the truck. The foreman asked, "So, what had that damn mutt so geared up, anyway?"

Hawkes held up a thin, round disk, smaller than a slice of bread. It was made out of a dull black metal, unpainted, with no markings of any kind.

"What the hell is that?" asked Keller, taking it from the ambassador's outstretched hand.

"They didn't have them when I was in the service, but I've seen them over the past few years." Reaching down to scratch Disraeli's head, he said, "It's a bomb, Ed. A very sophisticated one."

While the foreman turned the slim device over and over in his hands, Hawkes told the retriever, "Good dog, Dizzy. Good dog."

"Yeah," muttered Keller, still turning the bomb over and over in his hands. "Damn good dog."

6

Hawkes turned the explosive over one last time, then put it aside, setting it down on his nightstand. He had studied the device—rolled it over and over in his hands, just plain stared at it—long enough. Maybe it was time to let it be for a while, time to get out of his dirty clothes, steam himself off, and get some sleep.

Sure, sleep. Ought to be easy to sleep tonight.

Like the ambassador, almost everyone on the ranch was too excited—or too nervous—to sleep. Discovery of the bomb had unleashed an excited tidal wave of curiosity among Hawkes's workers. All of his people—wranglers, field hands, the cooks, gardeners, housekeepers—had wanted to see it, wanted to know where it came from.

He thought back over the pertinent questions that had poured out of them. Was it planted recently? Had it been there for years and no one knew? How powerful was it? Was it set to go off? Did it have a timer release? Electronic detonation? Pressure? Altitude? Who did it?

Accusations had followed the questions. It was the Deutchers. Payback time. No—Clean Mountain. With Hawkes dead, they could get the ranch easily. Hah—it was the damn government. The

ambassador was making them look bad by refusing to go to Mars.
That's this damn government's way. Doubt it—probably the damn
Martians. They don't want the boss up there. They just want to keep
bleeding the taxpayers dry so they can go on playing space cadet.
Big picture, ya, monkey—it's all of 'em . . . Deutcher probably
financed it, CME provided the men, Mars the bomb, and the damn
Senate approved it.

That's just crazy. You're nuts.

Am I? It's a Martian bomb, ain't it?

The field hand who had come up with the last theory, former
corporal Anthony Celdosso, had been right about that much, anyway—the bomb did come from a Martian factory. He had been
discharged only a year earlier and was up on what was current in
the national arsenal. Hawkes liked to hire ex-soldiers. He got along
well with servicemen and -women. They worked hard, knew how to
follow orders, and kept their distance from their commander. Benton Hawkes did not like people getting too close.

Bet you wished you had a few more friends now, eh?

The ambassador reached down next to his chair to stroke Disraeli's head. As a reaction to the voice within his head, he told the
dog, "Good boy. Good old, bomb-sniffing wonder dog. Was your
steak big enough tonight?"

Understanding enough of Hawkes's tone, the dog licked his master's hand. Starting to come up off the floor, the ambassador pushed
at him gently, discouraging him from rising. Disraeli was a loyal
dog, but an old one. It had been an exciting day and by rights the
retriever should have been asleep hours ago. Hawkes rubbed the
loose fold of skin at the back of the dog's neck, telling him, "No, no
. . . good boy. Go to sleep. Go on, go to sleep." His eyes drifted
back to the bomb, and he added softly, "One of us should get
some."

Reaching over, he picked the small disk up again and brought it
back to eye level for one more inspection. Tony had explained what
it was exactly, and how it worked. Officially named the Graamler

1OSA-11, it was affectionately known to those whose used it in the field as "li'l kick in the head."

A Graamler could be set off by fixed timer, electronic signal, altitude, even voice command. It had been set to detonate anytime the 4×4 descended to 1,500 feet above sea level—which meant the next time Hawkes left his property for anywhere at all.

And that detonation would have been the end of things.

The device had the power to incinerate the entire truck and anyone in it. It would have left a crater in the road approximately three feet deep and twelve feet in diameter. Everything present within the circumference of its aggravation range would have been incinerated—almost atomized.

Tony could tell that the device had not been present for long. It was too clean, for one thing. For another, it was a new type of toy— barely out of prototype development when the corporal had been discharged.

"So," mused Hawkes softly, not wanting to disturb the quietly snoring Disraeli, "someone wants me dead. The first question: Who? The second: Why?"

In his mind he ran through the list of suspects suggested by his hands after the Graamler had been discovered. Deutcher? Mars? Could it be CME? Could it? Or even someone within his own government? Possibly Carri, running some end game tied to a personal agenda to which Hawkes had no clue?

Getting up out of his chair, the ambassador took the bomb and crossed the room to his wardrobe. Pulling open the hand-carved wooden doors on the handsome oak piece, he slid the device back into his inner vest pocket. It was deactivated, it had spent most of the day there . . . it would be as safe there as anywhere else.

The bomb was not the problem. The real problem that worried Hawkes was what to do next.

So, he asked himself, whom do I alert? Someone tell me who it is I'm supposed to trust . . . whom I can call that I can be certain isn't working for whoever just tried to kill me. And even after I think of those who might be on my side . . . what about their staff, the connections leading away from them? Who out there is so secure that no one within the range of their voice can possibly be tainted?

It was the curse of playing the civil service game, one he had lived with for a long time: Who do you trust? No matter how secure an organization might be—no matter how respected or honorable or reliable—if you had just one enemy within it somewhere, or at some level it housed a single person who could be bought . . .

The ambassador knew how that game was played. He had turned plenty of people against their own kind in his time—it was his job. Office politics . . . any kind of politics. Hawkes knew how pitifully few dollars it took to buy men's souls. He had authorized too many of the receipts not to know. More than once, he had laughed out loud at how little effort, how few lies it took to blind people to facts they knew to be true simply by playing on fears they were too weak to ignore. It was only part of the reason he had kept people at arm's length since he had left the service—since he had entered the corps and become a creature of government.

But now he was on the receiving end, and it was damned uncomfortable. Certainly he had been there before . . . but not like he was after finding a bomb in his own home. That was a change in the usual rules. That was different.

Hawkes was not even sure he could trust his own workers. The Graamler had not rolled under the 4×4 and jumped up onto the axle. Someone planted it there. And that someone had either snuck across the miles of his ranch unseen, did his work and then slithered back out again—or he had no need to sneak because he lived there.

Like I said before, laughed the cynical voice in his head, bet you wish you had more friends now, eh?

Aww, God, shut up, he told himself, chasing away his depression. Leave me alone. I like things just fine this way. This is who I am.

Then, glancing down at the dark form sleeping soundly on the floor, Hawkes whispered, "Besides, I have all the friends I need right here."

The ambassador's gaze stayed fixed on the dog.

Poor Dizzy, he thought. Twelve years old already. How much longer will you even be with me?

Then what will you do? came the cynical side of his brain. Then what?

Before Hawkes could answer himself, a deafening roar thundered through his house.

1

Disraeli bounded up from the floor, his bark nervous and frightened. Hawkes staggered back to his feet, feeling somewhat the same. He had not even made it across his room before another explosion tore loose somewhere outside. This one went off much closer, blowing out the glass door to his raised porch and taking out the closest window. Flying glass filled the air. Shards embedded themselves in the walls and the ceiling, bounced off furniture, and rained down on the ambassador and his dog.

Hawkes slapped the retriever in the rump, aiming him for the door as he shouted, "Run, Dizzy! Run for it!"

Hawkes pulled open his nightstand drawer and grabbed out the old Ingram M-10 that had been there since he had come back from the war. A sudden memory flashed through his head that the weapon had not been cleaned since before he left for Australia. He reached into the drawer and grabbed the ammunition clips that always sat there with it, rammed one home, and shoved the rest into his pockets, casting aside the worry that the scaled-down submachine gun might be too dirty to fire. He had other things to worry about.

Who's doing this? he wondered, making his way to the door. This is twice. Twice someone's gotten over the fences: around the radar and the sensors. Past the guards. When the government had first insisted that he accept such elaborate protections, he had scoffed. Now he wished he had demanded twice as many.

"Who the hell are you people?" he shouted, taking the stairs two at a time down to the first floor. "And what the hell do you want with me?!"

Gunfire rang from the outside. Screams followed. Another explosion sounded and suddenly the ranch's power failed. Instantly the main house went black. Hawkes slowed his descent unconsciously, unsure in the dark of the number of stairs. The same heavy weapons he had heard before barked again. A hard line of terrible thuds slammed into the wood-and-stone walls of Hawkes's home, punching jagged holes close by, and filling the room with splinters and pebbles.

Over the din, Hawkes could hear the voices of the ranch's workers: some were shouting, barking orders; others were confused, lost—dying.

They're killing my people, thought the ambassador.

Lead smashed its way through three of the remaining windows in the massive living room. It gouged into the wood of the wall behind Hawkes, shattering the picture of his parents and knocking his Nobel Prize off the mantel. As he stood his ground for the moment, held helpless by the confusion in the air all around him, another explosion, seemingly louder than all the rest, rocked the grounds. The ambassador was thrown from his feet. He landed hard on the floor, smashing his left arm against the corner of the couch. Staggering to his feet, he snarled, "Maybe I should kill some of theirs."

The ambassador headed for the back of the house, Ingram still in hand. Coming into the kitchen, he could hear rough boots hitting the porch outside. Instinct told him they belonged to the attackers. Counting off the seconds he had before they reached the door, he headed for the large butcher's block in the center of the room and plucked up the cleaver hanging from its side. As he did, the door to his left flew open. Two armed men entered, one breaking left, the other right.

And welcome to my home, you sons of bitches.

Hawkes pulled back and hurled the cleaver end over end. Before it could dig into the chest of the man to the left, he let off a burst at the man to the right. Two of the three bullets tore into the attacker, spinning him around and bouncing him off the cold locker. The other took the full force of the cleaver hit. It staggered him slightly, but that was all.

Body armor, thought Hawkes. He could see the man shaking off the blow, his arm starting to come up. As time fractured into splinters of seconds, he pulled off another burst, and then another. The man fell backward, hitting the doorway he and his partner had just demolished. The dead man stumbled out onto the porch and then toppled off it. His body fell into the yard beyond, arms and legs awkwardly tangled.

The ambassador ignored him, hunching over the body that was still in the kitchen. Like his partner, he was dressed in sterile military fatigues. No marking to identify who he was, where he was from. Worse than that, the man's face had been bubbled.

Damn! Damn, damn, damn!

Bubbling was expensive. And if he had been bubbled that meant his teeth had been melted, his fingerprints filled, his retinas painted. It meant the invading force was most likely made up of mercenaries. It also meant that someone with money was behind what was happening. More than money—power. And suddenly, Hawkes knew what kind of fight he was in.

"One I'd better win."

Picking up the man's weapon, the ambassador was surprised at its weight; it was heavier than it looked. He recognized the Heckler & Koch insignia on the stock, but not its type. Not caring, Hawkes stood up, shoved his own, smaller weapon in his belt behind his back, and then headed for the door, holding the H&K at waist-high level.

The firefight outside had slackened off considerably. The ambassador instantly understood why. The ranch's power might have gone out, but fires in two of the outer buildings were lighting the area all too well. With the element of surprise gone, the invaders were digging in, looking for cover, searching for targets.

Yeah, and I wonder who that would be?

Inching his way out onto the porch, Hawkes gave the outer yard a quick scan, then covered the same ground again more slowly, searching for targets of his own. No one was in sight—no one was alive. He could make out nearly ten bodies on the ground within his field of vision. Sadly, he recognized far too many of them. Moving off the porch and down into the deep shadows cast by the service barn, the ambassador moved in that direction. He had a hunch he knew where at least some of the enemy were.

Setting private property ablaze was an old trick, one he had seen used on three different continents. Torch a man's house and he generally headed for a hose, not a rifle. Sizing up the angles at which the fires were set, it looked as if his attackers were looking to lure him and his people into the area near the large well in front. That meant they would be in the utility center, waiting to pick them off.

Hawkes crawled forward, toward the barn, the Ingram digging into his back with each shuffle of his legs. Drawing closer, he checked the safety on the unfamiliar weapon in his hands. As he made sure he was ready to go, gunfire erupted from the service barn. Screams of agony cut through the night. Before he could stand, another volley let loose, accompanied by more cries.

Getting to his feet, the ambassador rushed the back door. He felt his breath coming harder, could hear his heart in his ears.

Too old for this, he thought, mopping at his forehead. Supposed to be sipping my hot milk right now.

Getting to the rear of the barn, Hawkes threw himself against the wall. He pulled the H&K up against his chest and dug his back into the old wooden planks, making himself as small as possible.

He inhaled deeply, bracing himself. A new explosion rocked the ground, forcing the breath from him. Taking another, he said, "All right. Let's get this over with."

The ambassador let his hand fall to the door. He was counting on the fact that the darkness had probably kept the invaders from even spotting it. Slipping the latch, he opened it quickly and threw himself inside. Ahead of him, at the edge of the barn, he spotted five, maybe six figures. All those he could see clearly were dressed like the man who lay dead in his kitchen. All stood in a row, firing into the night at the backs of his people as they tried to reach the well.

Well, when in Rome . . .

Hawkes lifted the heavy weapon, squared it off at mid-chest height, and then opened fire at the left end of the row. He had meant to swing along the row and mow all of the gunmen down, but he had not reckoned on the weapon's recoil. The H&K had been modified to fire explosive shells, rounds that threw out an enormous back kick. The ambassador was able to keep his finger wrapped around the trigger only long enough to fire twice before being thrown backward, out of the barn.

The three invaders in the center of the line were instantly blown apart. The one to their right was thrown sideways, with gaping shrapnel wounds in his arm and thigh. The fifth escaped harm, however.

Taking advantage of the sudden drop in the volume of fire coming from the utility barn, several of Hawkes's wranglers triggered off again. The last of the five withdrew his position quickly, deciding to take his chances with whoever had attacked from the rear than with the men advancing on his position.

He hit the back door long before Hawkes had regained his footing. The ambassador had landed on his back. The blow had knocked the air out of him. The Ingram had torn into his spine, shooting stars of pain through his skull. Groping wildly, half-blind with pain, he was only halfway up when the fleeing soldier came through the door. The soldier spotted him instantly.

At once, the mercenary gripped the weapon tighter, swinging it around for a good shot. Hawkes desperately tried to do the same. Every move he made was far too many seconds behind his opponent, however. He was still trying to stand, still trying to bring his captured weapon around even as his enemy's trigger finger was tightening.

Then, seemingly out of nowhere, Disraeli hit the soldier solidly on the side, sending him flying. The man's machine gun discharged, barely missing Hawkes. The soldier hit the ground clumsily, landing hard on his side, cracking his head.

Wasting no time, the large black Labrador bit at the man's face, tearing his nose clear away from his head. Ignoring the wild, blubbering screams erupting from his victim, the dog drove his teeth into the man's neck, crushing his windpipe. Blood gushed from the wound. Not troubled by the warm spray, Disraeli bit harder, then jerked his head upward. A large chunk of the man's throat came away with the motion. The air filled with blood.

Holding his side, the ambassador looked down at the retriever and whispered, "Damn good dog."

And then gunfire erupted from the back door of the barn. The shooter toppled back inside, thrown over by his weapon's recoil. Several yards from Hawkes's feet, Disraeli lay still, cut in two pieces—dead instantly.

The ambassador stood frozen; his eyes stretched wide. Inside, he understood what had happened: the shooter who had been aiming for him hadn't understood his weapon any better than he had the H&K. The recoil had thrown his shot wild, killing Disraeli instead of Hawkes.

His teeth grinding together, his eyes unblinking, his body trembling from rage, Hawkes started for the barn. He entered without caution or subtlety, immediately spotting a figure moving several feet inside. He came up to it and stood over it. The man was unarmed, not even able to hold on to his weapon when the recoil had caught him.

The ambassador lowered his weapon to fire, and then something

the back of his mind had noticed forced him to stop. To look—to
see that whoever had killed the faithful retriever was not dressed as
the others. He wore regular clothing, clothing that Hawkes was
startled to find he recognized.

"No."

Tossing aside the H&K, the ambassador reached down and
jerked Daniel Stine to his feet. Holding him by his shirtfront,
Hawkes spun the corps-appointed aide backward and slammed him
against the side wall. Inside his head, a thin voice of reason whispered to him, pleading incessantly, Don't kill him. He knows who
did this. He knows why it happened. Where it came from. Don't kill
him. Don't kill him. He can tell us what's going on. He knows. He
planted the bomb. He knows. Don't kill him. He knows—he
knows—he knows.

Hawkes did not care. It did not matter what the man hanging
from his fists knew. The ambassador grabbed Stine's head in his
hands and smashed it against the wall. Once, twice, as hard as he
could. Again and again.

For twelve years he had one friend, one confidant, one being in
all the universe he trusted. Now he had no one.

Hawkes roared from deep within his chest, a numbing, echoing
bellow that tore his lungs and bloodied his throat. Still screaming,
he jerked Stine away from the wall and pitched him forward, toward
the front of the barn. The aide stumbled blindly, flopping wildly in
the flickering shadow-light cast by the fires.

The ambassador ran after the younger man, stepping on him
when he finally fell. Hawkes let his heel dig into the man's chest,
trampling him as hard as he could. In the back of his mind,
common sense still raged at him: Don't kill him—don't kill
him—

The ambassador's eyes cleared for a moment. In the background,
over the last of the gunfire, he could hear the roar of the blaze
taking his home to the ground. He could make out the voices of
some of his people trying to control the fires, trying to help the

injured. He could hear others crying, screaming as their pain pounded its way out of them, spiraling up into the night sky.

And then, out of all he could hear, his imagination created a noise for him, a sound resembling one of a tortured hound, dying by inches.

Without hesitation, Benton Hawkes reached behind his back, pulled his Ingram out of his belt, and fired, emptying his clip into the man on the ground before him.

8

The next morning found Hawkes in little better shape than when the fighting had ended the night before. In many ways, he was worse off. The ambassador sat in a chair on his side porch, folding his arms over the top pockets of his leather vest. His eyes simply stared off into space. As far as anyone who had seen him could tell, he had not moved since he had first sat down. Cook placed a mug of coffee in front of him, but he did not touch it. She came out later and slid a small loaf of freshly baked bread in front of him as well.

It sat next to the mug, untouched. Unnoticed. By that time, the coffee was cold, a thin film layered across its surface. A half hour later Cook came back out and removed both the mug and the loaf. She did not return. Hawkes sat throughout, thinking. Brooding.

He and his people had put out the fires. They had collected their dead—collected their attackers as well. For a short while they had debated whether they should radio anyone. It was the same paranoia that had stifled Hawkes's actions before. Whom could they call? And why? In the end, however, they chose people they trusted in the local sheriff's office.

It was obvious to Hawkes that whoever had authorized the attack would have to assess its level of success before making another move. It meant they were safe for the moment—but only for the moment.

Oh, yes, quite true, thought the ambassador bitterly, and that's contingent only on us having found *all* of their inside people.

Stine's betrayal had affected him badly. Yes, he had kept the man—boy, really—at arm's length. It was his way. It was how he treated everyone.

Get over yourself, Benton, he chided himself mentally in a brittle tone. You're not feeling betrayed. You're feeling embarrassed. You're getting old—old and foolish. You're starting to trust people . . . again. Remember what happened the last time you did that?

Hawkes's right hand curled into a fist. He remembered. All too vividly. He remembered the bodies that had been piled up that time as well. Because he had been open to his people. Friendly and trusting.

Not trusting. Weak.

The cynical side of him seized the moment to hammer again at the message it always held at hand for him.

Weakness. That's what sentimentality brings, it reminded him. Weakness and death. Look around you—at the broken windows and bullet holes and the blood on the ground . . . smell the smoke in the air. That's gunpowder and what's left of your home.

All right, he told himself. Leave it alone.

Certainly, Mr. Ambassador, he thought to himself in a mocking voice. Oh, but of course. You just sit there. Wallow. Have a good time. Don't worry about the men and women who died last night because you're getting soft.

Hawkes squeezed his eyes shut, trying to calm himself. It did not work.

No, no—I mean it, his mind continued. Don't give them a second thought. Or the fact that since you're still alive, whoever did this will probably be back. Don't worry about that, either. Just tell me one thing . . .

His body began to shake as the cynical side of him asked, Shall we have Disraeli buried, or just fed to the hogs?

"Shut up!" Hawkes screamed aloud, his body pulsing with rage. The ambassador slammed his fist against the arm of his chair— once, once again. The third blow shattered it, sending splinters deep into the edge of his palm. Cook came back out and stared as blood began to drip from his hand.

She was a short woman, standing no taller than five feet three. In her flats, her brow was barely higher than Hawkes's, even though he was still seated. Lowering her graying head a fraction to meet his eyes, she said, "That's what happens to men who don't eat. First they starts off by talkin' to themselves. Then they graduate to hurtin' themselves."

"Cookie, please . . ."

"Not you, though. You not one to beat around the bush."

"Cook—"

"Nooooo, sir. Unn-unh. You gettin' it all out of the way in just one shot. That's why you such an important man. 'Cause you know how to get things done."

Hawkes looked up at the old woman. She had fed him, as well as most of his staff and workers, for the last seventeen years. Ed Keller said once that she hadn't actually been born—that she had been cut from raw pig iron and brought to life by a lightning storm. She had taken it as a compliment.

Walking across the porch, hard and stiff, her tight face seeming more forged than human, she said, "Now I'm tellin' you, you've had enough time in that chair, playin' old man. You get up and get in that house and start figurin' out what happened here and start doin' somethin' about it."

"Why?"

"Damn you! Damn you for askin' and damn you for even needin' to ask. Who you think you are you can just go and give up like some nobody?"

"I am nobody."

"I believe you," she snorted, mad and indignant. Standing her ground, she reminded him, "But it's a big world out there. A lot of folks you still got conned. A lot of people in this world are stupid— they still think you care about doing the right thing."

Hawkes's head snapped around. His eyes crackling, he snarled, "I'm nobody special. I've never been any more than just another guy doing his job. I didn't ask for people to turn me into some kind of folk hero."

"Too bad," she answered him. "Everybody's got somethin' to live with. That's part of yours." Turning on her heel, the short woman marched back to the kitchen door. Holding it open, she turned her head enough to see Hawkes.

"Now, you goin' get in here . . . let me see to that hand of yours and feed you, or should I just find Ed and tell him to dig another hole so you can crawl in it?"

Hawkes held his place for a long moment. He was so tired. All he had wanted was to be left alone. He had done his duty all his life. When was it supposed to end?

He had done his job in the service, in the corps . . . Always. All it had earned him was a collection of enemies. He had done the right thing in Australia and effectively ended his career. He had done the right thing and gone to Washington to take his medicine, and now they sought to punish him by sending him to Mars.

Mars, he thought. You could send a dozen other people there, Mick—people who really know and care about the issues—who could do the job ten times better than I could. The only reason you want to send me is because you know how much I'd hate being there.

Benton Hawkes loved his world, his father's ranch and all the forests and fields and streams it contained. He had never even been to the Skyhook site, let alone the Moon or beyond. He had no desire to see any of it. Cruising in spaceships, charting asteroids, survey-ing unknown worlds—for him, none of it could compare to the simple pleasure of saddling up and riding out for a day in the woods.

And Mick Carri knows it.

But he also knew that Cook was right. Whoever had tried to kill him would try again. He stood slowly, pushing himself up out of his chair as if it were a grave. He looked around him as he did so. His keen eye took in the charred buildings, noted the smoke hanging in the air, the broken ground and trees and windows showing the lines of fire both sides had hurled at each other. The dusty outlines that marked where his people had fallen after they had been shot down.

And it'll happen again, he thought. The anger he had been denying, keeping capped off, finally broke through. As he walked toward Cook, a voice hissed in his head. Someone wants us to do or not do something. This all is just their way of saying "please."

As he reached the short woman holding open the kitchen door, Hawkes walked past her, saying, "Well, you want to get this hand looked at . . . stop standing around."

"What . . . ?"

"You gone deaf on me, old woman? Get in here and fix me up. Get Ed in here, too. And whoever's in charge of the official investigation."

"Now?"

"Yes, now. And get that stove going. I want a steak. Pan fried. Medium rare—in burnt grease gravy with mushrooms and onions."

"I know how to cook for you," answered the woman with a trace of indignation.

Hawkes continued on into the kitchen as if he had not heard her. Cook followed along, her pocket communicator already in hand. Keller and the local sheriff were in the kitchen before she had finished breaking out the first-aid kit. While she used the tweezers on the ambassador's hand, he told his foreman, "We're going to need some meat for tonight. I want you to get the boys over to the pen, pick out a good-sized hog, and get the spit ready."

"Don't need to, boss. We got three freezers full ri—" Keller stopped in mid-word. The look in Hawkes's eye reminded him that the ambassador knew what he wanted—at all times. Chastened, he said, "Um, ah, I mean . . . what, what time did you want it ready? To eat, I mean."

"Sundown."

"That's cuttin' it close, boss."

"Then get started."

Keller flashed Cook a look, wondering if the fire he sensed raging through Hawkes signified what he thought—hoped—it did. She
continued to dig at the wood embedded in the ambassador's hand,
pulling out one broken sliver after another. However, she took the
split second necessary to fill her eyes with the message that
Hawkes was indeed sending, and that Keller had better get about
doing what their boss wanted done.

The foreman's face broke out in a nervous smile. As he headed
out the back door, shouting orders, Cook smiled as well.

"So, Sheriff," Hawkes asked, trying to ignore the pain tearing
through his hand, "what do you know so far?"

Sheriff Bob Morgan was a middle-aged man with thinning, salt-
and-pepper hair. Pulling at his neatly trimmed beard, he answered,
"Mr. Ambassador, we got some facts, and we got some hunches,
and we got some stuff we've turned upside down and brought back
right side up that we can't make heads or tails of." Uncrossing his
arms from off his chest, he hooked his thumbs in his pants pockets
and then asked, "What order you want it in?"

"However it comes to mind." Hawkes winced as the last splinter
was pulled free from his hand. Cook poured more antiseptic into
the wound. Stinging white foam bubbled to the surface. As she
began to wrap it, the ambassador asked, "Sheriff, have you eaten?"

"I could share a plate, thank you."

"Cook, make that two steaks. And clear this table and get us a
couple of work screens. And bring the ranch layout file."

"Yes, sir," she answered. She pulled the last loop of bandage
extra tight. A little pressure to keep his hand throbbing, to give him
a bit of pain to chew on.

Gathering up the first-aid kit, she removed it from the table and
headed off to start filling the ambassador's other requests. As she
left the kitchen, her smile grew thin and mean. Hawkes was eating
and giving orders again. Someone was going to get their ass kicked.

"And, Cook, put on some more coffee when you get back."

"I only got two hands," she snarled over her shoulder. Her eyes twinkled as she headed back for the kitchen with the electronic work screens. She looked at Hawkes and Morgan, bent over the sheriff's hand recorder, studying his notes. She could see the heat coming off the ambassador—the tension in his shoulders, the hate growing in his eyes.

Oh yeah, she thought, satisfied. Somebody goin' get their ass kicked, all right. Real good.

Turning to her stove, she pulled out her biggest black-bottom skillet. Turning the heat up high, she threw a large margarine cube into it. Then she pulled out two steaks and started trimming the fat from them. As she spread the pieces out in the skillet, their juice began to merge with the margarine, all of it burning into a black grease.

Watching the pieces of fat shrivel into hard, brittle nuggets, she smiled again. Yeah. Real *damn* good.

9

The second half of the day passed quickly for Hawkes. He and the sheriff coordinated all the information found by both their teams. Unfortunately, none of it added up to anything that gave them either a solid conclusion or course of action.

Not yet, anyway, thought Hawkes, keeping himself under control. It will, though. It will.

So far, they had discovered a lot. Stine had managed to sabotage their home defenses by concentrating his efforts in only one area. Just thinking of the nearly fatal mistake he had made—harboring the traitor in his own home—made Hawkes's blood boil, but he contained himself. The sheriff had listed the aide's death as just a part of the slaughter, turning a blind eye to whose hand had been responsible for that part of the slaughter.

The damage Stine had done to their defenses had been purposely minimal. He had opened only a thin-line breach in the radar and motion-detection fields, but it was all the invaders had needed. They had hard-marched in, carrying with them everything they needed.

No vehicles had been discovered left behind at their entry point, indicating that the invaders had been dropped off. The ambassador's defense network had also registered entry into the ranch's airspace during the attack period. Most likely a pickup craft coming for the attackers. When it received no landing signal from any of the invaders it must have simply left.

That bit of information alone clued Hawkes to the fact that his enemies had known all their people were eliminated as early as the night before. The discovery of Morte chips built into the armor of the dead showed him that not only had their unseen foes known their troops were captured, they had known that they all were dead—even at what moment they had died. The chip signals had all been sent in the general direction of the intruding aircraft.

His people had tried to get a fix on the craft after it had exited Hawkes's airspace, but its pilot had looped out of the mountains to the south, into a several-hundred-square-mile area where no one had any tracking devices in operation. They could have gone off in any direction. Another dead end.

Tracing weapons, ammunition, body armor, uniforms: they discovered a great deal of information, none of which did them any good. All of the recovered equipment and uniforms were standard gear—nothing specialized, all of it bought on the black market. No matter what their sources were, they all traced back to stolen or smuggled points of origin.

Someone out there is pretty good at covering his tracks, thought Hawkes. Too good. There has to be something they missed, though. And we'll find it.

Body identification searches did not do them any good, either. Every one of the intruders turned up as having been officially listed dead years earlier.

The sheriff joked that time had finally caught up with them, but the discovery kept them from getting any further. Although they were able to identify all of the invaders, they could find no common thread to any three of them. Some pairs had known each other in the past, but not in a way that pointed any definite fingers toward a possible organization point for the attack.

The invaders had been of all sorts: Common labor pool, mostly ex-military from more than one country. Two electricians, several with bio-growth backgrounds. All skilled workers, but no geniuses. No one who would ever be missed.

Nor had they been for almost three years. One by one, each of them had disappeared from all the official records Hawkes's reach could access. The Earth records for more than 150 nations, those from Skyhook, Lunar Colony, and from Mars showed no mention of the men and women who had tried to kill him the night before after their "termination" dates.

They had also focused on Stine, but had no greater luck there. Stine was not cut from the same fold. He had still been officially alive the day before. But once investigated, his background showed no sinister connections, either: no hidden bank accounts, no large withdrawals that might show a pattern of blackmail—nothing.

All they discovered was that he was a loyal junior member of the nation's diplomatic corps. He was effectively clean—had no trails leading from him to anyone he should not have known. Nothing hooked him to Deutcher, to the Martian unions, or to their managers, either. Not to Senator Carri or Clean Mountain Enterprises . . . not to anyone.

Which, of course, is why whoever did this picked him.

Hawkes pushed his chair away from the table with a weary gesture. Sheriff Morgan did the same. As the sheriff got up and crossed the room to the stove, the ambassador thought, You've been set up real good this time. Somebody wants us out of the way—someone we can't identify, someone we can't even assign a reason to.

Morgan turned back from the stove. He held the coffeepot up in the air, holding it at an angle and tilting his head to ask Hawkes if he wanted another cup. The ambassador shook his head. After the sheriff had filled his own mug, he said, "That's about it. We've drug this thing around the yard about as many times as it's going to go."

"I know."

"And . . . I hate to mention it, but pretty soon I'm going to have to tell some more people about this. You being the target— that makes it federal all by itself. World court's going to want a piece of things, too. Media—they'll be trying to fry me for sitting on top of things." He took a long sip of his coffee, more to give Hawkes time to think than anything else.

"You're still an important enough guy that I can excuse a delay for a while," Morgan offered. "They can't lean on me too much, seeing that I've got your privacy request. Can't hold them off much longer, though. Especially the feds."

Hawkes rubbed at his eyes, breaking up the tightness pulling at them. He stared at the table for a moment, then looked up, sticking his hands into his vest's side pockets as he asked,

"How long until we get the autopsy reports?"

"Those should start coming in anytime. Why? You got some sort of hunch going?"

"No," Hawkes admitted wearily. "Just grasping at straws." The ambassador paused for a moment, then admitted to at least temporary defeat. "You go ahead and send out what word you have to. Try and tight-band it, though. I don't want the board flooding with reporters any sooner than it has to."

The sheriff moved off to broadcast the report items he had instructed one of his deputies to prepare hours earlier. After he was gone, Hawkes stood up as well. He moved around the kitchen, stretching his arms out, breaking apart the knots in his back. Finally, he stopped at the sink, splashed some water on his face, and went outside.

The sun had started to disappear almost an hour earlier. Heading for the barbecue pit, Hawkes played the night before over in his mind as he had a hundred times already. Nothing he could remember offered him any more clues.

He could see that his people had done a good job throughout the day. Much of the damage from the attack had been minimized, covered up in one way or another. The sight did not cheer him, however. As the hours dragged on, whenever he had come across anything that might have brightened his mood, he remembered Disraeli. The faithful hound's final moments, his last cry, all of it came rushing back to the ambassador with a frightening clarity.

Walking up toward the barbecue pit, he joined his workers who were not on guard duty. It seemed like a thin handful. Too many had died the night before. Too many people had perished, all of them innocent of any crime except for being employees of Benton Hawkes. The thought stirred rage within him. Bad memories slid to the surface, but he violently shoved them back down.

No, he told himself. *No.* These deaths aren't my fault. Not these. Don't lay this at my feet. I backed off. I left the world and drew my line in the sand. But that wasn't good enough for somebody.

Hawkes moved up to the edge of the fire pit, where nearly two hundred pounds of pork stood by the automatic spit, which had already been set up. The four-yard circle of hot coals sent out a searing wall of heat, keeping everyone back. All of the extra fat had long since bubbled to the surface and dripped away from the freshly slaughtered hog. The roast was as ready as it was going to get, filling the air with the thick aroma of juicy, heavy meat.

"Nice job," Hawkes told his foreman. Then he turned around to the crowd. He held himself rigid for just a moment, then said quietly, "Everyone here knows what happened. We lived and our friends died. Pure and simple. Is that where it ends? No. I don't think so. Not anymore."

The ambassador wiped at his brow. Even several yards from the fire, the heat was still intense enough to be felt.

"I thought I was out of things. That I was just going to retire and take it easy. Somebody else seems to think differently, though. Somebody else didn't want that. Why? I don't know. What they hoped to accomplish—well, I don't know that, either. But I'm going to find out. And we're going to have justice, one way or the other. You mark my words."

Those gathered cheered, their cries spreading far enough to be heard by those on outpost duty. Before the whooping and hollering could die down totally, however, Hawkes spotted the sheriff running toward the pit. Stepping away from the assembly to meet him, the ambassador asked, "Bob . . . what is it?"

"Autopsy reports started coming in. Thought you'd want to see some of these figures."

Hawkes took the printouts from Morgan. He scanned the entries: reticulocyte counts, red blood cell fragility figures, plasma volume, blood and urine electrolytes, protein counts, glucose levels, heart size, bone strength, calcium levels, cardiac output capabilities . . .

"See anything interesting?" asked the sheriff.

"These people . . . it looks like they've all been off-world." Hawkes looked at Morgan, then back to the pages. Eyeing the figures more closely, he asked, "They have, haven't they?" When Morgan merely nodded, the ambassador asked, "How long? What are the estimates on how long they've been gone?"

"Funny, I thought you might want to know that. I told them to check it out. Lab balanced the deterioration levels against a few factors. They said that, you know, you spend a week on a ship, that's as bad as two months on the Moon. Gravity differences and all. But they were able to measure the effects here against a varying timetable, and . . ."

"And . . . ?"

"They figure the corpses all had to have spent the last three years on Mars." Morgan paused, gave the information a moment to sink in. After he could see that it had all sunk in, he added, "They give it a plus ninety-nine that none of them have been back on Earth more than two or three weeks, tops."

Hawkes tried to contain his anger, but could not. Slowly, he began to shake. Fingers, hands, shoulders—the rage bubbling within him for so long finally took over completely, filling him. He hurled the printouts toward the fire. The pages burst into flames before they could even touch down on the coals. And then, without thought or reason, Benton Hawkes turned and followed them.

Marching across the open pit to the roasting pig, he could hear the leather of his boots sizzling. Heat ran up his legs, through his clothing, threatening to set them both on fire. Grabbing the blackened carcass, Hawkes jammed his face down into the meat then jerked his head back, pulling away a huge bite of flesh in a long strip. As he turned back to the others—chewing, swallowing, his face slick with grease—he thought, *Mars.*

Looking up into the sky, he walked back out of the pit. His boots hissed as they touched the cool ground outside the ring of fire. Downing the last chunk of meat, he felt his anger sliding away, being replaced by something colder—harder. Feeling the normally warm night air suddenly chilling his body, one word filled his mind: *Mars.*

Walking away from the pit, he left the sheriff, Celdosso, Keller, Cook, and everyone else behind. He had to. Life had proved to him again that wherever he walked, he had to go alone.

And now, he thought, he was going to Mars.

Heaven help whoever he found there.

10

Hawkes sat at the desk in his stateroom aboard the U.S.S. *Bull-dog*. He had pinned his usual travel picture of Disraeli up over the work area. The heavily armed merchant liner had left Lunar City three solar days previously. She had roughly eight days left in her voyage to Mars—eight more than the ambassador cared for.

After he had determined that he needed to head off-world to get to the bottom of his troubles, he had snapped instantly into action. Senator Carri had been alerted to Hawkes's acceptance of the Martian posting after the ambassador was already en route to Skyhook. If he did have active enemies in Washington, Hawkes wanted to leave them as little open time as possible within which they could act.

After a life in the corps, the ambassador knew what to take and how to pack it quickly. Twelve complete changes of clothing, color-matched sets appropriate for whatever different moods he might need to set. Dress suit, of course, formal boots, sword and scabbard, toilet bag, gross pack of beef jerky—everything was bagged in less than ten minutes.

A half hour after he had walked into the pit fire, he was in his 4 × 4 with Keller, headed for town in the same clothes he had been wearing for the past two days. The drive down the mountain in the dark was a long, slow process. The foreman commented several times on the fact that Hawkes had not changed, and the relative closeness of their quarters. The ambassador just smiled and ignored him.

Hawkes had other things on his mind. As they made their way to town, he used the trip both to make his travel arrangements and to go over what his foreman should be doing while he was gone. Not only did Keller have to run the ranch, as usual, but he had to do it with fewer hands. He also had to keep a wary eye on their friends at Clean Mountain Enterprises. As Hawkes told him at the airport, "Get me any information the sheriff or the feds come across. Whatever maneuvers CME tries, I want word on it at once. They're not taking our mountain, Ed."

"Not without a fight, anyways," the grizzled older man agreed.

The two shook hands on the runway. It was an awkward moment for them both. They had said good-bye to each other a thousand times in the past. None of the previous farewells had had the sense of finality that this one did, however. Finally, Keller stepped back toward the 4 × 4, announcing, "This is gettin' silly, boss. Like we was turnin' inta a pair of ol' women or sumthin'." Hawkes nodded, then stepped up into the small chartered jet waiting to carry him to the other side of the world.

"I'll be back, Ed," he told his old friend. Then, before either of them could say another word, he ducked his head and entered the jet. Seconds later, he was in the air. Once he was over the Pacific he put his call through to Washington, getting Mick Carri out of bed.

The senator had told him the Skyhook was booked weeks in advance. Hawkes had answered that if there was no room found for him by the time he arrived, he would make a press announcement that the American Senate was blocking his departure for Mars. By the time the ambassador landed in the Maldives, room had been found.

He spent the daylong ride to the synchronous orbiting elevator platform sleeping. Arriving rested with all his anger safely in check, he had exited onto the platform demanding instantaneous passage to Lunar City. He was told that nothing was leaving for three days.

"Nothing?" he had asked, yet with no trace of a question in his tone. "I thought there was constant traffic between here and the Moon. All the time. Every day."

"Yes, sir, Mr. Ambassador," the lieutenant posted to handle him had countered. "But it's mostly cargo flights. Not much for carrying passengers."

"Are there pilots? Crew?"

"Of course, yes. But . . ."

"Then find me some room on a ship and get me off this platform in fifteen minutes or be prepared to face a board of inquiry." When the man hesitated, Hawkes fixed him with a devastating stare and snapped, "My friend, someone's trying to keep me from getting to Mars. Now, my plan is to see to it that everyone involved ends up behind bars. You want to have to prove you're not one of them . . . you keep standing there."

In twelve minutes Hawkes was aboard a tug heading out with a load of empty sponge/mush barges ready to be strung back to the Lunar Colony for transfer back to Mars. Hawkes gave the lieutenant his compliments and boarded the old force beamer. Before he had his bags stored he asked the tug's captain what her best time ever to the Moon was—then offered her a thousand-unit bribe to break that record by an hour.

"When would you like to start marking time, Mr. Ambassador?"

"I marked time the second I came through the outside hatch," Hawkes had answered.

"Ah-ha. And who, exactly," asked the captain, taking a backward step, "would be paying any fines we might incur?"

"A diplomatic ship has no speed restrictions."

"Oh, then," answered the captain, turning to the nearest hand link to her bridge, "you won't mind if we skip a few of the usual formalities?"

Hawkes shook his head and smiled as widely as the captain. Eight and three quarters of an hour later, they were in lunar orbit. The captain was a thousand units richer and Hawkes was off demanding passage on the next ship to Mars. That ship turned out to be the *Bulldog*. It was a former warship, bought from the military when the newer Galvan engines had made everything else obsolete.

The Galvans could not go appreciably faster than the old ships, but they could turn a vessel much more quickly. The combat application of the new engines was readily apparent to all involved. Old navy vessels practically flooded the spaceway marketplaces several years after the Galvans' introduction.

The *Bulldog* had been converted into a merchanteer, one that moved both freight and passengers. Four other similar ships were berthed at the Moon at the same time, but the *Bulldog* was the first one slated to leave, and thus the only one Hawkes had been interested in. A series of additional, well-placed bribes got the 120,000-ton liner moving a half day early.

And now, Hawkes thought, sitting back in his cabin's only chair during the breakaway from the moon, all there's left to do is wait.

A knock on his door brought him a surprise. It was a lighter rapping than he would have expected from the captain or any of his crew. Deferential. Curious, he called for the unseen knocker to enter. She did.

"Ambassador . . . I almost didn't make it."

"What a shame," answered Hawkes. The young woman was tall, shapely, and unknown to him. She had dark hair cut short and eyes a shade of green that normally would have made him think the word *delightful*. Staring at the woman then, however, the only words that came to his mind were, "Why would I care?"

"I'm Dina Martel," she told him, a trifle flustered by his question. When he did not respond, she continued on in a questioning voice. "The corps sent me . . . I'm your aide for this mission."

Hawkes's eyes flashed for a split second. It was a slip—a break in his usual self-control—one she noticed. His mask back in place, he told her pleasantly, "I wasn't aware I needed an aide on this trip."

"Sir . . . ?"

"What about Daniel Stine?" he asked, curious to hear her answer, to see what she knew and what she did not. Or at least, what she would admit to knowing. "He's my assigned right arm these days. Why would you be sent to replace him?"

Martel's reaction was confusion. Somewhat flustered, she told Hawkes, "Sir, I was informed Mr. Stine was dead."

"Hmmm, indeed. Well, news does travel fast in this modern age. So, whose idea was it to replace him so quickly?"

"I don't know, sir—not exactly. Someone in the State Department, I would imagine."

"Oh, right," he said with a cold smile. "Who else?"

Hawkes had then dismissed the woman to go and find her quarters, telling her he would bring her up to speed later. That had been three days earlier. Since that time he had not brought her anywhere. After their first meeting, the ambassador had managed to avoid her at every turn.

Oh, he's polite about it, Martel thought, far too polite. I'm being kept at arm's length, and if it keeps up I'm going to get damn tired of it.

It did indeed "keep up." On the third day, Dina Martel had had enough.

"Come in," said Hawkes to whoever was banging on his stateroom door. As he saw the young woman enter, he said, "Why, hello. How are you enjoying the cruise?"

"I'm not, Ambassador. It's got me going in too many circles."

"I believe this ship is on an elliptical approach, Martel. Curved a bit, but no circles."

"There's something that has me going around in circles on this ship," she countered. "You wouldn't have any guesses as to what that might be, would you . . . sir?"

"None I'd care to offer," he told her. "No."

The young woman stood still for a second, pulling her strength together, rejecting her anger. When the moment had passed, she stepped into Hawkes's stateroom and asked, "Then could you please tell me what the problem is?"

"Problem, Martel? What problem?"

"The problem with me," she explained. "The reason you don't want to use me."

"I don't have any need of you. I wasn't expecting an aide on this trip—didn't plan on having someone underfoot. I've already taken care of everything. But if something comes up—if I need a battery recharged, a few files analyzed, or something—I'll call you right away. I promise."

Martel did not move. Hawkes watched her. He had reviewed her credentials. She had been with the corps for eight years. Had a clean, somewhat distinguished if uneventful record. Her schooling put her in the top of her class. She had brains to match her looks.

Stine had been handsome, too, he remembered.

Going cold inside, Hawkes remembered Daniel Stine's record. It glowed compared to hers. More years of service, better achievements—tops at everything. And someone had gotten to him, paid him, bribed him, scared him . . . did something to him or for him that had made him plant bombs, sabotage equipment, and lead murderers into Hawkes's home.

The ambassador's eyes locked onto the woman in his doorway. Barely able to keep his jaw from shaking, he said, "You want a job, you want something to do to pass time on the voyage, I'll give you a job. You tell me what's going on—who's doing what to get what. Find the names and dates and proofs I need to nail people to the wall."

"Which people, sir?"

"Which ones?" sneered Hawkes. "The ones who don't want me to go to Mars. Or maybe who do want me to go to Mars. The ones who want to steal my land. The ones who think I've gotten too popular, who want me out of the way because they're tired of the fact that I can usually cut through the crap."

The ambassador stepped away from his desk, moving across the cabin. Martel held her ground, though every instinct she had was urging her to back up. His eyes still riveted to hers, Hawkes snarled, "You figure all that out, then you tell me who it was that had my home attacked—who it is that's responsible for killing seven members of my staff . . . burning my home down . . . all the rest of it. You find out who sent the people who did all that. All right? You want a job, there's your job."

"Ah, okay . . . certainly, sir. If I might . . ."

Hawkes paid no attention to the words the young woman was saying. Closing in on her, backing her the rest of the way to the door with his presence, he snapped, "And I'll give you a little message to go with it: This whole business—the problems between the Martian Colony's provisional government . . . them and their Earth corpor/national sponsors and the unions forming up there and anyone else—all of it . . . I don't care."

The woman swallowed. It was a difficult gesture. Hawkes had rattled her severely. Pulling herself together, she asked, "You don't care about . . . about . . . which aspects, sir?"

"Any of it, Martel. Any of it. I'm going to Mars to find out who tried to kill me. Solving their petty problems seems to be the only way I can get my hands around the throat of the son of a bitch who killed my dog."

"But, Ambassador"—her voice came out weak and strained—"won't you still need someone to assist you . . . do your day-to-day . . . ah, everything?"

Hawkes pulled back a few inches, giving the woman a bit of room. Feeling the smallest bit of sympathy for her, remembering that he did not know if she was a replacement for Stine in any dark sense, he asked, "How is it you were assigned to serve as aide for me, Martel?"

The woman was caught off guard by his shift in tactics. She stumbled for a split second, then told him, "I happened to be on the Indian subcontinent when word came in that you were headed for the Martian Colony and that you were traveling unescorted. I was told to drop everything and to get to the Skyhook and rendezvous with you at Lunar."

"And why you?"

"Because I was the closest person to the Skyhook. They said that you were moving fast and that I would just have time to make it if I left immediately."

"So you just dropped your current assignment and jetted right down." The woman turned her eyes away for a moment.

"I wasn't on assignment, sir."

"Oh. You just happened to be in India . . ."

"I was on my honeymoon—*sir*," she snapped, suddenly tired of whatever game was being played.

"But you were willing to follow the call of duty—even then. How noble of you."

Martel's eyes opened wider. An almost overwhelming urge to strike back at the ambassador roared through her. Catching hold of herself, however, she said, "No, sir. It was not so noble. It's true that I'd like to see the Mars difficulties solved simply because the possibility of doing that kind of work is why I joined the corps in the first place."

More composed, fire building behind her own eyes, she spat, "But in this case, when I was told Benton Hawkes had accepted the Martian posting after all, and that I was supposed to accompany him. . . . You can imagine the thrill. What a coup—Mars and Hawkes on the same plate. Quite a feather in my cap, I thought. Doing the work of a lifetime at the side of a lifelong hero. Now there, I told my husband, was a wedding present."

Smoothing imaginary creases from her skirt and jacket, the woman continued, telling Hawkes, "I left with the clothes on my back. I rode in a car with mining replacement workers—standing room only. Eighteen hours on my feet with less than charming company. But that was okay. I had pulled the prize plum—Martian duty with Benton Hawkes. I missed you at the platform. The next ship out to the Moon was a troopship . . . which didn't leave for a half a day. But there was an asteroid tramper that was making a fuel stop on the Moon. Oh, yes, he was happy to get me there. Happy as a clam."

Hawkes put up his hand, cutting the woman off.

Well, he thought, judging the barely controlled passion in her voice, she's either innocent or a hell of an actress. Ready to bet your life on being able to guess which?

"Martel, you tell a sad story very well. Now tell me something else: Do you know *why* I need an aide? Do you know who you're replacing? Or why?"

"The news didn't get to me until I was able to do a message pickup on the Moon. I was told your last aide was killed."

"Do you know why? Or how?"

"No, sir . . . the memo didn't go into any detail."

"Oh, no? Pity," said Hawkes, making no attempt to mask his sarcasm. "Well, let me tell you. The last aide the corps appointed for me turned out to be a traitor. To me, to the Earth, I'm not sure which, exactly. But he allowed a party of murderers entry to my home and helped them try to kill me."

The woman's eyes went wide again. Hawkes noted the reaction, but he also knew it didn't really tell him anything. She could be shocked out of genuine surprise, or because she did not expect him to know Stine was a traitor.

"And, you ask, how did he die? I shot him myself."

"I see, sir," answered the woman, visibly shaken.

"Good," responded Hawkes coldly. Turning his back on the woman, he said, "So, as you now can easily understand, I'm just trying to keep one of us from getting shot in the back."

Before she could stop herself, the young woman asked, "Is that where you shot Stine?"

Hawkes's head jerked imperceptibly. Then, after a moment's pause, he smiled. He did not know if he could trust her, but he had to admit, he liked her spirit. Deciding to give the woman a chance to prove herself, he told her, "Let's just say I hit what I aimed for.

But, all that aside—what do you think? Would you like to turn around when we reach Mars and head back to your husband? I could invoke clause 34.Y: with one aide dead, I can just deem it too dangerous for any unnecessary personnel."

"I understand that you don't have any need for me—that you don't trust me or like me—"

"No, no. I never said I didn't like you."

"I guess that's something, isn't it?" she asked. Continuing on, she said, "Unless you have strenuous objections, sir, I would like to stay on. After all," she added, backing through the doorway, "you just might need those files analyzed, or some batteries charged."

Martel disappeared out into the hall, closing the door behind her. After she was gone, Hawkes stared at the door for a long while. Then, finally, he turned away, crossing back to his desk.

Maybe, he thought. Maybe.

Then he looked at the old picture of Disraeli he had posted over the desk, felt his hands tremble, and returned to his work.

11

The trip was almost over. The *Bulldog* was less than three days out from Mars. Of course, everyone on board was still buzzing over traveling with the famous Benton Hawkes. Martel had not helped the situation any, doing everything she could to pull him out among the other passengers. The ambassador had gritted his teeth and made most of the appearances under the heading of "playing the game." He did not like it, however.

Hawkes suffered through, trying to remain as pleasant as he could. Small talk with the business types, avoiding strategy discussions with the labor negotiators headed toward the same table he was, nodding his head as technicians spouted reams of jargon . . . etc., etc.

Normally it was all grist for the mill. But not this time. Hawkes had fallen into the worst place any diplomat could land: for the first time in his career he was caught in a situation he could not help but take personally. He tried to maintain a detached perspective, but he could manage to do so for only increasingly shorter stretches.

He found his nerves growing frayed. Rather than let them show, however, long before each affair ended, Hawkes simply managed to find some pretense that would allow him to retreat back to his stateroom. Staring into his mirror, Hawkes worked on his tie, thinking, I should just stay here . . . not even bother to go. Cut out the middle man. Avoid having to look for an excuse by just taking the damn tie off and going to sleep.

Or do another set of sit-ups or push-ups. Space travel kills tone, he reminded himself. Much better for us than more ship stores' processed pâté.

Well, then again, he reminded himself, you never know. The clue we're looking for might be out there in the dining room somewhere, just waiting to fall off some fumble-minded fool's tongue.

Oh sure, he chided himself, that's always been the caliber of people we get to deal with . . . fumble-minded fools.

Finishing with his tie, the ambassador silenced his mind, tired of the endless debating of his possible next moves. Whatever is going to happen is what is going to happen. So shut up and just get going, all right?

Stepping back from his mirror, he dropped his hands to his sides and inspected his look for the evening. Black three-piece, braid-and-ribbon fruit salad in place, tie straight, boots clean, creases sharp . . . "Ready enough, I guess," he sighed.

That night's function was dinner at the captain's table. Hawkes did not want to attend, but a lifetime of doing things he did not want to—with a smile on his face, no less—got him washed and shaved and into his formal suit. As he inspected himself in the mirror, he nodded with weary resignation. He hated everything about being on the *Bulldog*—about being in space—everything except the fact that being there was getting him closer to the answers he wanted. Trying to shove aside his hate, he buckled on his ambassadorial sword, thinking, Even still remember how to use one of these?

His palm around the grip, Hawkes grinned at himself in the mirror, daring himself to withdraw the blade. Taking the challenge, he pulled the weapon from its scabbard with one quick motion.

His hand extended the blade automatically, sweeping the air in front of him, extending his field of safety. His eye sighted along the blade's fuller groove, his mind using the image to replay past sparring partners for him. He lunged, stepped back, lunged again. Feeling his blood rush, he made a sweeping cut across the room, doubled back before an enemy could take advantage, then filled the air with a series of carving figure eights.

Then, in full extension, he stopped short. Holding himself and the blade rigid, he felt age in the muscles such activity called into play, muscles not called upon for these things in too long. The ambassador dropped his pose and then repeated the set of movements. He felt heat under his collar. His breath came in larger gulps.

Stopping abruptly, Hawkes's fingers found the end of his scabbard. Bringing his sword hand up past his head, he reversed the weapon's direction and then thrust it back into its usual home. Turning to the mirror again, he smiled to himself, then asked, "All right by you? Good enough?"

"Good enough," he answered himself. His mirror image assumed a sarcastic look, then added, "For an old man with no dog."

Hawkes's face darkened. Suddenly he hated the thought of the dinner again, of leaving his room, of doing anything except finding out who had set him up.

Taking one last look into the mirror, he told himself, "You know, I don't see you being much of a comfort to me in my old age."

And then he simply turned and left the room, giving his reflection no chance to retaliate.

Well, thought Hawkes, looking around the table, I've been to worse functions in my time.

"Okay, Mr. Ambassador, let's hear it. How does our table here on the *Bulldog* stack up?"

"Captain," Hawkes answered, "I'm a bit of a culinary dabbler myself, so I'm always willing to take into account every factor for or against a chef."

"Uh-oh," interjected Carl Jarolic, an environmental researcher. "This sounds bad, Captain."

"He's going to tramp you, Captain," joked Pensaval, a cost containment expert headed up to check over some of Red Planet, Inc.'s less productive branches.

"No, no," the ambassador offered. "Quite the contrary. On one of my first excursions around the ship, I inspected the *Bulldog*'s galley from top to bottom. Seeing what our chef was up against, as far as I'm concerned, preparing anything beyond beans and mush down in that hole would take a genius and a saint." Hawkes lifted his glass, giving the captain an honest nod of the head.

"I compliment your kitchen crew, sir." The ambassador took a sip of his drink, then added, "If I didn't have my own genius and saint, I might try to steal yours."

The captain beamed, saluting Hawkes with his glass before taking his own healthy slug. Resting his glass on the table, the captain then said, "I'm glad to find you like the food, Mr. Ambassador. But tell me, what do you think of the trip so far?"

"Tranquil," answered Hawkes diplomatically.

"Is that a euphemism for 'slow'?" asked Glenia Waters, the wife of a Red Planet manager returning from a stay on Earth.

"I guess it could be taken that way," Hawkes admitted with an honest grin.

"I see the ambassador is straining to get to Mars and down to business," said Colin Harrod, one of the *Bulldog*'s officers.

Tracey Sherman, another officer at the table, asked, "What do you think, Mr. Ambassador? Does it look as if you'll be able to settle this quickly?"

"You want my honest answer, Mr. Sherman—or the one that would look best in print?"

"Oh, please," interjected Jarolic, "favor us with a bit of honesty. Fresh air is so rare in space."

Hawkes nodded and gave the researcher a thin smile while everyone else laughed politely. Having spent no small amount of time during the trip so far going over the facts as they were known to Washington, the ambassador summed up how he felt, telling the assembly, "No, Mr. Sherman, Mr. Jarolic . . . I don't think a quick settlement is possible."

"Why not?" asked the captain.

"I'm sure the facts have shown Mr. Hawkes that the workers are too unreasonable to be dealt with quickly."

"Actually, Mr. Jarolic," answered the ambassador, a tiny bit taken aback by the man's bitterness, "I've found my information so incomplete that I plan to put a great deal of time into assessing the situation for myself."

The researcher pursed his lips, put off by Hawkes's answer. Before Jarolic could comment, Hawkes added, "To be perfectly honest, I'm not sure I trust much of the data I've received so far. This is a new kind of situation for me. I'm used to having everything at my fingertips. Instantaneous communications. Now I'm working with reports that are weeks old. Weeks. Coming from people whose honesty I can't even begin to gauge . . ."

"Because they're just low-class labor, Mr. Hawkes?"

"Because they're from a culture I've never encountered before. They live on another planet, Mr. Jarolic. And another thing . . ."

Hawkes had been surprised by the environmentalist's attacking statements. He had wanted to answer, but before he could, Waters cut him and everyone else off.

"Oh, now, stop. Stop. I'm going to hear nothing but this kind of talk once I get back home." Staring at the others imploringly, she said, "Dessert is on the way. Everyone has a drink. Let's not get on about business." She gave everyone a moment to turn her words over in their minds, then added, "Let's play a game."

Jarolic smiled. Hawkes held himself from sighing. Martel and the captain shared mixed feelings.

"Let's play Quote."

The crowd reacted with varying degrees of enthusiasm. When Hawkes protested that he did not know the game, everyone agreed that it was easy and fun and that he should try. Martel said, "The rules are very simple, sir."

Hawkes nodded, adding his own commentary: "They always are," he told her. His first reaction was to call it a night, but suddenly, something within him changed. The little voice inside he always trusted told him to stay. His mind thus changed, he said, "All right. Somebody explain these simple rules to me."

"Certainly," Jarolic offered, something in his manner seeming less hostile than before. "We pick a topic—nature, God, taxation—whatever. Then, one of us will throw out the name of a famous person. Let's say the subject is . . . 'the enemy,' and the first name called is Richard Nixon. Everyone then tries to come up with a quote from Nixon on that subject. Whoever comes up with one gets the point and gets to throw out the next name."

" 'Those who hate you don't win unless you hate them—and then you destroy yourself.' " Mrs. Waters beamed at the others. Jarolic recognized the quote and smiled.

Then he put his hand to his brow and nodded his head, saying, "Very good. I'd say you've been practicing."

"Oh, you know, so little to do, so much time to do it in." She turned to Hawkes, telling him in an apologetically explanatory voice, "I have a lot of time to read on Mars."

"I think Mr. Jarolic is applauding your formidable powers of retention," the ambassador retorted pleasantly. "Which certainly have me willing to throw in the towel here and now."

Hawkes feigned rising to leave, but Waters stretched out her hand toward him, begging, "Oh no, please stay. Please try."

"Come on, Ambassador," the captain added. "After all, you can't win them all."

"Well, now there's a bitter truth," answered Hawkes, his eyes narrowing. Deciding that perhaps his little voice was right and that he had stayed in his room a bit too much, he continued, saying, "But I suppose a round or two wouldn't hurt. If you promise to go easy on an old man."

"First topic, diplomats and diplomacy," said Mrs. Waters quickly. When Hawkes made to protest, she said, "Now, Ambassador, you asked us to take it easy on you. How much more generous could we be?"

Hawkes smiled. The woman was somewhat younger than he—he guessed her age to be somewhere in her mid to late forties. She was plump and had worn more jewelry than the night called for, but something within her easy manner and sincerity had touched the ambassador. Raising both his eyebrows to her in mock surrender, he said,

"Well . . . diplomats it is."

"Oliver Herford," said Pensaval immediately.

" 'Diplomacy: lying in state,' " offered the captain.

Everyone at the table applauded politely. Pensaval nodded, conceding the point to the captain. The older man nodded, then threw out a name of his own. "Alexander Woollcott."

" 'Babies in silk hats playing with dynamite,' " Hawkes responded. Again the table applauded. Hawkes shut his eyes for a moment, then said, "Peter Ustinov."

Everyone stared blankly. Sherman scratched at his head as if he had an idea who the person named might be. Hawkes gave them all a hint. "He was an actor from England . . . died about sixty years ago."

" 'A diplomat these days,' " started Martel, haltingly, " 'is nothing more than a headwaiter . . . who's allowed to sit down occasionally.' "

Everyone laughed politely.

"Close enough," the ambassador granted. His aide smiled, then offered a name of her own.

"American president John F. Kennedy."

" 'Let us never negotiate out of fear,' " responded Jarolic, " 'but

let us never fear to negotiate.' " When Martel conceded that the
environmental researcher had taken the point, he smiled and threw
out another name: "Trygve Lie."

Everyone stared blankly except Hawkes. He gave the table a polite handful of seconds, then said, " 'A real diplomat is one who can
cut his neighbor's throat without having his neighbor notice it."

Everyone clapped politely again. Hawkes gave the table the
name James Reston to chew on. Jarolic swallowed the bit, respond-
ing, " 'This is the devilish thing about foreign affairs: they are
foreign and will not always conform to our whims.' " Not even
waiting for acknowledgment that he had gotten the quote correct,
Jarolic gave out another name: "Admiral Bill Kimball."

Not waiting either, the ambassador responded immediately,
" 'He lied, I knew he lied, and he knew I lied. That was diplomacy.' "

Waters gave out a gasp at the speed with which the two men were
playing each other. The rest of the party settled back, seeing the
obvious, changing over from participants to observers. Having
taken the point, Hawkes offered, "Joe Stalin, Soviet dictator during—"

Jarolic cut the ambassador off, answering, " 'Sincere diplomacy
is no more possible than dry water or wooden iron.' " The environmental researcher took a quick breath, then threw out, "Daniele
Vare."

" 'Diplomacy is the art of letting someone have your way.' "

Hawkes watched Jarolic's face as the man granted the ambassador his point. He had known the nasty quotes would have to start
coming sooner or later. The art of diplomacy was not one well
understood by the general public. Like politicians and lawyers,
abuses by the worst members of the profession made everyone
suspect.

But Hawkes was not worried about having to dance around some
outsider's snide attacks. Fencing with loudmouths and bullies was
standard operating procedure for any career corps person. Every

formal dinner managed to produce at least one. Perhaps, thought the ambassador, Jarolic's just this party's designated boor.

As lightly as he wished he could take the game, however, Hawkes had a sneaking suspicion that there was more to it than that. The ambassador had attended too many dinners and battled verbally with far too many opponents to not have a better understanding of such situations. Jarolic seemed openly hostile. The corners of his eyes were too meanly crinkled. His smile, his eyes, his rate of breathing—everything indicated to Hawkes's well-trained mind that the man was on the attack.

Why? wondered the ambassador, staring at Jarolic. What's your problem?

Hawkes nodded politely as the researcher granted the last point to the ambassador. At the same time, one of the captain's officers came up to the table. Immediately Hawkes's attention was stolen away. Although no one else at the table seemed aware of it, there was a tension in this man's approach that no member of the crew had displayed throughout the entire trip.

Everyone waited politely for the captain to receive his message. The others around the table were all curious, of course. Far beyond curious, Hawkes felt himself slipping over into apprehension as he watched the captain's face. The man was trying hard to keep himself from betraying what he was being told. He was not particularly good at it.

It's not internal, thought the ambassador, watching the two men talk in whispers at the other end of the table. This is nothing he and the crew can control. It's external.

Hawkes ran over the possibilities in his mind: communications interference, meteors, a distress call, a comet . . . he knew it was none of those. Watching the captain tighten his face and narrow his eyes, the ambassador's fingers curled around the hilt of his sword.

Pirates, he thought.

"Ladies and gentlemen," said the captain, standing from his

chair, "I'm afraid I'm going to have to ask you to return to your quarters." Moving his head a fraction of an inch to the left, then back to the right, he indicated that his officers were to join him, saying, "Pensaval, Sherman, Harrod, you're all with me."

And then, they all suddenly found themselves on the floor as the first explosion sounded.

12

"**G**oddamnit!" the captain roared, cursing as he fell and hit the floor, and again as he scrambled back to his feet. When his officer had first approached the table, the captain had tried to minimize any panic that might ensue. Now, with the lights flickering and people screaming all about him, his only thought was to get down to tactics. His personal link in his hand before he was standing, he barked, "Swelver! Status—now!"

"We've got a single ship off the port. Distance . . . mark eighty-seven kilometers and closing."

As the captain began to cross the room, he noted a panicked knot of people in front of the door, banging frantically on it and clawing at its controls. Realizing what that had to mean, he stopped instantly, asking, "What the hell'd they hit us with? Flash pulse?"

"Yes, sir," Swelver's voice responded over the hand-link. "Planted it right in front of us. Precision spread. Caught our attention right off."

"Can we hit them back?"

"Sorry, sir. It was a right proper hit. External weapons have been shorted. Their pulse fried about a third of the electrical systems shipwide."

"At least," agreed the captain. Moving across the dining room to an unassuming console in the corner, he said, "People can't get out down here. Rather than waste any time on the door I'm going to plug in command from station D-four."

"Acknowledged, sir. We'll transfer all command control immediately."

While the captain moved off to the auxiliary post, Glenia Waters wailed, "Mr. Ambassador, what's happened? What was that explosion? What's going on?"

Hawkes debated whether he should tell the woman the truth, wondering if she could handle it. Not seeing any real option, he said, "Apparently, we've attracted visitors."

"Pirates?" The woman asked the question with fear measurably thick in her voice.

The ambassador merely moved his eyes to suggest that, yes, this was a possibility. Waters began to reach out to him for support, but Hawkes had other things on his mind. As Martel approached the pair, he pushed his aide to the task of comforting the woman, then moved off toward where the captain and his officers had grouped.

Hawkes knew better than to interrupt a commander at the beginning of a battle. Catching Pensaval's attention, he lowered his voice to ask, "What are we looking at here?"

"Depends on what they want, sir." The ambassador waited. Pensaval continued. "If they wanted this vessel, they should have tried to cripple us in a way that did minimal damage to the ship, but that would have killed all of us. If they were after cargo, any kind of plunder, really . . . same tack."

"Then what went wrong?" questioned Hawkes.

"Don't know, sir. They might have miscalculated."

"I doubt it, Mr. Pensaval," the captain interrupted. As Hawkes rotated his attention, the captain continued, saying, "My people have diagnosed their bow shot. Too neat to be anything but a prelude to boarding. Especially considering their present approach pattern."

"Boarding?" asked Hawkes, already knowing the answer to his next question. "And why do pirates bother to board a ship in space?"

"There are certain prizes they'll fight their way on board for," the captain replied. Trying to ease up to what they both knew he was about to say, he added, "Some cargo is too easily damaged in a killing attack. Deep space piracy also carries heavy penalties. Mass murder is something some of these sons of bitches try to avoid."

"And . . . ?" asked Hawkes.

"And," admitted the captain, "sometimes their goal is kidnapping . . . or target-specific murder. At this time, I would not rule out a direct threat to you. In fact, considering what we're carrying in the way of cargo . . . I would think it almost a certainty."

The captain turned and looked at his board again, reviewing the information being sent to him from the bridge. Bringing his attention back to his ship, he asked his people, "Where was our marine contingent when the lights went out?"

"Most of them were in their quarters, sir. I've already sent them to stations. I took the liberty of diverting one man from each squad down to the approaches to the dining room."

"Good," answered the captain. "Keep to the square. Try and get systems up and get a shot off at that son of a bitch. I assume the fighter bay is shorted out . . ."

"Dordman says it'll be at least fifteen minutes before he can get a ship out in the open, sir," came the thin voice over the hand-link. "And apparently that's going to involve him and his crew pushing one out into open space by hand."

Hawkes watched a thin smile curl one side of the captain's mouth. It told him instantly what kind of person the unseen Dordman must be.

"Relay my wishes for success to Mr. Dordman," ordered the captain. "And from here on, Mr. Swelver, our time being as fractured as it is, I'm giving you free rein to follow your own initiative."

"Thank you, sir," came the thin voice once more. Not bothering to answer, the captain asked,

"What's their ETA?"

"It looks like we have two minutes to contact, sir. Maybe less."

"Then—" But before the captain could continue, the main door to the dining room suddenly surged open. Instantly people began pouring out into the hall, even as the marines, who were assigned to their safety, tried to make their way inside.

Over the ensuing noise, the captain shouted, "Mr. Swelver, counsel Mr. Dordman that I'll be joining him down below. You keep the helm and do what you can about getting us out of this from your end."

"Yes, sir."

Communications were cut. The captain stood away from the auxiliary command console and met the ranking officer approaching. Before the marine could speak, the captain barked out orders for the entire group.

"Thornton, Esposito, you're with me. The rest of you, get these people out of here. Try to avert panic, but keep them moving." Singling out one bulky sergeant, he added, "Wagner, you're with the ambassador."

And then, without another word, the captain was gone. His officers began working with the crowd, clearing the room, trying to keep people moving in a somewhat orderly fashion. As Dina Martel came up alongside them, Hawkes turned from her, asking the sergeant, "So, Mr. Wagner, what do you suggest?"

"If the scum runners are on schedule, I'd say they're already on the ship. Any second now they're gonna breach one door or another."

"Ambassador," said Martel urgently, "shouldn't we be headed below like everyone else?"

"Plenty of time for that," answered Hawkes, suddenly turning on his heel and walking toward the bar. Wagner and Martel followed. Grabbing up an overturned bottle of brandy from the counter, the ambassador said, "Sounds to me like going out into the hall right now is just asking for trouble."

"I'm just a sergeant, sir," answered Wagner. "But I'd say if these nut grinders are actually after you . . ." Hawkes's left eyebrow went up. The sergeant noticed, adding, "News travels fast, sir."

"And rumors faster," agreed the ambassador. "And I'm not one to argue." Lifting the bottle, Hawkes inspected the label, asking, "So what are we going to be facing here?"

"Hard to tell, sir. When they board, they like to move fast. Get your target, get out. You know the drill. Nobody likes to fire off rounds in space; no matter how deep inside a ship you are, you can never tell what you might damage. Boarders come in with pikes, swords, shock sticks . . . maybe a few low-caliber weapons. . . ." The large marine turned his own electronic staff over in his hands. "For the most part it's usually a hand-to-hand operation."

"But what makes you think the ambassador is their target?" asked Martel. "If they wanted to kill him, why not just destroy the ship?"

"Can't trust a deep blast. Single target can always escape in a lifeboat. Awfully hard to track down in deep space. Contract kill needs confirmation." Martel turned away, taken aback somewhat by the marine's cold logic.

Ignoring their conversation, Hawkes asked, "You ever been in one of these fights before?" Without waiting for an answer, Hawkes reached out and righted an overturned glass. Then he caught it and another nearby tumbler in two fingers and dragged them both across the bar. As he filled the first one, Wagner admitted, "No, sir." The ambassador handed him a glass, saying, "Well, me neither." Picking up the other, he clinked it against the marine's, saying, "Here's to our second one, eh?" Wagner smiled, saying, "Aye, sir."

Both men threw back their drinks as a scream pierced the air of the dining room. It came from the hallway, and was followed by a chorus of other shouts. The first had been a death cry, the others merely the panic of the witnesses. Setting his glass on the bar, Hawkes said, "I'd offer to buy you another, Sergeant, but I think the bar is closing."

The marine casually flipped his glass over his shoulder. Hefting his staff, he narrowed his eyes, testing its weight in his hands, and said, "Sir, it's just possible I might have a bottle in my own quarters."

The sound of more screams came to the two men. There was no doubt that people were dying. Martel looked from Hawkes to Wagner. The ambassador's hand dropped to his sword as he said, "Well, then, Mr. Wagner . . . you lead the way. We'll be happy to follow."

Two men in light armor came through the door into the dining room. Both held bloody-edged weapons. As they moved in fast, the marine started to cross the room. Holding his staff in a tight across-the-body defense, he hunkered down into a concealing crouch. Without turning, he said, "I'll pick up this check, sir. You watch my back."

Wagner and the first two pirates clashed. The big marine came out of his crouch less than a yard away from the closest target. Swinging his right foot back, he moved sideways, allowing the pirate to run past him. Then, quickly bringing his staff up behind the man, he made contact at the base of the pirate's skull. The blow loosed a devastating electrical charge into the man's body. The pirate screamed. Spittle flew from his mouth and the air went heavy with the smell of burning ozone as the pirate dropped his weapon and fell to the ground.

The second invader shifted direction to cross in front of Wagner. The marine maintained his stance and snapped his left hand out, driving the other end of his staff into the approaching pirate's face. The invader was lifted off his feet. His face plate, along with his nose and the left side of his skull, shattered. The sergeant had to twist and then jerk his weapon to free it from the man's head.

"Ambassador!"

Hawkes reacted to Martel's shout. Three more pirates had entered the dining room from somewhere behind the bar, and a half dozen more poured in through the front door. Seeing that Wagner was going to have his hands full with his own half dozen, Hawkes left his aide near the bar, and moved forward to block the trio attacking from the rear. He drew the British Pattern sword and held the blade before his face, sizing up his adversaries.

"There's the target," said the middle man, pointing at the ambassador. Hawkes pursed his lips, thinking, Well, that settles that.

The first one to reach him swung for the ambassador's midsection with the blade of his halberd. Hawkes blocked it with the flat of his sword, then, before his opponent could react, ran his hand swiftly along the pole and cut into the man's fingers, shearing three of them away despite the man's reinforced gloves. He immediately broke away, pushing the wounded pirate into the closest of his fellows. Hawkes completed his turn, coming up short in front of the third man—also armed with a sword.

His new opponent favored a western style, a straight blade designed for its ultimate thrusting power. The ambassador's sword had a slight curve, a compromise design meant for both cutting and thrusting. The two men warily circled each other for a moment, then the invader lunged.

Hawkes backpedaled—one, two, three steps. The pirate followed. The ambassador bluffed his enemy again, retreating another two steps. The invader smiled, following once more, sensing an easy target. Hawkes feigned a stumble, trying to act surprised as his back touched the bar. The younger man sighted and lunged. The ambassador parried and returned, letting the pirate run himself through on his blade as he rushed forward. Blood sluiced down along the sword's fuller groove, splattering against the weapon's protective basket.

Hawkes lifted his foot and planted it in the man's chest, sending him reeling backward with a well-placed kick. He was instantly replaced by another pirate, this one also armed with a sword. He came in slower, more cautious. He had seen the fate of his mate and did not wish to share it.

Taking the battle to the enemy, Hawkes charged forward two steps to gauge the other man's reaction. The pirate smoothly moved back, then bounced forward a step, thrusting his blade. The ambassador had already moved to the side in anticipation. His sword came up and clanged against his opponent's. Both men broke instantly.

The pirate took advantage of their close quarters to aim a chest strike. Hawkes brutally parried it, slapping it aside. He hurried to follow with a cut of his own. The man dodged, spun around, and came in for another strike. The ambassador blocked and attacked, only to be parried himself.

The moment had come where both men knew they were evenly matched. Each had taken stock of the other and discovered that no easy victory would be forthcoming. Instantly they fell to the attack, locking in to a steel rhythm. The two men lashed out at each other, slashing back and forth through the air, and probing each other for the eventual misstep one of them would have to make sooner or later.

It came sooner, and it was not Hawkes's. The ambassador feigned another stumble, and suckered his opponent in. The maneuver did not work as well as it had previously. He managed only a downward strike along the man's forearm, creasing his armor and drawing blood.

It was enough, however. In the split second the pirate needed to switch hands, Hawkes stabbed out and buried his blade in the man's abdomen. The ambassador had no time to congratulate himself over his victory, though. No sooner did his opponent fall away than another moved forward, yet this one wielded a shock staff much like Wagner's.

"Make it easy on yourself, old man," said the grinning invader as he advanced on the ambassador. His voice sounding tinny through his suit's mike, he added, "I'll do you quick and painless as possible."

"How thoughtful of you," answered Hawkes.

The invader lunged and the ambassador sidestepped. Hawkes brought his sword around, cutting for the pirate's head, but the man brought his staff up, blocking the attack. The antique weapon clanged along the steel/titanium length. The ambassador went with the motion, sliding his blade along the staff and trying for the man's hand. He came close, but a split second before Hawkes's maneuver could catch him, the invader loosened his grip.

The pirate pushed off awkwardly, forcing the ambassador to step wide. Hawkes spun around and tried a long, angling thrust, but it fell short. The invader pulled his staff in close, then pushed it out and up, just managing to deflect the ambassador's next strike.

Hawkes pressed ahead, swinging wildly, trying to force the pirate back. The man made two awkward retreating steps, but then, as the ambassador followed, the pirate stopped short and made a wild swing of his own. The staff managed to break through Hawkes's defenses and touch his sword arm.

The ambassador stumbled badly. Even though the staff's touch against his arm was brief, the current blasted through him, shocking the sword from his hand. Hawkes fell to his knees.

"Sorry, Mr. Hawkes," said the pirate, stepping forward, setting his staff to full charge. "Job's a job."

The ambassador fumbled for his weapon. It was only a few inches from his hand, but it seemed several miles away. Hawkes reached for it, pawing the ground pitifully, but his eyes could not focus properly, could not discern which of the several images he was seeing was the real one.

And then the pirate set his staff to full power and stabbed down at the ambassador's body.

13

A roar of thunder ripped through the dining room. The bullet it had propelled slammed into the pirate's chest plate, through his body and then his back, and finally flattened out against the inside of his rear armor. The man gurgled, losing his grip on his staff. It fell away from his fingers and flopped toward the floor, almost hitting Hawkes.

The pirate wobbled, struggling to stay erect. Martel made it to the ambassador's side. She could help him up with only one hand; the other still held her gun. Closing the fingers of his left hand around the hilt of his sword, Hawkes struggled to regain control of his body. His eyes focused on the automatic in Martel's hand, and he stuttered, "How—how? You have, have, have . . . a gun?"

"Later," she answered, putting all her strength into getting the ambassador back on his feet.

Hawkes grabbed the pirate's staff with his left hand, using it as a crutch on which to stand, and then closed his eyes and took a long, deep breath. Inside his head, he summoned all his reserves to help him sort through the confusion in his brain and banish the last scrambling electrical pulse that remained from the pirate's weapon.

He felt his mental faculties returning, although he knew he was still weak—still almost helpless.

Opening his eyes, Hawkes could see more pirates swarming in the door toward Wagner. The bulky sergeant had gotten a table between himself and the latest wave of attackers. With his staff still crackling at full power, he swung back and forth in wide arcs, keeping his three current adversaries in check. Yet as he caught sight of the two coming up behind, he shouted out, "Lady—can the ambassador be moved?"

"Yes," Martel shouted back.

"Then move him out of here," called the marine. Two pirates blasted at him simultaneously but he caught the energy from their weapons in the containment field of his own, and slung it back at them. The move killed one of them instantly, and gave the other second thoughts about firing again.

"Do it while you've got the chance."

Still weak, Hawkes protested.

"We can't leave. Can't leave Wagner behind. Mustn't . . . ."

Martel shoved forward until the ambassador's arm lay over her shoulder, and pushed Hawkes back toward the bar. Forcing his steps, she told him, "Forget it. If we don't get moving like he said, we'll be as dead as he is."

"But he's not dead," Hawkes answered vainly.

"He's close enough."

As the pair got behind the bar, they heard the marine's weapon discharge again. Screams came from the invaders' ranks. With that one shot Wagner had taken out a third of the pirates in the room. Unfortunately he had had to deplete half his weapon's energy to do it.

"Go! Go on, *gooooo!!*" he screamed.

Martel could hear the marine's voice urging them into further retreat as she got the ambassador to the back door leading to the galley. Pushing him through to the other side, she worked feverishly to get the doors blocked. The desperate aide had managed to get only two of the eight batten locks in place when she heard another massive discharge from Wagner's staff. The sound was muffled by the closed doors. So was the marine's dying scream that followed.

"Shit."

Throwing herself to the floor, Martel got to the other doors, slamming their base locks into place. Then she stood quickly, slapping the remaining two lock bolts upward into their ceiling plugs even as the first of the pirates slammed against the other side of the doors. Martel jumped back, startled, even as Hawkes moved forward to get her.

"Come on," he growled.

His voice was thin, tired, but he was able to move and think again. It was all he needed. As quickly as he could, the ambassador slid his sword back into its scabbard. Then, still carrying the dead pirate's energy staff, he pulled his aide through the kitchen. Pointing to anything holding liquids throughout the galley, he yelled, "Break all the magnetic connections. Spill everything you can."

Martel watched as Hawkes shut down all the safety magnets he could, deliberately emptying all the cooking pots, storage bins, and sinks within his reach onto the floor. His aide helped him as best she could, not knowing what else to do. Behind them, an ugly noise tore at the doors.

"Sir," she cried, "they're going to be through any minute."

"Then let's get finished, shall we?"

His dress uniform covered in a dozen layers of slop, the ambassador splashed through the messy ruin he had made of the floor. Martel saw him heading for the drop hatch and hurried to follow him. As she joined him at the crew emergency exit, she found him working with a dinner knife on the controls of the pirate staff.

"Drop through," he ordered. "I'll be right behind you."

"But, sir . . ."

Hawkes pried open a panel in the weapon, immediately digging into the wiring below.

"Don't argue with me, woman. *Jump!*"

The aide's eyes darted across the littered room, now a dripping mess. She could see that the doors at the far end were going to give any second. She could see also that the ambassador was bracing for his own jump. Before he could order her a second time, she stepped into the escape slide.

At the same moment, two of the doors at the other end of the kitchen burst open. Shouts and curses flooded the room. Hawkes probed farther into the staff's circuitry. He could hear the invaders' heavy, armored boots splashing through the galley. Then, suddenly, he heard a hissing click inside the staff.

A split second later, the weapon went into overload, burning the ambassador's hands. Hawkes hurled the staff as far as he could, stepping into the drop exit. The sparking weapon hit the floor, sinking into wet slop just as the ambassador's foot left the floor.

Electricity shot across the deck, through the spilled soup and drinks and dishwater, up into the metal tables, and of course, into the pirates as well. Hawkes dropped down below eye level just as the room began to fill with smoke and the smell of burning flesh.

"**M**r. Ambassador," shouted the captain over the overwhelming noise filling the area, "I really don't think you should be down here!"

"With all due respect, sir," answered Hawkes, "if we don't get that ship out there, it's not going to matter much where I am. I won't be alive to appreciate it."

"Your opinion is noted, sir," answered the captain. "You two can join the rubble line. That's our top priority."

The ambassador and his aide moved over to join the ranks of crew and passengers working to clear the debris clogging the main fighter debarking tunnel. The massive bay area was a noisily echoing nightmare—one filled with blowing steam, flashing lights, and the smell of escaping hydraulic fluid. As Hawkes and Martel joined the work force, they saw Jarolic in the same lineup, but no one else from dinner.

The ambassador and his aide had found their way to the fighter bays without too much trouble. Hawkes's first assumption had been that if the pirates had indeed come aboard looking for him, his best bet was to go where they were not. His second was that most of them would head for the passenger areas and the lifeboats. So far, both assumptions had panned out.

Finding places in line, the two diplomats immediately got down to work, hefting their share of the clogging rubble. They helped pass it all along—large pieces of form plastic, burned lengths of wire and cable, chunks of steel and glass, and anything else handed to them.

Taking a moment to wipe the sweat from his eyes, Hawkes analyzed the problem there in the launch bay. Not only had the exit door been blocked by debris from the pirate's opening shots, but the aiming track had been filled as well. As one group of workers toiled to clear the exit door, another small band crawled along the track running from the first fighter, working to pry loose the smaller pieces wedged within it.

"So," asked Martel, shouting over the increasing din, blowing a wayward strand of hair away from her eyes at the same time, "is your life always this exciting, sir?"

"What do you mean?" asked Hawkes in return, turning his head from left to right in mock confusion. "This little tiff?"

The woman frowned for a moment, then suddenly snorted a stream of air through her nostrils. A short burst of appreciative laughter followed.

"Oh, yes," she said, dropping a forty-pound hunk of twisted metal in his outstretched hands. "You're good."

The ambassador passed the hulk to the next person in line, then told his aide, "I'm the best."

In the distance, Hawkes could see one of the ship's crew making an inspection run down the fighter bay. The ambassador's aide figured her job was nearly completed, considering all the time she was making. In another half minute, the woman stood up and signaled the captain. He signaled her back, waving her and the rest of the workers away from the area.

"All right," he bellowed, "That's it. We've done all we can afford to do. Clear this area."

As marines and crew started ushering the passengers in the bay to the exits, Hawkes crossed to the captain's side of the launch chamber. He got there just as an officer he took to be the previously mentioned Mr. Dordman said, "The track's clean enough to make a drag, Captain. That blister still piled around the door—the fighter'll blast through that easy enough."

"I hear a tone in your voice, mister."

"Yes, sir. It was my thought that as soon as we start to raise the hangar door, our playmates are likely to take another shot at us."

"My opinion exactly," answered the captain, reaching for a voice-link. Taking a deep breath, he indexed for the bridge, then shouted, "Mr. Swelver!"

"Yes, sir."

"We're about to engage the fighter bay. Can I assume our friends have been keeping an eye to that area of the ship?"

"Yes, sir. As per your back call, I've spun us three times since you got below. Just drift kicks to make it look like a tidal effect—nothing suspicious. But they've rounded to keep a forward aim each time. They've got you under trigger lock—no doubting it, sir."

"Can't you get a shot at them?" asked Hawkes.

"No good. By the time we could turn for a good shot they could cut us in half. That's why we need to launch a couple of buzzers. With a wing or two out there to give them trouble, we might have what we need. But . . ."

The captain made a shrugging gesture. As Jarolic came up behind them all, Martel shouted, "Isn't there some way you could distract them, even for a minute?"

"We wouldn't even need a minute," roared the captain as the

noise in the bay suddenly increased. "A few seconds is all it would take. But what . . ."

"Where's the water supply on this ship?" As everyone stared at Jarolic, he explained, "If there's a place where we could blow a large enough stream of water out into space . . . it would become visible instantly as it froze, even at a distance. Wouldn't something like that distract . . ."

The captain cut the environmentalist off with a wagging finger. Grabbing Dordman by the shoulder, he shouted, "That doesn't sound half bad. What do you think, mister?"

"Aft section eighty-five," answered the officer. "Just opening the intake valves would do it. Suction would probably rip that whole section of hull away."

The captain bent over a subspace screen showing the positions of the *Bulldog* and its attacker. As he did, Dordman added,

"Of course, we wouldn't have much water left for the rest of the trip."

"Anyone who doesn't like the taste of their own piss can take me up with the actions board," roared the captain. Wiping at his brow, he shouted, "Mr. Dordman, find me a pair of volunteers. We may have just found a way out of this hell."

And then, before anyone could move, a score of pirates poured into the bay area. Not worried about explosions in the heavily armored bay area, they came in with their sidearms drawn and extended.

The very first projectile explosion that went off killed both the captain and Dordman. Seconds later, the bay was in bloody chaos.

14

"**S**welver!" screamed Hawkes into the bridge link. "Answer me, mister!"

"Who is this?" came the officer's voice.

"This is Ambassador Hawkes. The captain and Mr. Dordman are dead."

The ambassador ducked behind the console as the fighting in the bay intensified. Martel and Jarolic squeezed in beside him, along with several other noncombatants as another round of explosions blanketed all other sounds. Out in the bay yard beyond, the marines and crew tried desperately to hold the line against the invaders.

The pirates had gained a large advantage by leading with an explosive attack. Dangerous and unexpected, it had turned the tide of the interior battle in their favor. Smoke and the smell of burning plastic and metal filled the air. Grabbing the arm of the officer who had been standing nearest to him and the captain a moment before the attack, Hawkes shouted, "Listen, did you hear the plan the captain was outlining?"

"Yes, sir."

"I want you to implement it." Turning to Jarolic, he yelled over the intense noise in the bay. "Think you can find this section eighty-five?"

"Sure," answered the environmentalist with a determined grin. "It's aft, right?"

"That's what the captain said." Turning back to the officer, Hawkes grabbed a hand-link out of the console, shoved it into his sash, and then shouted, "We're going to try and release the water. We'll let you know when we're ready. It'll be up to you to get the rest done."

"Aye, aye, sir," answered the young lieutenant. Reaching under the console for a thick wrenching tool, he said, "We'll handle this scum."

Hawkes then turned to Martel. Putting his hand on her shoulder, he sucked in a deep breath, then reached out to push a strand of her dark hair away from her eyes. Giving her a smile, he squeezed her shoulder, then said, "Care to cover our escape, deadeye?"

"Certainly," she answered. Pulling the automatic she had used earlier to save the ambassador's life, she chambered a round and asked, "Would you say things have gotten past the *tiff* stage yet?"

Another explosion went off, sending three bodies flying through the air. Their wounds were so severe it was impossible to tell which side they had been on. His eyes following the grim sight, Hawkes answered grimly, "Yes. I think they have."

The ambassador turned to Jarolic, who only gave him a curt nod. Hawkes returned it. He looked from the environmentalist to his aide, then said, "Let's go."

All three stood up at the same time. The others who had been next to them on the floor immediately slid into their safer position behind the console. Hawkes and Jarolic ducked low, squinted through the rolling smoke, and then broke in the direction of the rear exit.

Martel held her automatic ready, sighting along the barrel, skipping from target to target, watching only for those of the enemy who might notice the ambassador. Then, after Hawkes and his compan-

ion had disappeared from sight, she started over again . . . this
time pulling the trigger.

The first thing Hawkes noticed as the exit door sealed behind him
and Jarolic was the silence. Since the attack had started, the noise
in every part of the ship had escalated with every passing minute.
The aft access passages seemed completely quiet, however.

Hawkes was grateful for the respite, but its totality made Jarolic
suspicious. As the two men worked their way down the pipe-filled
hall, the environmentalist whispered, "Ambassador, can you hear
me?"

"What?" asked Hawkes, his voice slightly louder. Not quite able
to understand what the ambassador had said, Jarolic repeated his
question, speaking even louder than Hawkes. It took them another
round before the environmentalist's fears became apparent to
Hawkes.

"All the explosions—the fighting and shooting," Jarolic explained in a louder voice. "It's deafened us. We think it's quiet, but
it's not. Not this quiet. If we're not careful we're liable to walk right
into some of the enemy, or let them sneak up on us."

"Point taken," agreed the ambassador. "You keep an eye on
where we're going. I'll watch where we've been."

Jarolic smiled and nodded sharply. Exercising greater caution,
the pair returned to making their way to their destination. Each
tried to keep moving as fast as possible. Both men were aware that
every minute they wasted brought more death to the rest of their
shipmates.

How many have died already? wondered Hawkes. He had already seen the captain die, and his aide Dordman—both good men.

Just like Wagner.

The ambassador thought of his last sight of the big marine,
holding the invaders back so that he and Martel would have time to
escape. Another loyal innocent killed by an unknown enemy.

Just like Dizzy.

Hawkes could feel himself going cold inside. Too much suffering. Too many dead.

For what? For whom? What the hell is at stake here that people are willing to go to these lengths—to spend this kind of money?

The ambassador rolled it all over in his head. Buying off Stine, sending in the mercenaries who had attacked his ranch . . . now a full ship-to-ship battle in deep space. And those were only the things he was aware of.

Someone is pouring money out by the truckload. Why? What are they after? And what in hell do I have to do with it?

"We're here."

Hawkes turned at the sound of Jarolic's voice. He noted the large 85 painted on the metal wall ahead of him and nodded. The ambassador was struck by the large black number. He remembered his days in the service, when the "innovators" had tried to replace such things with digital readouts, voice boxes, and a hundred and one other technological enhancements. It had not taken long to prove to everyone involved that spending money as an end in itself was not a good thing, and that gimmicks did not necessarily mean progress.

Jarolic led the way inside the water-containment area. The ambassador asked him, "Does this type of system look familiar to you?"

"It will if I can find a dump release," answered the environmentalist as he eyed the machinery before him. "Or at least a semblance of a feeder-rejection series."

"Well, then," said Hawkes, slumping back against a wall, "I'd keep looking."

The ambassador let Jarolic move off into the room. His line of work gave him a chance to find what they needed and get their job done. Hawkes's plan at that point was simply to stay out of his way and try to catch his breath.

The pair had been lucky not to run into any more pirates on the way. Both men were tired and more than a little nervous. Both would have been willing to admit that armed combat was not their preferred line of work. They were out of their league and they knew it. The ambassador shut his eyes and mopped at his brow as he thought, We've been awfully lucky so far.

He felt the throbbing in his sword arm. It had been a long time since the British Pattern hanging at his side had been used as anything but an ornament.

Awfully lucky.

"Ambassador . . . ?"

"Yes?" croaked Hawkes, opening his eyes again. He listened to the harsh sound of his voice—realized he was more tired than he thought. "What?"

"Better get ready to signal the bridge. I think I've found what we need."

Hawkes pulled the hand-link from where he had stuffed it inside his sash. Unwrapping the length of fabric, he used it to wipe the drying sweat away from his face and neck. As he did, Jarolic called out again, "These old ships, they have conduits for taking on and discharging liquids from the big station globes. I'm betting we can flush a big enough drop at one time to get the effect we're hoping for."

"How is it you know about this kind of thing?"

"In my line of work, you pick up a lot of facts about moving water around."

Hawkes opened a line of communication to the bridge. Swelver answered immediately, letting him know that the fighter bay had taken heavy casualties, but that they were ready to follow through. "Just tell us when, sir."

The ambassador called out to Jarolic, asking, "How much longer?"

Up above, trying to familiarize himself with the dump controls, the environmentalist continued working as he shouted back, "One minute . . . five, maybe. I know that's not very precise, but I can't be sure. . . ."

And then Hawkes heard the scuffling out in the hall. Instantly he reached for his blade. His arm moved slowly. It was stiff—sore. Tired. Closing his fingers loosely around the hilt, he withdrew the weapon, pulling it to the ready. His sash and hand-link in his other hand, he told Swelver, "It could be any time—keep watch. We've got com—"

Hawkes jumped backward as three pirates entered the room. Each of them was armed and ready. His sword came up just in time to knock back the charged staff of the closest one.

"Get him!" ordered the one in the rear. "This has been too much for too little. Kill him, and let's get this X'd and off!"

The narrow confines of the hall gave the ambassador a small advantage. As long as he could hold the three back, he would have a chance. However, if the pirates could force him back the few yards to the main chamber where Jarolic was working, they would have him.

Forcing away his fatigue, Hawkes turned himself sideways, presenting as thin a target as possible. His sword extended, he fenced with the staff wielder as best he could. It was not the best way for the staffman to use his weapon, but it did extend his reach over the ambassador's, and it was the only way he could manipulate the long weapon in the narrow hall.

The two parried with each other twice more, twice again. The charged staff crackled with power. Several times Hawkes tried to slip his blade past the pirate's defenses, but he could not break the man's stabbing pattern. Worse than that, each exchange forced the ambassador to take a backward step. The staffman was herding him, using his longer reach to push Hawkes back into the larger room.

"You'd better hurry," the ambassador shouted over his shoulder.

"I'm almost there," answered Jarolic desperately. "You've got to keep them back a few more minutes."

"It might not be up to me," Hawkes told him truthfully.

The staffman grinned and spun his weapon. Hawkes lashed out in both directions, knocking the charged rod against one wall and then the other. The pirate, younger and possessing the advantage, pressed it again, bringing his weapon back from the wall before the ambassador could reach him with his blade.

A drop of sweat fell from Hawkes's hair, rolling down his forehead and dropping into his eye. He blinked it away, fury and desperation flooding his mind. And then, suddenly, the drop reminded him of his sash, still hanging from his bracing hand tucked behind his back.

Instantly he whipped it around and up into the air, aiming it at the end of the staffman's weapon. The wet end of the sash snagged the rod and clung to it. The pirate lifted his weapon desperately to break the connection. Hawkes let his end go, never intending to try and break the staffman's grip. Instead he lunged forward, stabbing the pirate directly through the heart.

Blood sluiced out of the invader's body and into his shock armor through the breach made by the ambassador's weapon. The protective panel shorted instantly, sending a rush of power through both the pirate's and Hawkes's body. The ambassador was flung in one direction, the invader in the other. Hawkes landed badly at the very edge of the larger room. The pirate was thrown into his two mates.

The pair of invaders brushed their dying companion aside and started forward for Hawkes. Stunned for the second time during the battle, the ambassador had yet to regain his feet. The armor shock had not been nearly as severe as the staff jolt he had taken earlier, but combined with his fatigue, it was almost enough to render him unconscious.

"You've been a lot of trouble, Mr. Hawkes," said the closest of the two advancing invaders.

"Now, that he has," agreed the one in the rear. "Far too much."

"But," said the first, ignoring his partner—his eyes carefully watching Hawkes, "your head is worth a great deal of bank to me and me mate here . . . so you won't mind if we just gather it and then take our leave."

The ambassador could not answer. Gasping for air he could not keep in his lungs, shaking spasmodically, he could barely keep his knees together under him. His sword hand was flat against the floor. Hawkes knew if he moved it he would only fall over.

The ambassador fought for control of his muscles. He willed his damaged nervous system to respond, to fight back, to defend him before everyone who had died ended up having died in vain. With all the energy he had, Hawkes turned his head upward, staring at the approaching pirates. With his last remaining strength, he got one foot under himself and picked his sword up.

The pirates stopped for a moment—not out of fear, but a combination of amusement and pity. The one in the lead looked at the trembling, shaking weapon hanging weakly in the air before him and sighed. Then he brought his own sword up in a clean move and knocked the ambassador's weapon out of his hand.

"You're a brave man, sir. But you've come to the end."

Before anything else could be said, a small egg-shaped object flew from behind Hawkes and struck the first pirate in the chest. Instantly, micro-thin lengths of wire shot out of the egg and enveloped both the man and the one behind him. As the wires wrapped around the pair, they constricted and cut deep into the two pirates.

Before either man could even scream, their bodies exploded. Blood gushed, splashing both walls, pouring over the floor, and coating the ambassador. A spraying cloud of metal and cloth and bone and organ fragments followed, flying everywhere at once. The bits and pieces splattered everything within an eight-yard radius.

Hawkes sputtered, gagging on the death of his enemies. He wanted to wipe the gore away from his face. He wanted to know what had happened . . . where the egg had come from, who had thrown it, what had become of Jarolic . . . and the ship.

The ambassador wanted to know everything, but he was helpless. He was too tired—had been pushed too far. Hawkes sighed and his eyes closed.

Whatever happened next was in someone else's hands.

15

Hawkes sat back from the large, polished fiber table that separated him from the various Martian delegates. Staring out at them, letting the flurry of questions, requests, and demands wash through his mind, he could not quite believe what was being asked of him.

And you thought surviving the pirates was tough, he thought, letting the cynical voice sound in his brain, trying to amuse himself.

Surviving the pirates had been tough. But he and the remaining crew and passengers had done it. The plan to distract the attacking vessel's bridge crew by releasing the *Bulldog*'s main store of water had worked. The moment's diversion had allowed the liner's marine contingent to launch their counterattack effectively. Ultimately, they had not been able to destroy the enemy completely, but they had driven the pirates' mother ship off, a burning, smoking cripple, which everyone decided was good enough.

Yes, more than good enough, thought the ambassador, especially considering the alternative.

The last three days of the journey, desperately trying to get to Mars, had been an incredible hardship for all. Passengers filled in for the crew; all those who were still alive and uninjured struggled to clear the debris, watching over those few pirates abandoned by their fellows, living on a water ration of only one cup a day, and gathering the dead from every corner of the ship. The work had continued around the clock for everyone until the *Bulldog* finally managed to limp into its usual lunar orbit around Phobos. There had been more than a little trouble just getting to the moon itself, let alone trying to establish a proper orbital approach and final pattern. But the makeshift crew had done it—sometimes with their fingers crossed—but they had done it all the same.

From there Red Planet, Incorporated's shuttles took over. A replacement crew was brought up to tend to the ship while all the survivors were transferred to the planet below. Standard procedure in such cases called for the prisoners to be taken away for separate interrogation while everyone else was looked at by the corpor/national's medical staff and then interviewed by their security people.

After that, the survivors were finally allowed to get in touch with their families, their employers, or whatever else had brought them off-world in the first place. Most took no more than a few minutes to meet their Martian contacts before they went off for a shower or a meal or just to sleep. Benton Hawkes was an exception.

Forgoing any of the hospitalities Mars might have planned to offer its new governor-regent, the ambassador called for a meeting of all interested parties within a half an hour. Almost every one of the representatives waiting for Hawkes registered surprise. Many protested, some of them quite loudly. The ambassador merely frowned. Waving his arms for silence, he announced, "Ladies, gentlemen, you've been looking for an answer to your problems for some thirty years. I've been enmeshed in your struggle for a few weeks and people have already tried to kill me three times. I'd say we've all been at this long enough." Hawkes stared at his wristlink, pretending to check the time. Raising his eyes, he made his face a dark scowl as he said, "Anyone who isn't seated at the tables in a half an hour isn't going to be seated at all." Looking out at the stunned faces on the crowd of managers, owners, workers' reps, and

various other concerned parties, the ambassador had to hide a
smile. Turning away, pretending to check his papers, he threw over
his shoulder, "There are twenty-nine minutes remaining, everybody. If you have anything you want to present to me then, I suggest
you go to get it now."

None of the representatives remained in the chamber when
Hawkes turned back again. This time he did smile—for a moment,
anyway. Then he glanced down to the table before him, locking
onto the half dozen trays overflowing with report chips. He picked
up a handful of the peanut-sized electronics as Martel entered the
room. Letting them pour through his fingers back into the tray, he
said, "Do you believe this? There must be six weeks' worth of
reading here."

"Mr. Ambassador, what are you doing?"

"At least six weeks. My God, I haven't seen anything like this
since they sent me down to South America to mediate that six-way
war . . . when was that? Fifty-two."

"Ambassador, everyone expected you to get some rest." Martel
stood in front of Hawkes, her hands on her hips. She had been on
her way to bed when she had been made aware of his announcement. "They thought you would at least want to clean up a bit. No
one thought you were . . ."

And then, sudden comprehension flooded her face. After a few
seconds she remembered to close her mouth. As she began to
apologize, Hawkes smiled, telling her, "Forget it. Let it be a lesson.
Stopping for anything except getting down to work just gives your
enemies time to get their next move organized."

"But how can you . . . I mean . . . to start a round of talks
now." The young woman cocked her head to the side. Then, in a
voice filled with serious concern, she asked, "Aren't you tired?"

"Exhausted."

The aide closed her mouth again, trying to think instead of
simply blurting out the first thing that came into her head. Hawkes
could see the effort in her face. Approving of thinking, he decided
to sit back and wait to see what she said next.

"Sir, permission to be confused?"

"Permission granted," answered the ambassador with a grin. Taking pity on the bone-tired woman, he told her, "Go ahead. Ask your questions. I won't spin you."

"Thank you. That's the nicest courtesy you've shown me so far." Hawkes nodded, actually amused enough despite his fatigue to grin. Ever since Martel had saved his life he had found himself growing quite fond of the young woman. Too fond.

Damn it, he told himself, you're here to do a job, not rehearse Romeo. Leave the Shakespeare for someone with nothing better to do.

He stared at her as she moved across the room, freezing a nondescript look onto his face as he also reminded himself, And, in case you forgot . . . she's married—a newlywed—and, oh yes, in case you needed anything else to keep you from getting distracted these days, there are people trying to kill you.

Hawkes waited as his aide turned and then pulled up a chair of her own. Easing her weary self into it, she said, "You're twice my age, so I'm going to assume that after what we've been through you're at least as tired as I am."

"Ouch. Thanks," he answered with a mock show of wounded pride. "Let's just say, 'point granted.'"

"Thank you again." Pushing at her short, dark hair, Martel took a deep breath to help her stifle a yawn. Then, she bit her lower lip, exhaled through her nose, and finally asked, "Sir, how can you think of opening negotiations without any rest? We've been through so much. . . . How are you going to be able to do it—keep your guard up—especially when the hours start to drag on?"

"The hours aren't going to drag on. I didn't call for an opening to the negotiations. I just called a meeting."

His aide stared for a long moment. The woman was tired, as exhausted as everyone else that had come off the *Bulldog*—more so than most. Her mind raced over her conversation with Hawkes, searching for the piece she was obviously missing. Finally, knowing she was walking into a verbal trap, but not knowing how else to get the answer, she conceded, "Okay, sir. You win. I'm just too wrung out to keep up with you. All I can see is you making people angry. You want them to run off, grab all their materials and run back here, and then you don't intend to start negotiations."

The aide let a thin smile cross her face. It showed a delicate mix of helpless surrender and "I'll get you later." Hawkes liked it. Before he could say so, however, Martel added, "If a humble battery fetcher can be privy to the workings of genius . . . could you please tell me what you're up to?"

"All you had to do was ask." Hawkes raised both eyebrows mockingly. His aide felt like sticking her tongue out at him but refrained, settling for a simple scowl instead. Paying off his last comment, the ambassador told her, "We have a small advantage here. No one expected us to sit down to the tables now. We're half-dead, thirsty, tired." Hawkes feigned sniffing his armpit, then added, "We smell . . . well, *I* smell. But then you know what they say about diplomats. You, maybe . . ."

Martel laughed despite her fatigue. Hawkes smiled. After the past three days, he felt the serious young woman needed a good laugh.

"All right—motion passed. The entire corps smells. Anyway, we came in with everyone working under an expected given . . . no one was going to be in any shape to do any work. So, since no one expects us to do anything, no one's totally prepared. They don't have their arguments in place. Like I said, I didn't call for an opening of negotiations, I just called for a meeting."

Hawkes sat forward in his chair, his hands checking his vest pockets for something he could not seem to find. As he did so, he realized he had on the same clothes he had left the ranch in, the same outfit he had been wearing when Disraeli had found the bomb, when his home had been attacked; when he had killed Stine. Suddenly, whatever he had been searching for was forgotten. Leaning forward out of his chair until he could rest his forearms on the table between himself and Martel, he told her, "I want them all to go grab up their half-prepared statements. I want to see what they have to say before they get a chance to polish it up and craft it into wording that hides what they really mean to say."

The woman nodded, more to herself than to Hawkes. She was used to functioning with formal, by-the-numbers types. She had never seen someone like him in action before. And then, a sudden thought seized her. Emboldened by the ambassador's style, moved to speak in a fashion she would not have thought proper with anyone else in the corps, she asked, "Excuse me, sir, but what would you think of someone who came to the table with nothing prepared?"

Hawkes smiled again. The woman was good. His mind flashed back to the *Bulldog*, focused on the pirate stabbing for him with his electro-staff, saw Martel's bullet blow open the front of his chest.

"What would you think?"

"At this point, Mr. Ambassador, I'd think anyone who wasn't prepared to start negotiations would be someone who thought you weren't going to get here to lead the negotiations."

Hawkes's smile split his face. He was too tired to hide his feelings as he normally might. Besides, not only is she right, he thought, but the woman saved your life. You can give her some of her due.

The ambassador's mind raced. In a moment, a hundred thoughts crowded through his brain. In that flashing split second, his guard down because of his weariness, because of all they had been through together, because she was beautiful and trusting and they were strangers alone in a world unknown, he almost forgot about everything. For a second she had no husband, and he had no reason to keep her out of his life—the way he had everyone for so long.

But the moment ended, and he remembered who he was, and who she was, and why they had gone through all they had in the first place. His all-too-reflexive restraint choking back his sparking feelings, he told her in a low voice, "Well, all I can say is"—the door to the chamber opened to admit the first of the returning negotiators—"if you thought something like that . . . you'd be right."

And then, despite his safeguards, their eyes met. Before he could stop himself, volumes of feeling passed from one to the other as Hawkes's defenses slipped and let the woman see at least a part of who he was. Martel did the same, willing to give as much as she got.

Then, finally understanding each other, the pair turned to face the incoming delegations.

16

Hawkes set aside the hand screen he had been studying for hours and then stretched his arms out to both sides, as far as he could. It had been two days since he had reached the surface of Mars. If he thought he was tired then, he had forgotten what kind of energy it took to stave off angry civil wars. He was bone tired—more weary and drained than he had ever been before in his life.

His opening gambit had succeeded well enough. None of the parties to the negotiations had been totally prepared. The management of Red Planet, Incorporated, and those designated to speak for the workers had brought the most material to the table. The Earth League monitor, the representatives from Lunar City, and those picked to audit the proceedings for the Asteroid Workers Federation came with far less, but that was understandable. They were there mainly as observers in the first place.

All five groups had been a bit miffed when Hawkes merely gathered in the materials they had brought, thanked them politely, and then dismissed them. But he had gotten what he wanted, and that was all that mattered. As he had explained to Martel later, "They're all annoyed with me right now. Hopefully that's good. Mad

at me, they might not take it out on each other—yet. It might keep
the lid on things for another few days."

"But," she countered, "isn't it possible that someone might think
you're just going to stall everyone and go ahead and step up some
violent plan they have?"

Hawkes had nodded in agreement, admitting, "Chance we take."

After that, he had sent his aide to get some rest, and then had
done so himself. Twelve hours later, after two showers, two meals,
and as much sleep as he could manage with all the reading he had
to accomplish, the ambassador sat down with the head representatives of each faction and had a far less dismissive meeting than the
first.

He blamed his manner from the day before on a desire to get
down to business, combined with a level of fatigue he found he
could not combat. "I have to apologize. Never having been through
anything like the last few days, I simply didn't realize how great a
toll everything had taken on me. Before you know it, I'm going to
have to admit I'm not twenty anymore."

He was gracious and humble, stepping back from his gruff attitude the day before. Putting everyone at the table more or less at
ease, he then proceeded to solicit their opinions on how fast things
should progress, what everyone felt were the most important points
to cover, and in what order they should be covered. He allowed no
arguments, gently reminding everyone that in the end all decisions
would be his.

Finally, after several hours, Hawkes declared that he had everything he needed to proceed. Assuring the assembly that he would
be ready to meet with them again in two days, he bid them all
farewell. To those who protested, he mentioned the mountains of
reports, statement records, briefs, complaints, and declarations
they had all given him.

"Do you want a spectator or a mediator? Or, more important,
which of you wants to take the chance that your position papers
might be the ones I don't get to?"

The protests ceased abruptly.

Settling in, Hawkes and Martel had read throughout the rest of the day. Of course, she ran everything through the computer net provided to them first. Hawkes had given her a list of key names and points to correlate. Using the computer to sift through the millions of screens' worth of material, Martel had pulled together the different parties' slants on each key person involved in the negotiations and how the viewpoints, demands, and objections mixed and matched with one another.

It still left Hawkes with several thousand pages to read. Now, after hours of staring at the hand screen glowing gently off to the side, the ambassador turned away from it. His eyes were so tired he knew another shot of Strain-Break would be counterproductive. He had already dosed himself with more than twice the recommended limits.

Realizing he needed a break, Hawkes decided to work within his brain for a while, just to figure out for himself what he had learned. The first thing that came to mind was the fact that everyone at the table had seemed prepared. That had been a disappointment; he would have liked to find a link between one of the parties and the pirate raid.

The interrogation of the pirates taken prisoner—both on board the *Bulldog* and subsequently on Mars—had yielded nothing of value. Finally, with Hawkes's approval, standing Martian law was followed and the prisoners were taken away to Recycle.

Most of them had been quite stoic about the sentence. A few had cried out in rage and disbelief until they had been removed from earshot. Sitting alone in his chambers a day later, the ambassador could still hear them in the back of his mind.

Angrily, he silenced the sentimental side of his nature, reminding himself that they were mercenaries who had taken on the job of wholesale murder. He did think the pirate attack pointed a definite finger, however. He was beginning to feel that the source of the attacks on him had to be Earth.

The first two attempts on his life had been made on Earth. The third had been an all-out try to keep him from Mars, and must have seemed guaranteed to succeed.

I've been here awhile and no one's tried anything. It could just be that they spent big and now they have to regroup. But I get the feeling this is Earth inspired. The AWF—why? What would be the profit? The workers . . . how could they have paid for any of it?

Absently pushing aside papers and memory report chips, the ambassador closed his eyes, trying to squeeze the fatigue out of them. As he did, he thought, Earth League . . . there's the place to look for the kind of money it takes to orchestrate a deep-space assault . . . or, he added, remembering the attack on his ranch, recruit a mercenary force of supposed dead men, for that matter.

Feeling a bit more secure, Hawkes shoved aside his own concerns for the moment, deciding to get back to organizing everything he had learned about the Martian situation. As he did, he was actually surprised at just how much everyone concerned seemed to agree on.

Point number one . . . the colonists who first came to Mars had done so thirty-four years earlier. It had been understood that life would be underground and communal for the first decade. After that, family units would be made available for those workers who wanted to live privately. After another decade, domed areas were to be completed, in which people could live on the surface.

There was no disputing this. Everyone had copies of the first agreement. Unfortunately, the outer domes were now fourteen years late in being completed.

Hawkes thought for a moment of living in tunnels for thirty-four years. Of never seeing the sun, smelling fresh air, running through grass, feeling the wind in your face, eating an apple pulled down from a tree . . . ten thousand thoughts flashed through his brain in an instant, ten thousand images and sensations that could not be seen or felt or indulged in by those who had come to settle Mars.

By those who had been born on Mars.

Who had never known anything but Mars.

It was a horrifying feeling to him—the thought of children growing up in caverns . . . comfortable caverns . . . clean caverns with piped-in water and food and light, caverns with a television that would pour out entertainment of any and all sorts . . . *if* one could afford them. Which led Hawkes to point number two.

Another thing that everyone agreed on was that the pay was extremely bad on Mars. For years the rewards for meeting quotas had been cut over and over. Here the ambassador found his disagreements cropping up.

Red Planet claimed that their expenses had turned out to be much greater than those initially projected. It was true that now they were supplying more than half the Earth's food, and through the AWF almost half the Earth's raw materials. But the cost of building the colony—living quarters; factories; the vast, continent-spanning sponge/mush vats—had yet to be paid off. Red Planet had scaled back actual pay and, for decades, had been making up the balance with shares in the company.

What it meant was that the workers were rich, but only on paper. By rights, they all should be living like royalty. The problem was that until the colony's managing company began to turn a profit, their stock—sheltered separately from the Earth League's other holdings—was worthless. A good hedge against the future for the corpor/nationals, which had invested together to create Red Planet, but worthless to the people dying to pay off the ever-spiraling debt the company had incurred in the act of creating itself.

Red Planet's output seemed to Hawkes to be the third major point. Once again, there was no disagreement—Mars was feeding, clothing, and sheltering the Earth. The ambassador could not even begin to imagine what would happen if production on Mars were suddenly to halt. But that was what talk of strikes and revolt was threatening to bring about.

On Earth, a number of the corpor/nationals had begun to grow leery of their investment. For decades, blocks of Red Planet stock had been traded back and forth on a regular basis like any other recognized currency. Lately, however, people were beginning to find it harder to interest anyone in taking even a fraction of the stock load they would have in days gone by. Because of the talk of unrest filtering back to Earth, the corpor/nationals claimed that Mars was getting labeled as a bad risk.

Of course, standing on the outside of the game, it was easy for Hawkes to see the self-fulfilling-prophecy aspect of it all, but that did not do him or anyone else any good. If the Earth League partners could not be calmed down, their desperately growing desire to turn their stock into capital held the potential of creating exactly the same level of disaster that any kind of physical conflict on Mars might.

And, point number four, conflict on Mars was beginning to look all but inevitable. Every one of the surviving original colonists was still trapped below the surface of the planet, living like a slave. Their children, born in the planet's lesser gravity, were bound to the planet even more closely than they were. Even if they could buy their passage off-world, they could not survive more than a few months in Earth's gravity without a great deal of medication and physical therapy—costly medication and therapy. They might migrate to the Moon, but from all reports, life there was even harsher than on Mars.

Three generations of people were trapped by greed and were powerless to get what they wanted—what they had been promised—in any way except through force. And Hawkes could see that more violence was coming. Reports showed that riots sprang up constantly. Two-, three-, ten-person outbursts were going off at random whenever another battered soul snapped and reached out for the nearest blunt object.

So far, no major damage had been caused. But from similar situations throughout his career, the ambassador knew that such things were only a matter of time. Without false modesty, he knew that his reputation was the only thing keeping things quiet for the moment. And he also knew from bitter experience that he could count on that for only so long.

Which brought him to the fifth point: the fact that Red Planet management did not seem inclined to change their policies much. To them, strikes were illegal because any attempt to unionize was illegal. Red Planet had turned into a sort of debtors' prison, with the cost of food and shelter more than its inmates could work off. The corpor/national's employees had no constitution. They had no rights. Legally, the company could do what it wanted with them.

On the other hand, immigration had fallen off to a trickle. No one wanted to move to Mars anymore because—despite massive attempts to silence such information—over the years the consequences had become all too apparent. Thus, Red Planet—and by extension, the Earth League—did need to negotiate, but they insisted that the circle still brought them around to the same starting point: there was no money to give anyone, there were no domes to move into, and there was nothing left for the colonists but working until they died.

A wave of tired hopelessness washed over Hawkes. Unlike most of the diplomatic problems he had been sent into during his career, this one was close to pure tragedy. There seemed to be no real villains . . . just a lot of helpless, scared people on all sides, looking for the way out of a room without doors.

Sighing, the ambassador stretched again, then got up out of his chair. He was tired to the point of irritability and knew he needed a distraction. Realizing he had not yet really inspected the quarters the Earth League had set aside for him, he began to move around the chamber, stretching out his cramped back and legs. He had to admit that he was surprised. He had gotten used to the opulence of government lodgings; he had been surprised to find something so . . . standard.

Everything about the two small rooms he had been given boasted pure functionality. Clean, straight-angled, relentlessly empty, it was a proud barrenness, one that spoke volumes about the severity of life on Mars. Everything was well built—the walls smooth and seamless; the table and chairs, couch, and shower area all practical and useful, but utilitarian.

Hawkes's mind roamed for a moment, taking him back to the clean, open beauty of his ranch. Shuddering as he contemplated the differences, he muttered, "God, I'm just so tired of this. I'm tired of being used, tired of working my way around in useless circles, tired of everything I accomplish always going for nothing."

And his cynical side reminded him, I'm tired of waiting to get my hands on the sons of bitches who killed Dizzy.

Suddenly Hawkes could no longer stand the sight of his pair of spartan rooms. Too tired to continue reading and yet too keyed up to rest, he found himself being consumed by darker and darker thoughts. The talks to come seemed hopeless. He could see them going on for months—months that might lead on to years. Years trapped below ground—years living in tunnels, no meat, no sun, no . . . "Oh, the hell with this."

Stalking across the room, Hawkes kicked his slippers under his bed and then grabbed up his boots. Pulling them on one at a time, he said, "All right, so I might be here for a while. If that's the case, I might as well go out and start learning my way around."

On his way to the door, he grabbed up his portable screen—just in case he decided to sit down and start reading again. He checked his pockets to make sure he had all the usual odds and ends. Then he pulled two beef jerky packs from his luggage, slid them into his inner vest pocket, and headed for the door.

For some reason, he did not take a weapon. He would soon have reason to question that decision.

17

Even wandering as he was, it did not take Hawkes long to descend to the lowest levels of the Martian Colony. Not down into the factory levels, of course, but only into the bottom reaches of the living quarters—the Big Above, as many called it. Not much he saw made him want to stop.

Everything looked the same. It was all too orderly, every corner, wall, and angle too functionally oriented. Directional markers crowded out any attempts at aesthetics by the original builders, which had been few enough. The countless communications boxes and security monitors did nothing to cheer the look of the place, either.

The ambassador stared down at the ground. Every floor was painted with the same pattern of designational and classification stripes—constantly telling him where he was and where he was going.

And if you walk backwards, thought Hawkes bitterly, where you've been as well.

He had not been walking for a full hour yet, but already the look and feel of the colony had begun to depress him deeply. In his time, the ambassador had trod the ground of some of the world's poorest nations. He had witnessed desperate poverty in lands torn asunder by mindlessly horrific wars. He had seen corpor/nationals take over vast tracts of countries, evicting all their citizens. He remembered the forced marches in Africa when Inver-Comp had seized power—the tens of thousands on the march. No food, no water, dusty roads worn down into the veld by an army of marching skeletons.

This might be better than that, he grudgingly admitted to himself after a moment's deliberation, but not by much. And if things don't change, and change fast, I can see it all getting worse. Fast.

Hawkes came across the central park of the colony shortly after beginning his inspection. He was surprised to find no one in it. Of course, he also had been surprised by the fact that he had seen only one other person as he walked. But, to his way of thinking, in a place as desolate as Mars . . . how could people not be in the park? It might not be the only park in the Above, but it was known to be by far the largest and most elaborate. As he wandered through it, the ambassador winced inside, thinking, God help these people . . . if this is the best they have. . . . He glanced from side to side, misery creeping into him with every second. . . . This. *This.*

The cold, logical part of his brain was willing to be impressed. Not only was the park on a formerly lifeless planet, but it was *inside* that planet, hidden from the sun. Everything being done was being done artificially. But still, the rest of him shuddered. It was a park without trees, without water, without birds or grasshoppers, without wind or ants or grass or even loose soil.

The entire park was actually a series of potted plants, mostly short, shade growers—stunted things, really. From one end to the other, he saw no flowers, no variation—no color except the same easy-to-grow dark green. It was the only life to be had for several levels, though, which made Hawkes curious as to why there was no one else about. Continuing on through the sad little acre, he chanced across a gardener trimming away dead and dying leaves. Curiosity driving him, he asked,

"Excuse me—but is this all there is?"

"What do you mean?"

"To the park? Is this all there is? Aren't there any trees, any-where? Any flowers, anything"—Hawkes waved his arms about somewhat helplessly, finally finishing by asking simply—"anything else?"

"No," answered the man somewhat sullenly. He did not know who the ambassador was, nor did he seem to care. He seemed interested only in performing his duties—whatever they might be.

Curious, Hawkes asked him, "Is this your job? Are you the gardener?"

"I signed on for a few hours a shift. All I could afford."

" 'Afford'? What do you mean?"

"Afford. Whadya mean, wha'do I mean? What're ya—deaf? A Jim's gotta make some extra bank to stay afloat in this crap hole. I get done down in the growth vats, I come here and do snip duty for the recyclers."

Understanding flooded through Hawkes. Suddenly he did not have to ask any more questions. There were no permanent garden-ers, just workers desperate for extra units. The man was trimming away dead growth and turning it over to the recyclers for who knew how little—would four or five hours' effort buy a meal? A stiff drink? The ambassador was too embarrassed to ask.

And that, he thought, is why there's no one else here. That's why I've seen only one person since I left my rooms. Everyone else is off working their own second and third jobs to try and . . .

He hesitated for a second, wondering what anyone would save for on Mars.

Work like a dog? Who cares? What does it get anyone? More worthless stock?

Suddenly he was seized by the madness of Mars. Why would anyone come there? Stay there? How could they? *How?* How did a person go on, day after day, after day . . . after day . . . after day? When every moment was spent stepping over more gray floor-ing, going past more gray walls, under more gray ceilings. When every bit of effort went to someone else's benefit. When every breath was as useless as the last?

Staggering slightly under the weight of the horror coursing through his mind, Hawkes reached out and steadied himself against a pole. The ambassador was a student of history; he knew about slave societies, from early Mesopotamia to the Soviet Union, which had dissolved less than a century earlier. In a sudden, frightening moment of clarity he realized that the only reason Mars was continuing to function at all was because it was peopled with men and women who had known no other life.

Their mothers and fathers came here to make a new life. They took on this hellish existence to give something better to their children.

The ambassador shuddered, suddenly feeling a horrible cold growing within him. Starting to move again, he whispered, "They sold themselves into slavery so the next generation could be free. And this is all they got."

"Excuse me?"

The gardener had come up behind Hawkes without his having noticed. The ambassador turned to him, saying, "Nothing. Just talking to myself."

"Hey, do what you want. I don't care what you were doin'. I just want to get through."

Hawkes noted the three huge bags the man was dragging. Noting also that he could barely move them all, the ambassador offered, "Can I help you?"

The gardener's eyes narrowed. "How much?"

"Nothing. I came out for a walk . . . needed to stretch a little. You take two, give me one, and I'll help you." Hawkes stared into the gardener's overly suspicious eyes, and then added, "People do that where I come from." As the man continued to debate accepting, the ambassador offered, "You'll owe me a favor. You can decide how to repay it."

Even with that, it took the man a few more seconds to make up his mind. Finally, however, he decided he could trust the ambassador with one of his bags of dead twigs and leaves.

Probably figures I'm too old to get away from him if I decide to make a break for it, thought Hawkes grimly.

As the pair moved down into the lower levels, the ambassador tried to engage the gardener in conversation. The farther they went, however, the less Hawkes felt like talking. Every level down seemed to grow grimmer. Each was older, less attractive. It was easily evident that the factory levels were not maintained nearly as well as the Above, a fact that saddened the ambassador to the point where he could not find it within himself to speak.

Noticing the difference in Hawkes as they trudged down to Recycle, the official bottommost depth of the colony, the gardener stopped to dig out his work release. As he did so, he told the ambassador, "You ain't never skipped down this far—got it?"

"Yes," admitted Hawkes, an overwhelming sadness choking his voice. "You've got that one."

The gardener stood back for a moment while the door to Recycle scanned his release card. His hands on his hips, he said, "You ain't never even been in red clay before. You're greenside, ain't ya?" When the ambassador nodded, the gardener suddenly reached out his hand toward Hawkes. Gently patting the ambassador's shoulder with sad understanding, he told him simply, "It's okay."

And then the man turned and grabbed up his three bags, dragging them in past the opening Recycle door. Hawkes caught a glimpse of its innards as the gardener entered: all tubes and steam and humming machinery. He had just started to turn away when the man stopped on the other side of the door. As it began its backward slide to lock again, the gardener freed one hand long enough to give the ambassador a short salute. Then, allowing the tiniest grin to cross his face, he said, "Hey, don't forget. I owe you one."

The door clicked shut, and once again Hawkes was surrounded with nothing more than the silent door and the black tunnel walls leading away from it. The ambassador allowed himself a small shudder, surprised at how lonely the narrow cavern felt once he was alone. But then he was not alone for long.

The man who had followed him from the Above was still behind him. He had thought to make his move in the garden, but Hawkes had started his conversation with the gardener, forcing him to wait.

But, thought the silent figure, watching the ambassador from the shadows, there's no one around now.

With practiced silence, he slid his knife free of its sheath and moved out into the light.

18

The assassin bolted out of the shadows in a rush, moving in a quick, straight line for Hawkes's back. Closing in, he screamed in a maddened voice, "Die, Eart'hog, die!"

The ambassador spun around, shocked at the sudden noise. Luckily instinct prevailed. Before he knew it, Hawkes had raised his arm just enough to lodge it under his attacker's, his wrist banging up against the descending knife arm. The two-sided blade stopped half an inch from Hawkes's head as the would-be assassin stumbled into him.

The force of the blow sent both of them reeling onto the tunnel floor, knocking the assailant's weapon from his hand. Both men grasped for it. Worry ran through the ambassador's mind. His opponent was younger by at least thirty years. He was a bigger man, and stronger.

Shoving fear aside, Hawkes replaced it with determination, and steeled himself as he crawled, trying to keep his foe from regaining his blade. The two grappled with each other every inch of the way—wrestling clumsily, striking at each other with awkward, flailing blows—each only trying to slow the other down as they crawled across the black floor, struggling to reach the lost knife.

Hawkes's mind pounded with confused questions as he fought his way forward.

Who wants me dead now? Is he from the same source as the attacks on Earth, or am I in someone else's sights now? There's big money at work here, just to kill one man.

No, he reminded himself. Not just to kill me. Nobody cares that much about me.

Heat coursed through Hawkes's body. He fanned his rage, feeling himself gaining on his attacker with each angry thought.

Me—I'm nothing. It's enslaving this planet that someone wants. It's my blood and the blood of a million others. A billion. A trillion—not that numbers matter. Not to them.

Hawkes felt his fingers balling. . . .

Kill off everyone—what does it matter? Ignite the universe just to light one of their cigars . . .

"No!"

The ambassador's fist came down in the small of his attacker's back. Forgetting the knife, Hawkes slammed his fist into the small of his attacker's back again and again. As the other man kept groping for the weapon, the ambassador dug the fingers of his left hand into his foe's side, twisting the flesh he found. His right caught up the man's longish brown hair and wrenched back with all his might, bringing a wailing scream from his would-be assassin's lips. As he pulled the man off the floor, Hawkes demanded, "Who are you? Why are you doing this?"

"Vat you, green thing. You'll sell Mars out for a shiny slug."

The knife forgotten, the two men were grabbing at each other, slapping each other's hands away, wrestling their way to their feet, each trying to topple the other. The ambassador hissed, "That's not true. I'm here to help."

"Stuff it. You're Earth. Earth bites our hearts out. You'll never side with Mars over Earth."

The two men suddenly pushed at each other in the same direction. The force of the maneuver sent them stumbling once more.

They slammed into the wall—Hawkes luckily on the outside. Gasping for breath, the ambassador said, "You're wrong. Whatever treaty I negotiate . . . it'll be the fairest . . . fairest one possible."

"Liar! No paper's ever going to free Mars! Fat Earth will *never* free us. But we will! The Originals didn't eat red dirt so you could drink their children's blood."

Hawkes could feel his hold on the younger man weakening. He had given it everything he had, but he was too tired. As the fatigue of days without rest started to eat at him, he struggled merely to maintain his grip, but to no avail. Sensing the loosening of Hawkes's hold on him, the assassin shifted his weight and then threw his arms apart, hurling Hawkes away.

Dashing to his fallen weapon, he screamed, "The Resolute don't listen to Earth lies. We reject you and all the green." Grabbing up his blade, the assassin turned back toward his victim. A cold sheen in his unblinking eyes, he began moving forward again, snarling, "Mars first, Eart'hog!"

But suddenly the Recycle area's massive door clicked open. The noise distracted the killer long enough for Hawkes to make it back to his feet. His enemy made another forward step, but as he did, a voice called out, "Hey! Whadya think yer doin'?"

"Stay back," cautioned the ambassador, recognizing the gardener's voice. "He's got a knife."

"Crunch it," replied the worker, moving up to Hawkes's side. Displaying his own weapon, one several inches longer than that of the now-outnumbered attacker, he said, "Everyone on Mars got a knife."

Shaking his fist at the gardener, the attacker shouted, "The Resolute won't forget this, bootlicker."

More people appeared in the Recycle doorway. As they began to step out into the hall, the foiled assassin ran off, his oaths fading behind him: "The Resolute don't forget!"

As the Recycle personnel began to crowd around the two figures in the hall, Hawkes leaned back against the wall. Safety was making him aware of his pains. Reaching out to the gardener, he rolled his eyes and gave the man a feeble smile, saying, "Thank you."

"I owed you one," the man answered matter-of-factly.

Ready to walk off, the ambassador caught his arm, holding him back. Reaching inside his vest, he asked, "Have you ever had meat before?"

The gardener looked at Hawkes with a puzzled stare. When he realized the ambassador was serious, he said, "No. No one in the family's seen meat since the grandolds."

Finally getting his inner seal undone, Hawkes got his hand into his pocket and pulled out the two beef jerkies he had taken with him earlier. The ambassador was almost embarrassed by the look in the gardener's eyes.

The man read the words on the outside of one of the packages. He did not know what a "kippered beefsteak" was, but he appeared willing to find out. As the small crowd gathered about watched, Hawkes took one of the jerkies back and then tore open its vac-uum-sealed package with his teeth. Peeling back the plastic outer coating, he bit into the barest end of the thick, red meat stick. Then he chewed up the bit he had torn free and swallowed it. Handing the packet back to the gardener, he urged the man to do the same.

While Hawkes went back to trying to regain his breath, the man did as he had been shown. He chewed slowly, rolling the shredding fibers around in his mouth. The gardener moved the small chunks around in his mouth, his eyes wide, his expression near rapturous. He swallowed as little of the precious mouthful as he could, forced into the reaction only by the fact that his mouth was filling with saliva at a rate he had never known before.

Then, suddenly, he became aware of the reaction of the crowd around him. Neither embarrassed nor gloating, he slid the un-opened jerky into his pocket. Then he folded the plastic wrapper down over the one Hawkes had opened and slid it into his pocket with the other. He took a step closer to the ambassador, smiled, and said, "I guess I still owe you one."

19

The next night, Hawkes and Dina Martel sat in one of the low-energy people movers that buzzed about through all levels of the Martian Colony. Little more than a golf cart with a primitive robotic brain, the small three-wheeler quietly carried its passengers toward their destination.

"Do you think this is a good idea?" asked Martel, worrying at the strap of her gown.

"It was my idea, wasn't it?" Hawkes raised an eyebrow at her in amusement. "Yes, I think it's fine." Reaching over, he helped with her dress. "But you'd like an explanation, wouldn't you?"

"As to why you're showing such favoritism this early in the game? Yes."

"That barely deserves a response, but as my old commanding officer used to say, 'You can't be expected to play along if you don't know the game plan.' So, let me ask you: What do you think we accomplished today?"

"We opened negotiations," she answered. "We got everyone seated at the same table and we got them talking to one another."

"Were we in the same room?" asked Hawkes with mild sarcasm. When his aide was silent, he reminded her, "We didn't get anyone talking. We baby-sat a bunch of children. We listened to the same useless gaggle of threats and demands and accusations we spent our first two days here reading about." As their vehicle slowed to enter the elevator to the next level, he continued, "No one was *talking* to anyone else—they were just blaming each other for how lousy their lives are. You and I—we think we know what the story is, that we know what everyone's grievances are. We don't know anything."

Martel's eyes narrowed and she focused her attention on Hawkes. She knew he was leading her somewhere, but she also knew that it was an important part of her job never to think something was a good idea simply because it had come from the great Benton Hawkes. The ambassador needed more than that from her.

"We don't know who's telling the truth—any kind of truth beyond the self-serving type that everyone believes. If we're going to help anyone here, then we're going to have to go out and get a few of the facts for ourselves."

"And so we use poor Glenia as our patsy?"

"To answer your question," answered the ambassador, "yes—we certainly do. We use anyone to get the job done to the best advantage of the greatest number of people." His voice going a bit softer, he added, "I like Glenia Waters. She was sweet and charming. We're not going to hurt her. We're simply going to use her to try and get this whole process moving forward. Maybe you're thinking of settling down here—I'm not."

The elevator doors suddenly opened again. As the silent cart moved out into the residential area set aside for the upper management of Red Planet, Inc., the ambassador lowered his voice and said, "We met Mrs. Waters on the *Bulldog*. We all survived the pirates together. Now we've accepted her invitation to dinner. We're not taking sides—we're taking dinner with an old friend. We're diplomats—we're allowed."

As their carrier slid to a quiet halt near a doorway labeled with the number they had been watching for, Hawkes noted that the entrances to the various apartments on the management level seemed fairly close together. Storing the fact away for later consideration, he whispered, "After all, I had dinner with one of the working class last night, so you can hardly call this taking sides."

Martel started to make a retort, but was forced to stop as the door opened. Glenia Waters flowed out of her front door. She was all smiles and open arms, calling to them, "Come in. Come in. My God, I haven't seen either of you since we left the ship, and that was only for a moment across a crowd." Taking Martel's hands in her own, the woman added with genuine warmth, "Of course we all heard that the ambassador hadn't been harmed . . ."

"Well, nothing permanent," Hawkes interjected with a tone of mock pride.

Rolling right past him, Waters continued, "But really, Dina, I hadn't known whether or not you survived until you accepted my invitation."

"I'm fine. But what about you, Glenia? Did anything . . . ?"

"No, no, not an old warhorse like me. Someone pushed me backward into a crew locker. It was uncomfortable, but considering the alternative . . ."

The trio made silent agreement that they were lucky to have survived. Before any further comment could be made, a man roughly the same age as their hostess arrived at the door, making a final adjustment to his tie. He was tired looking, his eyes dark, and his skin tight and sallow. But he was as happy as his wife with their guests, and immediately asked why everyone was in the hall when the party was inside.

In the Waters living room they ritually were introduced to the children, who were then sent off to amuse themselves while Glenia went to attend to things in the kitchen. Samuel Waters took over as host, first serving drinks, then picking up a tray of hors d'oeuvres. Extending it to his guests, he said, "Every bit of it grown right here on Mars. This is no reconstituted sponge/mush. This is the fresh act. The real deal. And maybe it's just hometown pride, but I think dehydration just kills the taste." He gave Hawkes and Martel each a moment to make a selection, then asked, "What do you think?"

Martel's eyes opened wider as she bit into the canapé she had selected. Holding it away from her mouth, she exclaimed, "This is very good—it really is." As Waters's head turned toward Hawkes, he agreed, saying,

"Yes. I must admit I've never had anything quite like it."

"It's the parsley and the peppers," called Mrs. Waters from the kitchen.

"Now, honey," complained her husband lightly, "don't give away all my secrets."

"Peppers? Parsley?" questioned the ambassador. "I thought you folks only grew smush here."

"For export," offered Mr. Waters. "Pretty much everyone keeps some kind of home 'ponics system. Good as fresh smush is, who could eat it all the time?" When Hawkes merely smiled and nodded, not bothering to mention that that was all he had been fed throughout his stay so far, his host rose to his feet and offered, "Come on, let me show you our setup."

Alerting his wife that he was taking their guests into the back of their apartment, Waters led Hawkes and Martel into a tunnel carved into the solid rock of Mars beyond the clean lines of their home. The rough ceiling was covered with a sophisticated series of grow lights. Rows of hydroponic equipment hummed silently below. Tubes of water hung from the ceiling with plants growing in them: root bases curling about in the fluid, long vines flowing down into the room. Examining a length of potato vine growing in one of the tubes, Martel said, "I had no idea there were private setups like this here."

"Oh, my," Waters answered, "everyone has them. We have to." As his guests waited politely, he continued, explaining, "Every apartment as it's built is set up with a 'ponics unit. Having plants everywhere throughout the colony keeps up the oxygen levels. People grow whatever they want."

Pointing to a long rope of eggplant curling down a pegged pole, the manager said with pride, "The seeds for these came from Earth almost forty years ago. It was about then that the vat central fellows started trying to figure out what to do with the fibers from the sponge/mush plants."

"I beg your pardon?"

"Oh, sorry, Mr. Ambassador, I'm getting ahead of myself. One of the big problems we have is keeping the plants trimmed back. I'm sure you realize the smush growth is a self-replicating body. What most people aren't aware of is that after the meat is harvested from the stems, and the pulp from inside them, there isn't anything we can do with a lot of the stem fiber. We can only recycle so much. The stems are pretty acidic . . . takes a lot of other waste to balance them out."

As his wife appeared in the entranceway, Waters took on the look of a man who had suddenly realized he was rambling. Getting himself back on track, he said, "So, anyway, to down a report into a memo, the Originals decided to try and find some personal uses for the leftover fiber. There are some who make pillows—strip the fibers down to weaving strings. Others carve stuff, build furniture, so on. But one of the first uses was as compost. Just took it home and threw it in the corner to have a smell that wasn't paint or ore oils. Anyway, a lot of things grow in acidic soil . . ." Waters spread his hands apart, finishing, "You can guess the rest."

As the trio turned toward Mrs. Waters, following her back out into the finished section of the apartment, Martel asked, "And every management apartment has one of these caverns dug back off of it?"

"*Every* apartment has one," corrected Waters easily. "Workers have to eat and breathe, too, you know."

"Those workers you were cursing over the bargaining table to-day, Samuel?"

Hawkes and Martel shot each other silent looks as the husband answered his wife.

"Yes, dear . . . those workers."

"A lot of them are our friends, you know."

"If they were our friends, they'd understand that I'm not the one keeping them from going outside." Turning so that all of the others present could see his face, Waters asked earnestly, "Does everybody think *I* want to live like an ant?" He paused for a moment, as uncomfortable as everyone else in the tiny bubble of silence, then asked again, "Do they?"

Before anyone could answer, the front monitor announced, "Carrier dropping off. Vincent Pebelion approaching."

Mrs. Waters moved to the front door. Indexing the lock, she slid the door open and ushered a couple and their two children inside. Hawkes's face opened into a smile as he greeted the man personally, saying, "Well, hello. I didn't think we'd be seeing each other again so soon." Turning to Martel, he said, "This is the man who saved my life last night."

The woman next to him smiled widely. "That's my Vinnie," she said.

Almost blushing, the man downplayed his role, saying, "I just came out the door and yelled. I had to do it, anyway—except the yelling, of course."

"Then," said Hawkes, extending his hand, "let me introduce you as a man whose sense of timing is one I appreciate."

Pebelion handed a covered dish he was carrying to Mrs. Waters so he could shake Hawkes's hand. As the ambassador introduced the part-time gardener and his family to Martel, Waters told them, "We're still trying to track down that Resolute fellow who jumped you. No luck so far, from what I hear. But anyway, after you reported the incident, I made it my business to find out who the hero was." Walking over to Pebelion, Waters punched him in the shoulder with obvious affection, saying, "Should have figured it was one of my chief vat-kickers." Then, turning back to the ambassador, he added, "When it got to me that it was Vinnie, I didn't see where you'd mind if we invited him to join us."

"No, of course not," answered Hawkes. "You never know, it's

been a few hours. Someone must be out there getting ready to make another try for me."

Mrs. Waters laughed, telling her husband, "Didn't I tell you he was droll? He was like this the whole trip."

With that, the two wives sent the newly arrived children off to join the others. At the same time, turning his attention toward the covered dish Pebelion had handed Mrs. Waters, the ambassador asked, "And what's this?"

"It's a pot pie," answered Hawkes's savior. "Wheat crust, potato filling, sunflower seed topping."

"There's something more, isn't there, Vinn?" asked Waters, a trace of puzzlement crossing his face. "I mean beyond spice. I smell something . . . something good . . . but I, I . . . what is it?"

"I was going to let it be a surprise, Sam. Shoulda known I couldn't get past that nose of yours." Reaching toward Mrs. Waters, Pebelion pulled away the lid from the dish he had given her. As its contents' aroma filled the air, he said, "It's meat." Hawkes stared as he watched the looks that came over the faces of both Sam and Glenia Waters. As both of them simply gawked, Pebelion told them, "That's right—meat on Mars. The ambassador gave me it for savin' his life."

"Glenia's told me about meat," murmured Waters, his eyes locked on the covered dish. "She's managed to try it a few times when she's been off-world. I, you know . . . I mean . . ."

"It's really not good for you, you know," added Martel, somewhat embarrassed by everyone's amazement.

"Neither's this," added Pebelion, pulling a flask of clear liquid from his hip pocket. "But what's a party without the best of everything?"

The chatter broke down into the normal civilized responses friends make toward each other for sharing their best. All of which did not escape Hawkes's careful eye. As everyone moved to the apartment's dining area, he could not help but wonder,

If what he was seeing was the way management and labor

thought of each other on Mars, then what was all the arguing about? If what he had just seen was the truth, then where were all the lies he had been reading coming from?

There at dinner, smiling, nodding, joking, sharing both families bounties, he stewed over the question nagging at him. He knew he could find no answers then, but things were beginning to make sense to him. Between what he had learned the night before and what he was learning there at the Waters family's happy table, he was beginning to fit some of the pieces together.

Now, he thought, if I can just live through the next few days, maybe I can shed some light on what's really going on around here.

20

The next few days' negotiations were more of the same. Hawkes presided over the different factions, maintaining order between them, listening to them squabble, barely able to keep his patience. It was not that the ambassador had lost any of his skills. Hawkes was as much in command as ever. He simply could not believe how little there was for the concerned parties to debate, and yet how many times they could go around in the same circles.

After a week of getting absolutely nowhere, Benton Hawkes had had enough.

On the fifth day of negotiations, the ambassador came to the meeting room ready for blood. The attempts on his life were coming a little too often for him. He was beginning to feel as if even his luck could not hold out much longer. He had not taken to walking with a bodyguard yet. It was no sense of false bravado, he simply knew how many points a show of fear would cost him, and how little good armed escorts ever did anyone.

Besides, he thought, his fingers edging their way toward his gavel, if I have to listen to this bunch much longer, I think I might welcome a good fight.

Across the table from him, Ace Goth was covering the

same ground he had the last fifteen times he had been given the
floor.

"To hell with your proposals. I'm telling you right now, the workers of Mars aren't going to put up with much more." As everyone
groaned he brushed his long sandy hair back behind his ears, then
raised his voice, claiming, "Hey! I don't want to hear it. The corpor/
nationals haven't lived up to their contract—any part of it—and
everyone knows it."

"Mr. Ambassador," started Herbert Marrow, head of the Earth
League delegation, "once again I have to state the obvious . . . so
what? These people"—his hand waved in Goth's direction—"don't
even have a legal right to be represented at this table—Red
Planet's charter invalidates the creation of any unions. We *all* know
this."

"I'll tell you what I *don't* know," growled Goth. "I'm not sure
what you're so hot under the collar for, Marrow, bein' how this is
supposed to be between us and Red Planet. But just in case the
League has some stake in this I ain't been imprinted with yet, let
me remind you that there is no union. You're the one that keeps
talkin' about a union." Goth allowed his statement to undercut the
League head's anger, then added coolly, "Of course, the failure of
your management company to meet the points of your contract,
those're the kinds of things that just might get some people to start
up some unionlike activity."

"Like strikes?" demanded Marrow.

As Sam Waters tried to intercede, reminding everyone that no
one had mentioned a strike, Goth roared back, "Maybe someone
should mention strikes. Maybe that's just what we need around
here."

"Strikes?" thundered Marrow. "Strikes are illegal, and you
know it."

"Then maybe we'll just settle for a mass walkout."

"Do it," dared the league head, "and I promise that anyone who
leaves his job will be fired . . . cut off without pay and without

access to company housing or benefits." Hawkes shut his eyes, tired of the never-ending circles. As he began to lift his head, Marrow snarled, "You people want to live on the surface of Mars so bad, go ahead . . . walk out. That'll be the only place you'll be able to afford to live."

"Genocide," cried Goth. "That's their answer. Work our fathers and us and our children into the ground—then kill us off." The angry workman stood up so suddenly he sent his chair flying. "Genocide!"

"Not genocide, simply union busting." "But there is no union, you bastard." "That's what you'd like us to think. We're supposed to be idiots who can't interpret talk of walkouts." "And we're not supposed to recognize the fact you don't intend to do anything on Mars except cultivate a race of slaves—"

"That's enough!" All heads turned toward Hawkes. "That is all, absolutely *all* I want to hear from the lot of you." The ambassador stood, staring at both Goth and Marrow. It took only a moment for them both to slide back down into their seats.

"I've had enough of this. Enough—do you hear? Ace? Herbert? Do you? This is it. This is the end. We've heard this same sloshing round robin day after day. Well, not tomorrow. Let me tell you about tomorrow."

Hawkes sat back down. His back ramrod straight, his hands on the desk before him, his arms looking as tense and strong as hydraulic lifts, he said, "Tomorrow everyone comes back here in the morning, ready to negotiate. Negotiate. Understand? Not argue, bitch, complain, moan, bicker, quibble, quarrel, rant, boil, or brawl. Negotiate. And . . ." turning his attention squarely on Marrow, he added, "I'd like you to understand that I don't appreciate your team's stalling tactics. True, it makes sense—as long as the workers keep working, who cares what happens? But, no matter, I want it stopped." When their team leader assumed the properly wounded expression, Hawkes told him, "Nice reaction. A little insincere around the eyes, but eyes are tricky, aren't they? There

isn't a lot of time between now and tomorrow to practice, so if you
don't want to look so wounded when we reconvene in the morning, I
suggest you begin to answer some of the questions posed rather
than simply keeping the circle going."

Before any of the assembly could break away, the ambassador
warned the remaining delegates, "And, please, don't any of the rest
of you get the idea that I think the rest of you are angels. You're all
simply bickering rather than even beginning to attempt to work out
any kind of agreement."

Closing his eyes, covering his face with one hand, Hawkes
paused for a moment. Then he opened his eyes again, glaring out
over his hand, saying, "Frankly, I'm tired of it. And so I'm warning
all of you, if I don't see some kind of real effort being made tomorrow, I'm going to wash my hands of the lot of you."

His eyes narrowing, Hawkes focused his attention on the back
wall, glazing his eyes in just the right manner to make every man in
the room think he was staring directly at him. Then, filling his voice
with dark, raw threat, he told them all, "And if any of you thinks
that means you'll be free to do what you want, to strike, to bring in
troops, to wash the entire planet with blood and plunge the Earth
into desperation as food and raw materials disappear, think again.
You people remember . . . I'm the governor here. If I don't see
some attitude adjustments in the morning, I'm going to start issuing
some executive orders. And if that happens, I promise you there
isn't a one of you here who will be happy with the results.

"Not one."

And then Hawkes turned and walked out of the room, putting as
much steel into his stride as possible. Half of the move was directed toward showing those at the table that he had become as
rigid as he could. The other half was simply to keep him on course.
He knew if he bent at all, he would turn around and lash out at the
assembly, telling them what he truly felt in the most basic terms.
That would be very counterproductive.

Martel followed him quickly, not allowing a trace of what she felt to show to the group. Catching up to him in the hallway outside his chambers, she said, "I know since it was your idea that the answer will be yes, but I thought I'd ask anyway . . . was that a good move back there?"

"Maybe," answered Hawkes, his tone a subtle mix of confusion and anger. He indexed his door open, motioning for Martel to precede him, saying, "It was the best I had to offer."

"Sir, you've kept other warring factions from each other's throats for months on end. We haven't been here a week and a half and these people have you climbing the walls."

Martel entered and took the seat she had begun to think of as hers. Crossing her legs, she bowed her head for a moment, then pulled it up again, asking, "What's so different here?"

"Dina," answered Hawkes, surprising her by using her first name, "I wish I knew. I really do. Oh, I can guess. Maybe I'm just getting old and can't suffer fools as gladly as I used to. Maybe I don't want to be remembered by history as the man who destroyed civilization throughout the solar system."

"I don't think—"

"Don't think what? That war could come out of this? Interplanetary war? Ships being launched against each other—not across rivers or lakes or even oceans . . . but across the gulfs of space? Don't you realize what we're talking about here?"

Martel shrank back slightly in her chair. Hawkes had grown loud, his nerves raw. He had not frightened her, but in her concern she pulled in on herself, giving him the stage to work out his fears. Curious and a bit frightened by what he might say, she sat back and listened as he continued.

"This wouldn't be like any kind of war we've ever seen," he told her. "If the Martian supply chain gets cut off, forget the raw materials. Forget the steel and plastic and thread and glass and everything else. No one'll even notice that. And do you know why? Because they'll be too busy trying to find something to eat."

The ambassador crossed the room, heading for his luggage.

Reaching down under his shirts, he pulled out the single bottle of Jack Daniel's he had packed back on Earth that until then had remained untouched. Staring at it for a moment, he put it aside and said, "If the food barges stop shipping—if the colonists stop production, or explode the vats—there'll be no stopping it. We've both read the projections . . . even at their best, it won't take two weeks for every scrap of food to disappear from the face of the Earth. Millions will be dead by the end of the first month. Billions by the end of the second. *Billions!*"

Hawkes took another look at the fat, square bottle of sour mash next to him. Turning away again, he said, "Worldwide plague, along with cannibalism, will be the least of what we can expect. Don't forget, we're talking about out-of-atmosphere warfare. For the first time in over a century, for the first time since we discovered their true horror . . . man will feel free to use nuclear weapons again. Why not? For once, the enemy doesn't even breathe the same air as we do. Who cares what happens to bastards like that?"

Martel stared, saying nothing. There was nothing she could say. She had no arguments to hold up to Hawkes's logic . . . not even any suggestions. It had been a century and a quarter since mankind had exploded a nuclear device to take life—well over half a century since anyone had had any serious fears about their ever being used again.

Now, she thought, those fears were going to be coming back. After just a moment she realized, *Going* to be coming back? They're already here.

Feeling her skin going cold, the aide looked from the ambassador to the bottle at his elbow and, despite all that had been learned about the effects of alcohol over the past century, she had a horrible insight into why its popularity had never diminished.

21

"**D**o you really think this is a good idea?"

Hawkes and Martel stood inside one of the thick-pour containment bunkers leading to the outer surface of Mars. The ambassador had changed from his formal attire back into the clothes he had worn when he had first left the Earth. His aide had changed as well, accepting his judgment that rougher clothing might be more appropriate for exploring the outside of the planet than their duty suits.

Standing in front of the hatch to the decompression chamber that led to the smallest of the outer domes, the two stared forward, not quite certain exactly what to do next. Glancing over at the ambassador, Martel followed up her question, asking, "I mean—*really?* No one is supposed to be up here. No one is supposed to enter the domes."

"But why?" responded Hawkes, still staring at the door. Turning toward his aide, he repeated, "Why not? We both read the same research. These domes have been standing for decades. What's wrong with them that no one is living in them? Why don't people visit them?"

Reaching his hand out toward the control box, the ambassador depressed the heavy yellow button that opened the inside of the decompression chamber. A loud click snapped the quiet, and then the large, thick metal hatch began to roll slowly sideways. As the interior of the air lock was exposed, Hawkes took a tentative step forward, telling Martel, "This is what we need to know. When we reconvene the talks tomorrow, if things start going around in the same familiar circles, we need something to shake things up. If we've got some facts—any facts—something that proves people *can* live on the surface, or that they *can't* . . . it might force one faction or the other to give in a little."

"I have to admit," said the woman, "at this point, even 'a little' would be something."

"Well, then, my dear," answered the ambassador, bowing to allow Martel access to the decompression chamber, "let's go see if we can find some."

The woman picked up the pack bag next to her by its twin handles and then stepped inside. Depressing the black button on the inner door panel as she passed it, she moved next to Hawkes as the heavy door slowly rolled back into place. The two diplomats waited patiently, both of them scanning the meager contents of the chamber while they waited for the hatchway to seal itself again.

Whoever had erected the dome had not left much behind to impress later visitors. A trio of old compression suits hung off to the side, with a few power attachments and oxygen packs scattered at their base. Nothing else. No messages scrawled on the walls, no papers, no clues of any kind to identify the men and women who had worked on that site. Hawkes studied the silent suits, their black faceplates reflecting back his probing eyes.

As he stared, he remembered the severity of Mars's recycling programs. Suddenly he was not wondering why there were not more signs of the past in the chamber, but how even the few there had survived. The ambassador spent the next few moments checking the outer levels, making certain the dome beyond contained a breathable atmosphere. And then the hatchway behind him and Martel finally clicked closed, signaling that they could proceed.

"Well," he said, feeling a strange dread curling through his system, "ready?"

"I guess so," she answered, sensing his apprehension, and sharing it.

"Then," he began, pausing for a second as his hand reached out for the control button to the last door, "let's go take one of those giant steps for mankind."

His finger pushed against the heavy control button. The outer door ground with protest, snapping the hold of inertia. Slowly it rolled back, sliding away into the wall of the bunker. At first glance, all that lay beyond was the ribbed plastic of the extension tunnel leading out to the dome.

At first . . .

"My dear God . . ."

The words came out of Hawkes in one breath. He and Martel moved into the tunnel slowly—not out of any lingering trepidation, but from wonder. It was their first view of the Martian surface, and they were as stunned as any other person who had ever seen it.

The first thing that caught their attention, of course, was the sallow cast of the sky. They could not take their eyes off it, craning their heads upward and in every direction.

Yellow, thought Hawkes. Yellow.

He remembered a pair of sunglasses he had been given that had been fitted with yellow-tinted lenses. At first he had been fascinated. They had made everything seem clearer, more sharply in focus. But after a short while, he had begun to realize something else.

The yellow glass leached more than just pinks from the visible spectrum, it took away everything warm—everything human. All around him, everything appeared cold and autumnal, as if the blood had been drained from everything in preparation for a winter that would end all of existence. Even looking at his own hand through those lenses had unnerved him. He knew it was his hand, but still it had appeared foreign—alien—to him.

And now he found himself on a yellow world, an entire world designed by the cosmos to drain everything warm from a scene, to leave things stark, devoid of all humanity . . . foreign . . . alien.

Well, thought Hawkes with a shudder, it's not like this isn't exactly what you expected.

The pair continued to walk through the long, plastic-bag tunnel. They began to pick up their pace after the first few minutes, slowly becoming accustomed to the utter strangeness of their surroundings.

Both of them began to notice little things around them, such as the descending layers of footprints in the sand that showed someone had been coming out into the old dome on a regular basis, no matter what the official reports said. Or that it was warmer inside the tunnel than it had been in the air lock, or that tiny beads of moisture were running along the plastic roof above them—often collecting in a central area to form actual drops.

Ducking the occasional drip, Martel began to unpack some of the equipment she had brought with her, while the ambassador merely looked out through the walls of the tunnel at the barren landscape beyond.

The scene outside was one of ancient, undisturbed desert drift. One boulder in particular, much larger than all the other rocks around it, caught Hawkes's eye. It was coarsely granular, banded in at least two directions. From what he could tell from a distance, it appeared to be a breccia fragment. He thought it might have been the central remains from a meteoroid impact, considering the ring of smaller, similar fragments that seemed to surround it.

While his aide moved on ahead around the curve in the tunnel leading into the dome, Hawkes maintained a slower pace, still fascinated by the view. He had seen all of the great deserts of the Earth, had spent considerable time in the Mojave Desert and the adjoining Death Valley region. But neither of them had struck him as did Mars. Sliding his hands into the side pockets of his old leather vest, he moved at his own pace, unable to break away from his view of the outside world.

It was true, he told himself; the deserts he had known all had their own striking colors and irregular formations, but they could not compare. Even the worst parts of Death Valley had some small traces of life here and there, even if only the remains of long-dead weeds—there were still clues that life was possible. Mars, however, held no such traces. Nowhere in sight, from zero to the horizon, was there the slightest glimmer of anything except sand and rock and lifeless soil.

Nowhere.

Hawkes continued on toward the dome. His pace began to pick up, his strides growing longer and quicker. Beyond him—beyond the relatively thin plastic wall holding in his atmosphere—the Martian landscape lay dully. Unmoving—uninspired—only the wind stirring up ancient layers of dust and desiccated soil. The single thing still of interest to him was the quirky way the browns and yellows outside blended to give the view its strange, orangish tint—what for centuries had granted Mars the distinction of being known as "the red planet."

It was only a mild diversion, however, and quickly forgotten when Martel suddenly called out to him. "Ambassador, there's something here I'm pretty sure you'll want to see."

The tone in his aide's voice caught his ear. Anxious for anything that might break the monotony of the Martian surface, Hawkes hurried his pace. Coming into the domed area, he found what he was looking for.

"Good Lord . . ."

"Maybe," answered the woman, taking soil readings in the center of the dome. "But something tells me he might have had some help here."

The ambassador crossed the sandy, broken floor of the dome, staring at its central point. Martel stood off to the side taking soil readings, but Hawkes barely noticed her. His attention was riveted by the flourishing wealth of life she was studying.

"I don't believe it," he muttered, trying to convince himself that the tangle of plants before him was not just a product of his imagination. A thousand questions flooded his mind: Who had done it? Why hadn't he been told? Why hadn't anyone been told? This was the kind of thing that could have eased a lot of the tension that was tearing the colony apart. Why was it being kept a secret—and who was doing the keeping?

Hawkes studied the mass of intergrown stalks and vines. The dome was roughly a thousand meters across. He estimated that the living circle in its center was somewhere between one hundred and a hundred fifty meters in diameter. Ivy and other creepers had been coaxed up old stanchions. Broad-leafed varieties littered the dome floor around them, surrounded and intergrown with numerous trailers such as aurea and traveling sailor.

"Someone found a use for Sam Waters's leftover fibers," Martel murmured.

"He had started telling us about the problem they had in the old days with disposing of the excess sponge/mush fibers. Someone's been dumping loads of it here, and mixing it with the right chemicals to negate its overly acidic qualities. The Martian soil seems to have something to do with that as well."

"They must have worked the area, smuggling excess water out here on their own until they got enough of a hothouse effect going to get their own little atmosphere recycling." Pointing toward the ceiling, she said, "Look."

Hawkes stared up, seeing the hundreds of thousands of hanging droplets waiting to grow fat enough for gravity to release them. But before he could comment, a loud "whooshing" sound swept through the air, followed by a violent ripple that shook its way across the dome. Thousands of drops broke free from the ceiling at one time, raining down on the ambassador and his aide.

Rubbing the water from his eyes, Hawkes looked up again. What had happened? he wondered. What was wrong?

It took him only another moment to realize what had happened, and fear made his heart skip a beat. Turning back toward the tunnel, he screamed,

"Run!!"

Even as he charged for the tunnel's entrance himself, he could see the compression door to the chamber beyond sealing shut. Without looking up again, he knew the ceiling was slowly beginning to lower . . . knew that the dome was collapsing.

22

"**K**eep running!!"

Hawkes's boots tore gouges in the Martian soil as he raced back toward the tunnel entrance. He was no more than a few meters from the opening when the much younger Martel caught up to him. As she slowed to pace him, he shouted,

"No! Go on. Go on. Get up there. Get the door open again."

"Okay," she shouted. Moving off, she offered, "It must have closed automatically in response to the drop in pressure."

"Maybe," he shouted after her. "Maybe not. They move so slowly. And that one's already closed. I don't know . . . but . . ." The ambassador went quiet for a minute, trying to catch his breath. Still running, he yelled out, "I don't think this was any accident."

Martel did not answer, save to pick up her pace. As she ran ahead, Hawkes felt himself going slightly dizzy. The tunnel was so long, the bunker so far away. Both of them were trying desperately to run a three-minute mile. Soon they would be running it without oxygen.

The ambassador continued to struggle, making the best time he could across the sandy floor of the tunnel. He saw his aide reach the rent in the passageway's plastic side. Air was being sucked out at a horrifying rate. Hawkes watched as she stumbled, trying to pass by the pull of the outward stream. Then, lowering his head, he narrowed his eyes and pushed forward, telling himself, Move, old man. Move! Keep running. Keep moving. Crawl if you have to, but keep going. Don't let them win. Whoever these goddamned bastards are . . . *don't . . . let . . . them . . . win!*

Hawkes threw his legs out in front of him, one after another, again and again, forcing energy into every step. Halfway to the end of the tunnel, water splashing down on him with every new shudder of the rippling plastic sheets above him, he had almost reached the hole when Martel shouted, "It's . . . locked!"

"What?" Hawkes puffed in disbelief.

Hanging off the bunker, holding her aching side in exhaustion, the woman sucked down a deep breath and screamed, "It's locked! Someone's locked it from the other side."

The ambassador saw the sabotage point at that moment, and realized what had happened. A small oxi-candle had been triggered near the base of one panel. It must have taken the flame generator at least five minutes to burn even the smallest pinprick through the plastic wall. Once that had been accomplished, however, vacuum pressure had done the rest, and the panel had been split from top to bottom by the explosion of escaping atmosphere.

Hawkes stumbled through the escaping stream. The whipping air whipped the dust and sand of the floor up in violent swirls, filling his eyes, choking him. The current tore at the ambassador, dragging him away, along with all the oxygen. Fighting it all, Hawkes hung on, thinking grimly, Damn you. Damn you, bastards.

He thought of the miracle of the garden behind him, already dying without ever being seen except by him and Dina and its unknown creator. Enraged, he forced himself through the gale. His vision going red, he thought, You're willing to kill every chance this planet has, just to get whatever it is you want. Well . . . you're not killing me. Goddamn you all to hell—you can kill the whole universe . . . *you're not killing me!*

Reaching Martel's side, gasping for air, Hawkes stabbed at the heavy yellow button. There was no click, no noise at all—only the harsh scarlet of the legend SEAL IN PLACE glowing in the readout area of the door controls. He stabbed it again and again, punched in the black button next to it as well—all with the same results.

"What're we going to do?" shouted Martel, panic flooding her eyes. "What *can* we do?"

"We can think," said the ambassador, gasping. Falling against the door next to her, he reached up, grabbed her shoulders, and said, "We can act. We can try!"

Then, desperately looking around the area for something with which to force the door, trying to purge the sound of the escaping atmosphere from his ears, he asked, "What are you carrying? Do you have anything we can use to get the panel open?" Slapping at his own pockets, checking every lump he felt, he continued, "Maybe we can play with its wiring . . . get it to—"

And then his hand closed over the round shape in the upper left-hand pocket of his vest. The form had been there for so long—so much had happened—he had almost forgotten about it. Praying he had found what he thought he had, he grabbed at the zipper over the pocket, fumbling to get it open. He tore at it in desperation, jamming it halfway.

Roaring in frustration, he grabbed at the half-open pocket and tore it away from his vest. The Graamler 10SA-11 he had carried there since the night his ranch had been attacked fell out into his hand.

"What's that?" asked Martel, already panting from lack of oxygen.

"Hope," answered Hawkes.

Blinking at the stinging dust filling his eyes, he searched the smooth dull black metal for the proper controls, trying to remember everything Tony Celdosso had told him. Praying he had remembered correctly, he slapped the bomb against the lip where the door met the wall and then threw himself against Martel, shouting, *"Down!"*

The pair had no sooner hit the ground below when the Graamler exploded, blasting the heavy decompression hatch inward. Pulling each other upward, the two struggled against the escaping atmosphere, pushing their way toward the twisted wreckage of the door.

Forcing his way into the air lock, Hawkes threw himself against the far wall. The escaping atmosphere continued to howl in his ears, sucking him backward. His hands aimed at the control box; he caught hold of it, slamming his index finger against the release button.

As Martel struggled to Hawkes's side, the ambassador slumped against the still-locked door. As he did, he revealed the readout panel of the door controls. The woman gasped in horror at the sight of the flashing red words: SEAL IN PLACE.

The cynical voice in Hawkes's mind sneered at him, Now what do you do?

For once, he had no answer for it.

23

"The suits!" screamed Martel, pointing wildly. "The pressure suits."

Hawkes followed the direction of his aide's hand as the woman started across the chamber. He saw the trio of suits flopping against the other wall, straining against their hooks as the dissipating atmosphere tried to suck them out of the ruined air lock.

The ambassador understood her meaning instantly. While she headed for the antique compression suits, Hawkes moved to intercept the pair of oxygen cylinders he saw rolling across the floor. He caught the pair of them, even as the first of the suits tore free from the wall.

"Benton!" Martel screamed in warning, but she was too late. The flying compression unit hit the ambassador square in the back—boots first, then the helmet. The faceplate shattered against the back of his head. The impact staggered him badly. Before he knew it, he had dropped one of the oxygen cylinders he had saved.

Blood sluiced wildly from a deep gash in the side of his head. Scarlet ribbons flew away from his head, disappearing past the compression door, following the lost cylinder into the tunnel—out into the atmosphere.

Hanging on to the remaining oxygen, Hawkes tried to unwrap himself from the flapping sleeves and leggings banging against him. At the same time, his aide reached the other wall and caught hold of the two remaining suits, holding on to them for dear life.

The ambassador forced his way to her side and immediately began screwing their single canister of air to one of the suits. As he did, he shouted, "Get in. Get in the suit."

"No," she screamed back. "You take the first one. I'll take the other."

"It's empty," he shouted back. "We've only got the one. Now get in."

"No!" As he felt the cylinder click into place, she continued, saying, "You're too important. You have to survive! Too much depends on it."

He wanted to argue, to tell her she was young—a newlywed—that she had her whole life ahead of her. He wanted to admit just how tired of everything he was—how he really would not mind checking out a little ahead of schedule.

But there was no time. All their air would be gone in a few minutes. Maybe in only a minute. The logical side of his brain silenced all argument; it forced him to look into her eyes. He could see her determination . . . could see that if he did not agree, she would simply release her hold and allow herself to be sucked away so that he would have no choice but to live on with more guilt than he could bear.

So what do you do, Hawkes? he asked himself. What do you do this time?

"All right. All right," he shouted. "Help me get in and get it sealed. Hurry!"

A loud, crashing sound tore away their attention. Outside in the tunnel, the loose cylinder had smashed through one of the passageway's support struts, tearing it loose from its mooring. As their atmosphere began to escape at an accelerated rate, the ambassador shoved his legs into the suit, screaming, "Hurry!"

His head pounding, black spots beginning to dance within his field of vision, Hawkes steeled his will, forcing his arms into the compression suit sleeves. Behind him, Martel shoved weakly at the back plates, desperate to align the magnetic seals properly. As she completed the last of them, the ambassador maneuvered his head into the large black glassed helmet.

And then, as the dark bowl snapped into place, he heard the rush of oxygen filling the suit. Sucking down a deep breath, he dropped to his knees, fumbling for the power attachments on the floor. Grabbing up the pile driver he had noticed earlier, he grappled with the awkward tool, trying to align its contacts so he could bring it to bear. Struggling to keep it sliding along its tracks, he prayed, Come on, you can do it. You can do it. You're not going to let that girl die. Not like the others. Not again. No one dies again. Come on . . . come on . . . come on . . . *come—*

The connection took. Instantly Hawkes moved back to his feet, forcing the ponderous compression suit toward the other wall with all his strength. He wanted to look back to see if Martel was still conscious, wanted to examine the voice controls to see if he could find the outer speakers, but there was no time.

The older compression suits had been designed as lifesaving equipment. Their basic design was simple enough that anyone could get one running—could keep himself alive just by getting into one. Anything else, though, took time to figure out. Mere seconds, split seconds, even . . . but Hawkes had no seconds to spare. The time it would take to rotate his head to look at the woman willing to sacrifice herself for him might be the time it took to sign her death warrant.

"Just keep moving, old man," he growled to himself. With sweat running down his forehead, he fought the dizzying fatigue that clawed at him, pushed away the internal suggestions his body was sending to his mind, growling again, "Just keep moving. Do it. Do it. *Do it!*"

Reaching the next door, he swung up the power attachment, slammed it against the curved lip of the heavy door, and then pulled back on the pile driver's trigger. Immediately the robotic arm piece began pounding at the hatchway's edge. Hawkes kept moving the slicing chisel edge back and forth, trying to get it wedged inside the vacuum-tight seal.

"Hang on, Dina," he whispered, alone inside his helmet, not knowing if the woman was even still alive. Once inside the suit, his senses of hearing and touch had been completely shut off. Now he had no idea if the air was still rushing away . . . or already gone. Ignoring the grim possibility, he continued to work, still praying, "Hang on. You can do it. You've *got* to do it."

Monstrous sparks arced away from the end of the arm piece, bouncing from the ceiling to the walls and floor. Ignoring them, blinking at the sweat filling his eyes, tasting the blood running down the side of his head, Hawkes worked at calming his heart rate and keeping the pile driver aimed correctly. As recoil tension tore through his arm, he gritted his teeth against the pain and redoubled his efforts. He knew by now that alarms would be ringing below. There was no doubt he had enough air to last until help arrived.

Dina Martel's fate, however, was another question.

That thought firmly planted in the front of his mind, he kept ripping at the air-lock seal, until suddenly, *"Yes!"*

Broken chips of titanium steel broke away from the hatchway lip. In another second a spiderweb of cracks splintered outward from the ambassador's attack point. In another, his arm attachment broke through the hatch.

Instantly Hawkes was hurled onto his back by the fresh rush of air being pulled from the inside of the colony out into the air lock. Fumbling his way to his knees, the ambassador cursed the slow-moving compression suit as he struggled to turn around. After a handful of yearlong seconds, he had made his way to his feet, had turned the suit, had found Martel.

From the looks of the bloody tangle her body had made when it snagged against the opposite doorway, it did not appear that Hawkes's efforts had been completed in time.

24

An unshaven Benton Hawkes sat in the stiff-backed but comfortable woven-fiber chair off to the side in the white room. The ambassador had refused to leave the intensive-care unit, even though he had been assured repeatedly that Dina Martel would live.

Oh well, of course, she'll live, Hawkes had thought bitterly as the medical staff cooed their never-ending reassurances. He stared down at the slight, broken body in the bed before him with the death white skin. After all, all the damn machines you have attached to her say she'll live, so she'll just have to. Right?

The ambassador had dismissed the staff, saying that he would sit with her . . . by himself. Postponing the negotiations, he took his meals there, slept sitting up in the single chair, and washed his face off occasionally in the room's duty sink.

He did not hamper the medical unit's personnel as they passed in and out to perform their duties, but he was quite adamant about not desiring any company. His was a solitary vigil—except for the two security men outside the door, assigned to stay with him at all times for the remainder of his stay on Mars.

About time, his cynical side chided him. How long did you think your luck was going to hold out, anyway?

"Longer than hers . . . I guess."

Hawkes whispered the words with angry regret. He had chastised himself incessantly since two days earlier, when the last attack had been made.

What did you think you were doing? Where did you think you were? Bad enough wandering around in the middle of the night and almost getting yourself killed . . . but to risk her life . . . to risk *her*. . . .

The ambassador turned his head back toward Martel's bed. Her limp body was still pale, still unmoving. Hawkes turned away, ashamed of himself. It had been his decision to go out without security people.

Staring down at her, he remembered her face without any bruises—laughing, shouting, scowling at him, arguing—bright and glowing and filled with an energy most women could only dream of possessing. And then, staring down at her, suddenly he had his answer.

True, he mistrusted both Red Planet's and the Earth League's security people. But the real reason he had taken Martel and gone off without anyone else was simply because he wanted to be alone with her.

Ah, me, the noble Ambassador Hawkes, his cynical side sneered, lusting after another man's wife. Mick Carri would be so proud of you.

Hawkes turned away, but did not leave the bedside. For the ten thousandth time his mind replayed the nightmare of their escape. Blowing the door had flooded the air lock with atmosphere—sucking it up from the lower levels—and had immediately brought scores of emergency workers. He had saved them—saved her—by the merest of seconds.

Collapse crews had filled the ruptured door with a quick spray of plastic foam to stabilized the leak. Even before they were finished, Hawkes and Martel had been spirited down into the lower floors of the colony. Hawkes had stayed as close as he could the entire time they had worked on her, waiting out the desperate hours, fearing she might die because of his foolishness eating at him every moment.

Once her most obvious injuries had been treated, the worst part of the waiting began. The ambassador turned back toward the bed, wondering what the final outcome for the brave woman before him would be.

Brain damage? Possible—there was no guarantee she had received enough oxygen during the last moments of his assault on the door. Full use of her hands? Fingers? Legs? Who knew? Blindness? Deafness? Full or partial? No way to determine. Not in her present condition. The doctors all agreed there would be no way of knowing for certain until she woke up. . . .

If she wakes up. If I don't send her back to her husband a vegetable, or a corpse.

There was so much science could do—and so little of it had been shipped up to Mars.

Why bother? It wasn't like it was a world or anything. It was just a factory. Just another section of real estate owned lock, stock, and barrel by another band of banks and corpor/nationals. Not a place where people lived . . . just where they worked.

Worked and bred and died.

Hawkes stared down at Martel. With all the tenderness he could manage, he reached down and brushed a single loose hair back in place over her ear. Then, taking her hand in his, he whispered, "I'm sorry, Dina. I'm more sorry than . . ."

Hawkes froze. Feeling something moving in her hand, he shifted his eyes in that direction. Opening his fingers, he saw several of hers flex—once, then again. His breath stopped, choking in his throat. His head snapped back in the direction of hers just in time for him to see her eyelids flutter, to hear, "Ben?"

It was a soft, struggling whisper, but it brought air rushing back into his lungs, hope into his soul, as he whispered back, "Dina? Dina—are you awake? Can you hear me?"

"Oh, Ben . . ."

Her voice was weak, distant. Her words were not slurred, how-ever, and suddenly the ambassador had to restrain himself from shouting. Squeezing her hand, he asked with fearful excitement, "Can you feel that? Can you see me?"

His questions not registering, she said, "You did it. You saved us."

"How do you feel? Can you feel your toes? Your fingers? Can you move your fingers?"

"No," she answered weakly. "I can't move my fingers." After a moment's pause, she continued, "You're holding them too tightly."

He looked down at their hands, then shifted his gaze up to her face. He saw her eyes opening fully, saw the twinkle in them, saw the unsteady smile working to spread across her face. Releasing his crushing hold on her fingers, he smiled himself, asking, "Better?"

"I don't know," she answered with mock seriousness. "Think I'll be able to play the piano when I get out of here?"

"I don't know why not," he told her, knowing what was coming. He waited as she took a deep breath and then gave him the punch line.

"That's great," she said first, then added, "I could never play before, you know."

"I know."

"Oh," she teased him, her voice still faint. "You've heard that one before."

"That joke, dear girl, is older than radio waves. Everyone's heard it before."

"You're just a mean old bully," she teased him again, her voice even fainter.

"Yes," he agreed. "And you're in intensive care for a number of good reasons. So, let me ask—do you want anything? Food? Drink? Are you in pain?" When she shook her head in response to all his questions, he said,

"Then why don't you close those beautiful green eyes of yours

and get some more sleep?" When she started to protest, he scowled
at her, then said, "I won't go anywhere. You go back to sleep. We'll
talk again when you wake up."

Martel tried to summon the energy to disagree, but she could
not. Even as she told him no, her eyelids closed and she fell back
into unconsciousness. Hawkes noted, however, that the smile she
had worn since she had first opened her eyes and seen him standing above her did not fade. Patting her hand gently, he bent down
and kissed her forehead, then returned to his chair across the room.
The ambassador started to sit down, then suddenly stopped. Grabbing up the chair, he crossed the room with it, and placed it down
next to the bed.

Then he sat down. Finally certain that his aide would be all
right, he closed his own eyes and got his first real rest since enter-
ing the emergency unit. His own smile did not leave his face any
faster than Martel's had left hers.

25

"So," asked Hawkes, "how are we feeling now?"

"Outside of the pain," his aide responded, "I feel swell."

Martel had slept for another seven hours. When she awoke the second time, she felt much stronger and far more alert. She was surprised to find that Hawkes had not left the room, that he had abandoned the negotiations to stay with her. A notion crossed her mind, one that involved feelings between her and the ambassador—but she dismissed it at once.

Then, suddenly, her eyes met his and she saw something that made her call it back for further consideration. Looking up at him, she started to speak, but felt the words catching in her throat. It did not matter. She could tell by his reaction that he understood—that he knew what she was going to ask. She could see the awkward embarrassment in his face.

"Ambassador, back on the *Bulldog* I gave you a story about being the next person in the system rotation. You thought I was lying. You were right."

Hawkes's face did not move. Giving him a moment to think, she continued, "The next person in the rotation was nowhere near close enough. So when my boss heard what you were up to, he pulled the right strings to get me the assignment."

"That right?"

"Umm hmm. He sent me to the subcontinent on an over-the-ice-cap one-seat rocket shuttle."

"Spared no expense," interjected the ambassador. His mind was racing, wondering just where her confession was leading.

"If he couldn't get me the assignment, I was to get as close to you as possible, anyway—stay near your back." Still weak, the woman paused for a breath, then added, "Val said you were too impulsive for your own good."

"Val?" Hawkes's eyes lit up. Suddenly everything made sense. "Val Hensen. That's how you could catch up to me—that's how you were able to get a gun on the *Bulldog*."

"The commander is very thorough." Martel gave the ambassador a coded message from his old commanding officer, a string of words that would mean something only to a soldier from Hensen's former brigade. Hearing the words, Hawkes nodded thoughtfully, suddenly realizing a number of things.

"Then you're not married. At least . . . you weren't on your honeymoon."

"No," she said, holding back something not important at that moment. "No honeymoon. Val picked that story out. He said it was best to present a professional front that would keep some distance between us."

"Well, yes," answered the ambassador slowly, old sections of his past suddenly flooding his brain, "I suppose that was probably the best approach." Hawkes closed his eyes for a moment, fighting old pains. Opening them again, he said, "Val would know that better than most, I guess."

"I know it's not my place," said Martel, looking up out of her bed, tubes still running into her arms, disappearing under the sheets aimed toward her chest. "But if it was something . . . if you wanted to talk . . ."

In his mind, the ambassador could feel long-buried memories clambering up out of the dark corner to which he had relegated them so many years before. He could feel the hot wind blowing in off the desert, hear the explosions all around him, see the thousands of enemy shapes hunkering off in the dark night.

The taste of burned plastic and fried air came to him again. The feel of sweat trickling down behind his ears returned to him so realistically that his hand almost rose to wipe it away.

So reflexive had his instinct become to pull away from anyone who came close to him—to his past—that Hawkes found himself actually pushing away from the woman's bedside. His involuntary response tore at him, pushing up walls almost faster than he could tear them down. His fingers clawing into a fist, he steeled his will, then said, "It was a long time ago." The words felt awkward in his mouth. Pushing them out one by one, he continued, saying, "It was my last year in the service. Of course, I didn't know then that it was my last year . . . I just, I mean . . ."

Her hand moved slowly, dragging itself across the bed to reach his shaking fist. Her fingers closing over his hand, she closed her eyes and simply listened as he talked.

"I was, what? Twenty-one, twenty-two? A kid. A kid playing at being a man."

Hawkes could see it all again. Fire rained down out of the sky, drenching the reflector net, lighting the area. His remaining troops were illuminated—revealed for the pitiful handful they were. For eight days Hawkes had maintained the line he had been sent to hold. He had lasted longer than anyone else Hensen could have sent because he would go anywhere, carry out any order, and his troops would follow him. They knew he would always get them out, no matter what.

"I'd advanced pretty quickly. I kept trying to get myself killed, command kept giving me medals and promotions for it."

He could see the last night clearly again. To his right was Max Carnahan, his second in command, his best friend. On his left was Angie, Captain Angela Lodge, his reconnaissance and communications chief, his best officer, his fiancée. Neither of them was worried. They had followed Hawkes from the Aleutian campaign, through the Korean run, the Standard Oil/Sudanese conflict, and the food riots in Providence. They knew he would find a way to turn the tide.

Another flood of fire washed down at them, and then the final assault came. The robot tanks began their crawl across the sand, followed by the thousands of starvelings desperate to follow them to food. They came in ever-growing waves, and try as they might, Hawkes's troop simply did not have enough trigger fingers to aim at the never-ending torrent of bodies.

"The enemy just kept coming. The force had invested in machines along the perimeter. Thought the threat of death would be enough to hold back the border. Didn't think they needed more than a handful to monitor their automatic weapons. Well-fed bureaucrats in air-conditioned offices. Forgot what hunger does to people."

The ambassador shuddered as he relived the final assault. Explosions continued to light up the night sky, pounding at the enemy, pounding at his own encampment. While his people continued to concentrate on the unceasing line coming toward them—advancing constantly over its own dead—Hawkes continued to argue with his superiors, trying to force them to recognize the reality of his situation.

Finally, when they broke connection, demanding he stay in place, he had turned to give the order for withdrawal. Let the bloody fools come, he had thought. Let them take what they want. They were going to, anyway . . . he saw no reason to die to make sure a few more or less were stopped.

And then, just as he turned to order his people out, a lone shrieker burst through the reflector net. The chemical gas bomb had shattered a fried-out section of the silvered plastic screen directly over Hawkes. Carnahan and Lodge saw it before he did.

"A bomb—a burner—made it through our defenses. I didn't know. It was right over my head—couldn't hear it for all the other noise. But two . . . two of my people . . . they saw it. They both

moved before I knew what was happening . . . pushed me out of
the way. Took the brunt . . . they took . . . they, they . . ."

And then, the tears broke forth. The tears held back for more
than thirty years exploded out of him, shaking his body, washing
his face, dripping onto his chest. As Martel put all the energy she
had into holding his hand, the ambassador dropped his head forward, pressing it against the restraining bar on the side of the bed.

He closed his eyes as tightly as he could, but he could not hold
back the tears, or the horrible sight so long buried in his memory.
He saw them again, burning, screaming—the sticky gelatin paste
clinging to them, eating into their skin, charring them to the bone,
and beyond.

He had lost his mind then. Racing to the sandbag wall, he had
slaughtered those coming forward, throwing everything in his ar-
mory at them. The thin line of human decency, the pity he had felt
for his starving opponents, had unconsciously stayed his hand before. But that thin line had been crossed.

Gathering up control pads one after another, he set off every
mine, blew every shell, launched every missile, every rocket,
dropped every piece of sky-high he had on the approaching horde.
The charred smell of his burning friends in his nostrils, he set his
own defensive shields aflame, crashing his orbiters into the approaching line, did anything to kill as many of the tattered attackers as he could.

Then, when he ran out of electronics and ordnance to throw at
the hated figures in the darkness, he gathered up whatever equipment was closest at hand and stormed over the wall, disappearing
into the night.

His men found him the next day, wandering the smoking, ruined
plain, searching for victims. Once he had run out of bullets, he had
clubbed to death those he found with his empty weapons. When
they had splintered and fallen away into pieces, he had fallen back
to hands and knife, searching the dunes, killing those few he found
remaining any way he could.

In the end, he kept the people whose land had been stolen from them away from their own food. The world was almost shocked at the death count: 318,000 people killed in a single night. An entire country of starving beggars wiped from the face of the planet for the greater glory of the Sands/Bender Corporation.

Val Hensen protected Hawkes, did not allow him to refuse his medals, his promotions, his glory. He protected the haunted, shattered young major, forcing him to keep his temper, not to throw away his entire life in some empty gesture. Putting "the hero of the line" on forced leave, he had taken the anguished young man on a retreat, staying with him until he had regained what he could of the threads of his life.

Hensen had understood. He had known Hawkes's father, had known of the sacrifice the senior Hawkes had made for his son, and how the deaths of his best friend and fiancée would affect the young man.

Hawkes told Martel the entire story—what had happened to his father, to Carnahan and Lodge, to the marching enemy that only wanted to eat. The emotion of it all overwhelmed him several times, but each time, as soon as he could continue, he moved on to tell her more.

Martel found herself crying as well, unable to control her emotions as she felt the aching depth of the ambassador's sorrow wash over her. He stopped then, his voice choked. Finally, though, when he could control himself again, he told her, "I've been alone since then. Oh, I've had people to talk to, who know me well enough . . . but I've never let anyone get close to me again. No one except a pup my dad had wanted me to care for. I loved that dog, and for all these years I've had pups from her line. The last was Disraeli, the dog Stine killed. Dizzy had been my only friend for his whole life—and then that rat bastard killed him. . . ."

Hawkes felt the sentiment and tears welling within him again. Shoving them aside, realizing there was no longer any time for self-pity, he said, "Back before, though, after the battle, I was ready to throw everything aside, denounce the corpor/nationals, the ser-

vice—you know, make a noble speech, get a flash of media attention, ruin my career, end up a proud nobody." Hawkes paused,
taking in a deep breath. Looking down at Martel, he let the aching
ball his fist had become open into a hand. Letting her fingers slip
into his, he told the woman, "Val stopped me. He convinced me
that it would be a waste. That if I really wanted to avenge what had
happened, to make it right, to get back at the system . . . then I
had to wait. I had to put in my time and become a part of the
system—a part with enough power to throw the switch when the
time came and bring down the game."

Standing up from Martel's bedside, the ambassador absently
brushed at his clothes with his free hand. Looking down at the
woman, he gave her a slight smile and said, "I think it's about time
I tell the doctors they have a patient who wants to talk to them."

The woman blinked, then nodded. The two of them stared at
each other for a moment, searching for words that would allow them
to break away from each other. After an eternal handful of seconds,
Martel finally asked, "Do you think you've got the power now?"

Hawkes reflected on the question for a long moment, then looked
down again and said, "Yeah. I think I do. And . . . I think I
finally know where the switch is."

Smiling, the woman stared back up at him, then said, "Well,
then . . . go throw it."

Feeling lighter than he had in decades, Hawkes left the room,
finally ready to bring all his enemies low.

26

"Carl Jarolic . . . just the man I want to see."

The environmentalist entered Hawkes's quarters, leaving his marine escort at the door. Giving the ambassador a look that revealed little, he moved his head to indicate the security people behind him, saying, "Yes, so I gathered."

Understanding his inference, Hawkes filled his voice with a soothing tone, saying, "The marines—oh, please, don't mind them. It's just that after all the different attempts on my life, those security people I can trust are getting a little edgy."

"Those you can trust?" Jarolic's interest was caught by the ambassador's choice of words. "Am I being told something here?"

"Not really," answered Hawkes. "You seem a clever enough man, so I wouldn't imagine so. Obviously someone is out to kill me. I have my opinions as to why, of course, but for reasons of my own, I'd like to hear yours."

"Mine?" Jarolic was taken aback. As he hedged, not understanding what the ambassador was after, Hawkes cut him off: "I'd just like to know what you think is motivating these attempts. Humor me."

"All right, if it will help in some way." Hawkes smiled encouragingly. Trying to organize his thoughts, Jarolic finally continued, "I'd guess that someone doesn't want the Martian work force to organize. Since it seems reasonable they'll get some kind of concessions out of all this, if someone wanted that halted badly enough . . . killing you would be a good way to stop negotiations. And if they succeeded, I guess it would be smart to try and point the blame toward the workers."

"Interesting," said Hawkes.

When the seconds continued to drift by in silence, Jarolic asked, "Excuse me, but is that it? Is that all you wanted? I mean, I do have duties to attend to."

"Not for a while, you don't," Hawkes told him. "I've requested that you be released from your duties to assist me for a while."

"What?" Jarolic almost came out of his chair. Although he kept himself under control, both shock and anger could be heard in his voice. "What do you mean? Who do you think you are that you can do this?"

"Who do I think I am? Governor of this planet. Until someone succeeds in killing me off, I can do anything I want. And what I want to do right now is prove your theory. I want to find out who it is that's trying to kill me, and to prove that they're doing it because, for some reason that probably only revolves around money, they want to keep the population of Mars indentured slaves forever." The ambassador stared at his guest, his face hard.

"From our discussion on the *Bulldog*, I got the feeling you were the kind of man that would be sympathetic to such a goal. Having fought alongside you, adding in the fact that you saved my life, I figure I can trust you at least as much as anyone else around here. Now, if you don't have any interest in helping these people, or if I can't trust you . . . well, then, say so now, and go back to those duties of yours."

The environmentalist took a moment to pull himself together.

Actually giving his answer a moment's thought first, he finally answered Hawkes, telling him, "No . . . no, sir. I would like to help
these people. And, yes, you can trust me."

"Well, then, that's settled," responded the ambassador, standing
up from behind his desk. "So, let's get going."

An hour later, the two men found themselves fast approaching
the surface of the planet. As they ascended in the same elevator Hawkes had taken with Martel a few days earlier, Jarolic
said, "Almost there." When the ambassador seemed surprised,
Jarolic reminded him that his work had already taken him to the
planet's surface. Hawkes turned his attention to their security detail. As he prepared to don his helmet, he told the well-armed pair,
"We're going to go out to inspect the collapsed dome. Don't remind
me that the League and RP management have already looked
things over. I'm the one someone was trying to kill out there—I'll
take my own look, thank you." As the elevator slowed to a halt, he
finished, "I want you two to stay here at the elevator door and guard
our backs. I'm not making the same mistake twice. Contact us
through the coms if you need to tell us anything."

The security people nodded, then unpacked the sole weights
they had carried for Hawkes and Jarolic, and began sizing up the
refurbished surface bunker for the best places from which to stand
their watches.

As the two security officers attended to that, Hawkes and Jarolic
did up each other's helmet tabs, started their oxygen flows, and
then stepped into the weights laid out for them, all four of which
snapped easily into place. The pair then tested not only the boot
connections, but all the points on their pressure suits that could
possibly be breached. Then, once they were both satisfied, they
headed for the recently installed emergency lock.

The new air passage was a much simpler affair than the old
compression door. It had been installed not as a permanent fixture,

but only as a temporary necessity to allow access to the outside for the security teams that had combed the area. The doors were multiple layers of plastic membrane reinforced with embedded magnetic strips. Anyone visiting the outside would slide himself between the membranes as quickly as possible to prevent too much of the bunker's atmosphere from being lost as he passed through.

Once the two men were outside, Hawkes directed Jarolic's attention to the remains of the ruptured dome. As they made their way across the planet's rough surface, their weighted boots forcing them to drag their feet through the sand, the ambassador cued his com to Jarolic's wavelength, then asked, "So, tell me, what do you think of the Resolute?"

"Excuse me?"

"The Resolute. The Mars First group—the terrorists—the unionists—the underground that's been trying to get things jumping here."

"I'm not sure you can call them all of that."

"No?" questioned Hawkes, "Well, then, what parts would you say applied?"

"Why me?"

"Just making conversation." To prod the environmentalist, Hawkes added, "It's a long way to the dome in these boots."

After a moment, his companion answered, "I wouldn't know, really. I'd say it's possible they were behind some of the attempts on your life—before you got here no one really knew which way you were going to go—but, I must admit, from what I know about them I think that they have Mars's best interests at heart."

"But are Mars's best interests everyone's best interests? Mars's and Earth's combined?"

"I . . . I don't . . . I guess I don't know," stammered Jarolic. "Aren't you here to smooth things out for Mars?"

"No, of course not," answered Hawkes. "I'm here to smooth things out for *every*body. What would be in Mars's best interests would be to make Mars the center of the solar system and shift all power away from Earth."

"Reversing the way things are now," Jarolic interrupted.

The ambassador smiled, admitting, "Blunt, but not incorrect. Earth now has too much power, and Mars too little. To reverse the situation simply reverses the problems. No, what I have to do is find a place where all the players can stand with something like equal footing." Hawkes paused to take a deep breath as the pair approached the ruined dome. As they worked their way in through a rupture point in the now-useless tunnel, the ambassador continued, "To do that, I have to understand all the players. I can't steady the boat until I can figure out who's rocking it." Hawkes paused as the pair moved into what was left of the old dome. Pointing toward the ruined garden, dry and frozen and useless, slowly rotting in the center of the massive plastic bubble, the ambassador asked, "Do you think the Resolute are capable of something like this?"

Staring forward, his eyes filled with unbelieving shock, the environmentalist whispered, "Do you mean growing it . . . or destroying it?"

"You tell me," answered Hawkes.

As the two men moved forward, Jarolic muttered, "This is unbelievable—this is impossible." As the environmentalist stared at the wrecked remains of the once-lush garden, he said, "I hadn't heard about anything like this being on the surface. Who could have done this?"

The ambassador watched the other man's body language. Even through the bulky pressure suit, he could tell that Jarolic was truly surprised. Tapping the man on the shoulder to break his fascination with the ruined plant life, he said, "I don't know, but I wish I did."

"I can tell you this," answered the environmentalist, "I don't know who tried to kill you and your aide, but I can't imagine the Resolute allowing something like this to be destroyed, no matter what the gain might be." Hawkes said nothing, waiting for Jarolic to continue.

His voice afire with trembling anger, he said, "Plant life on the surface of Mars—I mean, this would have proved their case—that the domes were a viable place to live. You can tell just from the remains that whoever planted this had already attained a viable ecosystem."

The environmentalist moved farther into the dome, pointing excitedly. "Look," he shouted. "Up along there—you see that streaking on the inner curve of the bubble? This place was generating its own moisture. There was enough plant life here to offset a full-time community of at least fifty people. Easily. Perhaps a hundred. Especially if they introduced a further range of growth in their own personal areas. Lawns, flowers—you understand—for the oxygen/carbon dioxide ratio . . ."

"I understand," Hawkes said softly, implying more than he admitted to. Turning back toward him, Jarolic approached the ambassador, his arms moving wildly for emphasis.

"This is a terrible crime. Life—life growing on the surface of Mars—plants pushing down roots, going to seed, dying, decomposing, giving birth to new life . . ." The man's voice was wild and excited. His hands clutching Hawkes's shoulders, he said, "It was all starting. Someone had taken the first step. Moved toward . . . toward getting people up out of that damned hole in the ground back there. Up to the sun, to the sky."

"Yes," agreed Hawkes sadly. "And someone else destroyed it."

Suddenly, Jarolic went rigid. His mouth straightened out into a thin line. His eyes narrowing, he demanded, "Show me."

Hawkes led the environmentalist back to where he had first seen the oxi-candle used to destroy the dome. After a few minutes of searching, the pair found the remains of the device that had been used to put Dina Martel in intensive care, and had almost killed Hawkes as well.

Jarolic was well acquainted with the mechanism. He had used

similar candles to light many an underground site where their by-product of heat was as welcome as the light they produced. The oxi-candle was still in place where it had been planted, its securing spike deep within the loose Martian soil. Jarolic suddenly moved away from it. As he stared down at the candle, he said, "Ambassador, when you noticed the candle before . . . was it on the inside of the tunnel?" When Hawkes asked what Jarolic meant, the man simply said, "You humor me this time."

"Well, to be perfectly honest, I don't know. It appeared to have been set to burn a hole through the tunnel wall. By the time I got back to this point, the hole had stretched up, down, sideways. What's your point?"

"Okay. First, the trigger is pointing outward. That would mean whoever set off the candle shoved the trigger up against the wall. Much harder to reach that way . . . *if* they were on the inside." Hawkes blinked, his mouth opening in surprise. Before he could say anything, his companion continued in an excited voice.

"Second, look at the line created by the bracing beams to either side of the initial hole. If you look closely, you'll see that the candle wasn't set up inside that line."

Hawkes dropped to his knees. As he studied the scene, he had to admit that the environmentalist was correct. But then, even as he worked his pressure suit erect again, Jarolic noticed something else. Pointing frantically away from the tunnel, he shouted, "Look! Look at that." As the ambassador stared across the broken, empty plain, the environmentalist moved away from him, pointing at the ground as he did so. "Look," he ordered again. "Don't you see them?"

It took Hawkes a moment to note what Jarolic's trained eye had spotted. Eventually, though, he said in hushed amazement, "Tracks."

"Exactly," said the excited Jarolic. "Leading up to the tunnel from the other side of the bunker, and then back again that way—

out into the desert." Bending down to examine the ground more closely, the environmentalist added, "This is why you never heard anyone. Whoever tried to kill you didn't do it from inside the tunnel. They were *outside*."

And then, before Hawkes could say anything, the first shots flew silently in front of his helmet.

27

"**R**un!" shouted Hawkes, pushing Jarolic back toward the dome. Several more shots tore through the thick plastic of the tunnel, showing the environmentalist in no uncertain terms what had started Hawkes moving.

Jarolic reached out and grabbed the ambassador's arm. Jerking him back, he halted Hawkes's progress just as more tiny projectiles tore in front of him.

"Down!" shouted the environmentalist. Letting himself drop, he pulled Hawkes down along with him as another fusillade went over their heads.

"There's someone out there with a bearing launcher."

"What?"

"It's a compression weapon—kind that fires only small ball bearings."

"BBs," exclaimed Hawkes. "An air rifle. Of course! No oxygen needed for combustion. But judging from the holes it's putting through the tunnel plastic, BBs or not, it can rip a hole in our suits just the same."

"Right. And they've got themselves positioned somewhere out there between us and the door. We can't get back in, and security can't come out to rescue us."

Another barrage slammed into the sand drift to which Jarolic had maneuvered the two of them. Both he and the ambassador looked their situation over. It did not look good to either of them. They were a pair of slow-moving targets, a long way from safety. A few holes in their suits and they would be dead before they could get back inside.

They could not see the enemy—had only a vague idea of his position. And it seemed likely from the number of shots being fired that there might be more than one of them. Hawkes's mind rolled over all their options, wondering what they could do.

His first impulse had been wrong. Not used to life in a pressure suit, he had forgotten for an instant how slowly they forced one to move. Anything moving at that speed was an easy target.

Then the tactical section of his mind told him, Don't move at that speed.

A hard smile crossing his face, Hawkes indexed his wrist-link, putting himself in contact with the security team in the bunker. He quickly alerted them to the situation outside, then ordered,

"I want you to scope out their location, then lay down a pattern of covering fire."

"We understand, Mr. Ambassador. We'll signal you when it's safe to return to the bunker."

"That would be fine—if I planned on returning."

"Sir . . . ?" Hawkes did not bother to explain himself, answering only, "You have your orders, mister." Then, turning to Jarolic, he said, "First off, thank you for helping me put things together out here."

"Anytime."

"I might hold you to that. Second, though, thanks for saving my life—again. You're a handy fellow to keep around."

"Your point, Mr. Ambassador?"

"When the security people start firing back at our friends, I'm going to make a move toward bringing them down."

"What?" exclaimed Jarolic. "In one of these suits? You're not going to get very far very fast."

"I am," answered Hawkes, reaching down toward his left boot, "once I get rid of these." With a flick, the ambassador released the weight plate on that foot, then moved to his right boot and released the other. Turning to Jarolic, he said, "You with me—or have you had enough heroics for one day?"

"We wear these weights for a reason. If you don't keep yourself stabilized, you'll go down fast—helpless." His eyes flashing toward the broken rocks all around them, he added, "Which means you probably won't get up again."

Hawkes nodded. "It's all right. You stay here. I've been wanting to get my hands on this bunch for a while now."

The younger man stared through the dark glass of his helmet, straining to see Hawkes's eyes. As he did, he put a hand on the ambassador's shoulder, shook his head, and said, "You must have been a real hell-raiser in your day."

"You want to see some hell get raised—you stick with me. This day isn't over yet."

Reaching down to his boots, careful not to raise his head above the level of the protecting dune, Jarolic released his weights, saying, "Then, let's race to sundown."

Before Hawkes could reply, the booming report of the security men's weapons echoed across the barren plain. Raising his helmet just enough to see where their shots were landing, the ambassador calculated the kind of arc he and his companion would have to set to sneak up on that position. Then, steeling himself, he gulped down a deep breath of his suit's pure atmosphere and shouted, "Let's do it!"

The two men made their way to their feet and started bounding across the Martian surface. Both moved in staggeringly long leaps, covering hundreds of yards in just seconds. It was a speed unknown to either of them, helped in part by Mars's lesser gravity, in part by its atmosphere's lack of resistance. In less than a minute, they had raced down the length of the ruined tunnel and were rounding the dome.

Trusting luck, and not daring to decrease their speed, the two barreled around the end of the dome, charging straight on. Instinctively, both headed toward the point drawing the security team's main fire. Their weightless boots slid across the surface of the sand, forcing them to bob and weave to maintain their balance. A fall at that point would not only ruin their chances of surprising their enemies, but—as Jarolic had implied earlier—with all the brittle, sharp-edged cinders littering their path, might prove fatal as well.

Halfway from the curve of the dome, the two men split apart. They knew bunching together only gave their foes an easier target.

If they see you, Hawkes thought to himself. And the whole idea here is to not be seen—so, get moving, old man. Get moving, and keep moving, and don't be seen until you want to be.

The ambassador bent low, compacting his form, running all out. As he moved, he indexed his wrist-link, ordering the security men to cease fire. Jarolic saw the motion and bent low as well, pouring on the speed. Both men knew they would be at the dune protecting the enemy in a matter of seconds.

Then, thought Hawkes. Then we get some answers.

That mean you won't be killing them like you did Stine? his cynical side joked with him. A vision of Martel's body jammed in the doorway of the ruined compression chamber flashed through his brain. Again he saw her vacant eyes staring at him—the floating spheres of her blood escaping out the door—lived again the helpless horror of watching her die, unable to do anything more than pray and wait. Slamming the memory into the back of his brain, he snarled, "Oh, I'm going to kill them, all right. They just won't get off as easy as Stine."

And then he was upon them.

There were three figures camped behind the dune. Hawkes plowed into the largest of the trio at full force, lifting the man up and out of his crouch, sending him flying from behind the protective wall of sand. The man landed hard on his back, splashing sand and cinders in all directions.

Jarolic reached his first target at the same moment. He chose the same approach as Hawkes: simply running headlong into his target. His attack knocked loose his foe's pressure helmet. Before anything could be done, all the air stored in the woman's suit rushed out, and was quickly followed by whatever her tank supplied.

In a maddened panic, she scrambled for her helmet during the handful of seconds she had left. At the same time, the third member of the team turned, trying to bring his weapon to bear on either of the two attackers. He was able to get off a round of shots before Jarolic threw himself on top of him. They all went wild, however, managing only to further tear the panicking woman's suit.

Hawkes turned back from his first foe, watching the flying helmet land at his feet. Instantly understanding the situation, he scooped up the helmet and headed back into the fray, just as the last shots fired by the man on the ground tore through the woman's suit—and her body. As the ambassador stopped, holding the helmet out to her, the woman gurgled, blood splashed out of her mouth, and then she fell to the sand—dead.

When the first man Hawkes had hit did not rise, the ambassador inspected the situation, finding him dead as well. His suit—and his spine—had been pierced by a short, thick dagger of obsidianlike rock. Hawkes stared at the blood that soaked into the ground beneath the dead man's body, and leaked out of and around the woman's pressure suit, and, remembering the wave of it flowing from Martel, sadly whispered, "Maybe they weren't so wrong when they named it the red planet, after all."

Then, throwing aside the useless pressure helmet, he helped Jarolic drag their only living enemy to his feet. Roughly pushing the man forward toward the security officers, who approached from the bunker, he thought to himself, Now . . . now we put an end to this.

28

The prisoner refused to talk. He had spoken, of course. He had made prophecies of the colony caverns running red with blood, warned of riots, the mass murders of Red Planet management, the rape and slaughter of their families, other ramblings in the same vein. But as to who he was working for, why he had twice tried to kill the ambassador, what he hoped to accomplish, his only answer—over and over—was, "The Resolute are firm. All else shall be washed away."

Those facts had been only mildly surprising to Hawkes—certainly no more surprising than to discover that his attacker was the same long-haired man who had attacked him outside of Recycle. The ambassador had almost hesitated in turning him over to Red Planet security. On the one hand, he wanted to question the assassin personally. On the other, he still had his doubts about whom he could and could not trust.

But, he decided in the end, standing in the interrogation area with the security men who had accompanied him and Jarolic to the surface, if I can't trust these two . . . who can I trust?

Giving orders that the pair remain with the prisoner at all times, he retired for the moment. He had more than one reason. First, he wanted to check in on Martel. Despite her rally, he was concerned about her condition. Also, he wanted to consult with her on every-thing, especially his prisoner. He dismissed the man's rantings about being a member of the Resolute. His instincts told him that was a lie. Still, the captured assassin was the first concrete link he had found to whoever was behind what was going on, to whoever it was that was trying to kill him . . . and had killed Disraeli.

You just might be a little too emotionally involved to handle this guy. Besides, it's always best to be second.

Hawkes knew that Red Planet's people would play by the rules with their prisoner. Whatever he had to say under their gentle questioning, Hawkes would study the vids of it . . . then it would be his turn.

And I won't be so gentle.

The ambassador rounded the last bend before the intensive-care unit. In the distance he could see Jarolic in heated discussion with the two marines stationed outside Martel's door. As he neared, he asked, "Gentlemen, anything I can help with?"

"Our Mr. Jarolic here doesn't seem capable of understanding a no-admittance zone, Mr. Ambassador."

"Mr. Hawkes," started the environmentalist, "all I wanted to do was—"

"Please, please," said Hawkes, cutting Jarolic off, "everyone . . . we're all one big happy family here." Turning to the pair of marines, he said, "Ed, Dave, job well done. Thank you very much. I think in the future we can afford Mr. Jarolic a bit of latitude." Turning back to the steaming environmentalist, he said, "It's an old saw, but they *were* just following orders. My orders, to be exact. So blame me, and let's go see the patient."

The marine closest to the access panel stepped aside and then indexed the door open, allowing the two visitors to enter. As they did they found Martel, still flat on her back, stuck with tubes and attached to monitors, but with a highly amused look on her face. As they approached, she laughed and said, "Carl—I see you finally got in."

"Very funny," said Jarolic in a bitter tone. "Our shipmate's a comedian." Hawkes spread his hands, offering, "I rescued him for you. He's done it for me so often, I figured it was my turn."

Turning as best she could to face the two men, Martel said, "I could hear him outside—arguing and arguing. It was just so . . . so . . ." The woman stopped, alternating between gasping weakly for breath, then giggling again.

Jarolic rolled his eyes, offering defensively, "I came down to visit . . . and they told me to go away. I have to admit I really came down in the hopes of finding you, Mr. Ambassador, but . . . after they cheesed me I just bug-flipped. Guess it became one of those principle-of-the-thing bits. You know."

Raising an eyebrow, Hawkes noted, "You know, Carl, you get a bit colorful when you're miffed." Martel laughed again, covering her mouth out of pity for Jarolic but still unable to control herself.

Turning back to her, Hawkes said, "You'd better settle down, young lady. You keep on laughing like that and you might break something in your condition."

Then, turning back to his companion, the ambassador asked, "But you said you were actually looking for me. You sounded a little serious, too. What's up?"

"Ah, actually . . . it was . . . ah . . ."

"Unless it's something embarrassing, you can speak freely here. This is sort of a meeting of the Keep Benton Hawkes Alive Club. If the three of us can't trust each other . . ." The ambassador let the thought briefly hang in midair, then asked, "So, what's on your mind?"

"Sir, I've been hearing some very disturbing rumors ever since we came back in from our little expedition."

"The ones about riots, murder, management pogroms—those kinds of rumors?"

"Yes. They're spreading throughout the colony—fast." Jarolic moved toward the room's single chair. Grabbing its arm, he turned it slightly and then sagged into it, as if all the energy had suddenly drained out of him. As the environmentalist tried to pull himself together, Hawkes offered, "We were hearing the same thing from our prisoner."

When Martel asked what he was talking about, the ambassador quickly filled her in on all that had happened outside. By the time he was finished, Jarolic seemed a bit more steady. Turning back to him, Hawkes said, "Anyway, I'm not sure we have that much to worry about. The guy claims to be a Resolute slogan spouter. He was talking in clichés the first time he tried to kill me, and that's all he's been doing since we started to question him."

"I'm not so sure he's Resolute," said Jarolic. "And, I'm not so sure he's just spouting slogans."

"Carl," said Hawkes with a touch of calculated frustration, "the man's on file. His name's Ray Peste. He's a Martian—a low-level commander in the security force, no less. He's been here three years. He hasn't said much, but he does claim to be one of the Resolute. He says they have members at every level. He also said," finished the ambassador, forcing his voice to grow more serious, watching Jarolic's reaction carefully, "that he's their assassin, that it was his job to kill me."

The environmentalist stared for a moment, then lowered his eyes, breaking contact with Hawkes's. Closing his eyes, he took a deep breath, then looked up again and said, "Mr. Ambassador, I really wish I didn't have to say this . . . but I do."

"Carl," asked Hawkes, only somewhat surprised in the darkening shift in Jarolic's manner. "What is it?"

"I think there is something going on here no one knows about, and that it's going to blow wide open—soon. I think there's going to be some kind of outbreak . . . and that it's going to be a lot worse than anyone can possibly imagine."

"Carl . . ."

"That man is probably telling the truth about a riot, but he's not Resolute. He just wants the workers to take the skid for whatever happens."

Hawkes could see that something was upsetting the environmentalist, something he was having a great deal of difficulty getting into words. Taking a small step back, he tried to give the younger man the feeling of having more room. As he did, though, he asked, "Carl, how would you know these things?"

Jarolic twitched, and then stood to face Hawkes. Staring unblinkingly at the ambassador, he took another deep breath, and then announced, "I know he's not a member of the Resolute, because I am." Not trying to read the looks on either Hawkes's or Martel's face, Jarolic plowed forward, saying, "And I know he's not the man they assigned to kill you . . . because . . . that was my job."

29

"**W**hat?"

"I posed as a wire-service man to get onto your ranch. I'm the one who planted the bomb in your truck."

As much as he had expected the announcement about being a member of the Resolute, Hawkes had not been prepared for Jarolic's second bombshell. Grabbing tight hold of his will, he forced himself not to speak.

First rule, his mind thundered. *First*—let the other guy do the talking. Keep it all in, no matter what you want to say or ask. Shut up and let him talk.

"I was already in Lunar City when you arrived. You were moving too quickly, though—no opportunities there—so I booked passage on the *Bulldog*, figured I'd get you on the way home."

Ignoring his mind's cautioning, Hawkes asked, "What stopped you?"

"Listening to you. You might remember I went at you pretty good at the dinner table. But when I saw how you handled yourself, what you had to say . . . who you were—who you *really* were . . ." Jarolic twisted his head from side to side, biting at his lower lip. "I, I . . . I don't know. You weren't what we'd been told."

"And what was that?" asked Martel, knowing Hawkes wanted to know, sparing him the trouble of asking.

"The word was that you were just a stooge tool deep in the Earth League's pocket. That anything you did here would just be . . . for show, you know. To set us up for the clobber."

Hawkes moved past the younger man, heading for the room's single chair. Sitting down, he put his head in his hands, burying his face in his fingers. As he sat, wordless, seemingly the picture of dejection, Jarolic moved closer to him, pleading his case.

"I swear to you, the Resolute were only behind the bomb." Facing Hawkes, eyes steady, his voice rose as he insisted, "I know the rumors say the men who invaded your ranch were Martian, but they were not Resolute. We couldn't raise the money for something like that even if the colony went on another thirty years. It was all we could do just to get me to Earth."

"Oh, well," said Martel with sarcasm. "Good to hear you're too poor for any all-out violence."

"You're missing the point," Jarolic told her. "I'm trying to warn you about something. I just confessed to a crime you could have me executed for. Doesn't that tell you anything?"

"There's a man in custody here who apparently has pretty much the same story," she snapped back. "You both claim there are going to be riots soon, both claim to be part of the Resolute, both claim to be assassins sent to kill the ambassador."

"Well, yes," said Hawkes, lifting his head. "But I've actually caught the other guy making his attempts." Shaking off his mock depression, the ambassador faced Jarolic. "You might be a failed murderer, Carl, but I'm pretty sure you're an honest man. I believe you planted the bomb. I also remember some other things you've done for me, so let's say we're even. Also, there's a guy with long brown hair and a nasty disposition I've been itching to do a little dental work on. How about the Resolute assassin and the stooge tool join forces and go see what else that boy has to say?"

"All right, fine," said the ambassador, sitting across the large table from the man with the long, brown hair. His elbows on the table, he threaded his fingers, resting his thumbs against his chin. "You've told us fifty times. Excellent. Now, tell us for the fifty-first. Why has the Resolute planned these riots?"

"To show you greenie flips we mean business. To tell you to pack up your thieving overlords and head on back to Earth." The assassin banged his chains against the tabletop. The clatter echoed through the plain room as he shouted, "Mars for Martians, law! Martians in red clay—Greensiders in hell!"

"Oh, dear," said Hawkes with mock fright, "slogans. The rabble have slogans. Whatever shall we do?"

"Sir . . . ?" asked one of the pair of marines in the room.

"No, no," answered the ambassador. Holding up his palm as if to restrain the man and woman, he said, "We couldn't possibly use violence on him. That was outlawed decades ago."

"Ah, sir . . . ?"

"No, no, no beatings. No torture. No mind-altering drugs. We couldn't break his bones, or fry his cortex, or burn his skin, or run electrical current through him." His voice darkening, the false notes fading quickly, Hawkes continued, adding, "No tugging on his nails with pliers, no inserting thin glass tubes into his urethra and then bombarding him with sexual images until he goes erect and castrates himself. No, no, nothing like that."

Peste involuntarily moved back, pushing his spine deep into his chair's woven back. Seeing an uncomfortable dread growing in his eyes, the ambassador let his voice drop to an even more sinister level as he added, "No . . . marines, diplomats . . . we can't do things like that. Rub lye into someone's eyes, snip their toes off, break their teeth with hammers." Hawkes stood up then, moving his way around the table. "Sewing bugs under his eyes, slicing a forked path down the center of his tongue . . . or maybe," added the ambassador, his voice lilting with sudden surprise as he reached a finger out to touch the chained man's shoulder, "maybe just probing him with needles for a while."

Peste flinched violently, the force of his fear moving his chair several inches. The ambassador ignored the reaction, walking back toward the two guards as he said, "No, the law is the law. We just can't do any of that. Which is why you two will be leaving now."

"What?" shrieked the assassin. "You can't leave me here with him."

"Oh, come on now," chided Hawkes as he held open the door for the already departing marines. "You're in security—you know I can't stay. Against regulations for an outsider to be present when a prisoner receives visitors."

"Visitors?" sputtered Peste. "What're you talking about? Who? What do you mean?"

"Why," answered the ambassador as he held open the door for five silent figures who entered, each with a menacing satchel slung over his shoulder. "Your Resolute brothers."

Terror filled Peste's eyes. He was not stupid enough to miss what was being done to him. He was also not foolish enough to think Hawkes was bluffing. The men moved up to the table and threw their bags onto it, each one clanging with the sound of tools banging one against the other. The chained man, feeling the last of his resolve crumple, shouted, "All right, you win. You win."

"What?" asked Hawkes, stopping halfway out the door. "What do we win?"

"Whatever you want. Names, places . . . answers. I'll talk. But"—Peste regained some of his courage, putting it all into a single demand—"you have to promise to keep me alive. Your word, Hawkes. Your *word* . . . that you'll keep me safe, and that you'll get me back to Earth."

The ambassador pretended to consider the offer for a moment, then said, "Names, places, answers. In other words, just talk . . . your word against someone else's? No good. Not enough."

Turning his back on Peste, Hawkes headed out to the hall. Before he could let the door shut behind him, however, a sudden inspiration came to the chained man, causing him to scream, "Proof! I can give you proof!"

"What proof?" demanded the ambassador in a demanding snarl. "Spill it—now."

"I can take you," answered Peste in a shaking, frightened voice. "I can show you all you'll need."

"Well," said Hawkes, his voice suddenly light and chipper, "I for one love a good show. Let's go see what you've got."

30

Peste led the way for his two marine guards, Hawkes, Jarolic, Sam Waters, and the five silent Resolute members. They were deep below the Above in an old explorer bore—one of the wildly arching deep digs the Originals had sunk over half a century earlier. All in the party were heavily armed, just in case the chained man was a better liar than he seemed.

The group slowly moved along, lighting their way with hand torches. The tunnel was cold from the lack of both heat and any trace of human passage. As they moved through the almost frosty subterranean passage, Hawkes commented on how smooth the walls were. Jarolic told him, "That's because they were dug by directed lava flow."

"What?"

"The Originals. When they first landed, they dug down to a large lava sphere."

"That's right," added Waters. "My daddy told me about it. The Above was built mainly in the remains of an old lava pit. Then, when they broke in, they set up the equipment they needed to tap into the planet's core—where it's still molten. Then they set off mini-eruptions in the magma—"

"Actually they would have to drill and set the explosions off in front of the magma," corrected Jarolic. "Opening the rock up a bit to coax the molten rock to burn through in the direction they wanted it to go."

"My dad was a magmateer," said one of the silent Resolute members. "My mother told me the stories about the tunnels. Tunnels like these—they're all over the place—go all over. Remote boring isn't an exact science. The slap-cappers would take their best guess and pray." The man went quiet for a moment, then added, "Dad didn't guess right one day—got swept up when a hot flood rebounded for some reason. Plugged up and poured back. Eighteen magmateers . . . burned up in seconds. Just gone. Even their hard suits just melted down. They never found nothin'."

The entire party went silent again, mostly out of embarrassed respect. As they moved along, playing their lights across the walls and floor and ceiling, kicking up the reddish yellow dust that had covered the tunnel base over the decades, Hawkes asked, "Peste— where exactly are you taking us, and how much farther is it?"

"I don't think it's far. You have to remember, no one knows these tunnels that well. What I want to show you happened a good while back. I'm not exactly . . ."

And then, Peste stopped moving. Directing his light ahead, he saw that for some distance the floor was littered with pieces of broken glass and metal. Playing his light along the left wall, he noted a sudden pattern of wild breaks and chips in the otherwise smooth wall. Switching his light over to the right-hand side, he found the final off-branch he had been looking for. Pointing ahead with both hands due to his cuffs, he announced, "There. That's it."

The small band crowded in through a long-abandoned pressure doorway. Motioning to one of the Resolute members, Waters ordered, "Jerry, let's set up that dish now . . . get some light in here."

The man did as directed, taking only seconds to unfold the lightweight reflector lamp. When he clicked it on, the chamber was bathed in a high-intensity white. Except for two even smaller exits, and a heavy lever built into the back wall, there did not appear to be much to see. Turning to their prisoner, Hawkes said, "There doesn't seem to be much here."

"There's enough," answered Peste. "I led a clean-out party down here a couple months back. We had word a group of Resolute were going to meet to make final their plans for forcing a union on Red Planet and the League. My bosses didn't want that. I was ordered to stop it, break it up . . . get rid of them."

"Your bosses?" asked Waters, visibly distressed. "*I'm* one of your bosses. What the goddamned hell are you talking about?"

"You're not my boss, Waters," sneered the man. "You haven't got a clue as to what's really going on here."

The Resolute members started to whisper among themselves. Quietly the two marines slid in between them and the prisoner. While everyone waited, Hawkes asked, "But where's this proof you were talking about?"

"Here," answered Peste, pointing to a broken spot in the wall. He moved about the room, pointing to each additional section of chipped floor or wall he came across, adding, "And here, here . . . here. Here, too. Here."

The ambassador went up close to one of the spots. Inspecting the pattern of the breakage, he said,

"Shotgun patterns." Turning back to Peste, he said, "You shot up a room. So what?"

"Following our orders, we shot up a room full of people."

"And did what with them?" asked Hawkes. "There're no bodies, no blood, nothing. Holes in a wall don't prove much."

"We hosed the place." When the look on the ambassador's face remained puzzled, the prisoner added, "Recycle."

And then everything fell into place for Jarolic.

"The Cobbers!" He growled. Moving forward across the room, he continued to shout out names, his voice growing with each new one. "Samuels and Renker . . . Fennel, Smitty, Lara, Rabbit and Skuker! You bloody fucking bastard!"

Hawkes made a motion to one of the marines. The man quickly

put himself in between Jarolic and the prisoner. Jarolic struggled with the marine, screaming, "I'll kill you myself, you shit-fucker! You bastard!"

While the guard contained the environmentalist, Hawkes raised a hand to caution the other Resolute members to stay back. Addressing them all, he barked, "That'll be enough. We're here to keep the solar system in one piece. Not indulge our own feelings."

Standing back safely behind the ambassador, Peste taunted Jarolic and the rest of the Resolute, shouting, "That's right. We killed them, hosed them, distilled them, and sent their juice on to fertilize the smush."

Turning to the ambassador, he said, "It was justified action. They killed eight of my squad. That's the tracings you saw out in the hall. They blew the tunnel on us. What was left of us came in shooting. We recycled them just like any other corpses on Mars."

Jarolic burst past Hawkes and the two marines and screamed out, "Then why the buzz lies about a suicide pact? Why the cover-up?"

"Ambassador," said Peste, ignoring the environmentalist, speaking only to Hawkes, "we had a dangerous situation on our hands. If those people had been prosecuted as unionists, even posthumously, their children would have lost everything. We chose to spin the story we did to try and keep the lid on"—the prisoner cocked his head in Jarolic's direction, then sneered—"these fanatics."

"You make a nice case, Mr. Peste," said Hawkes. "Of course, you've tried to kill me twice, and I don't think you can explain that away in the line of duty."

"No," agreed the prisoner. "Not any duty you'd agree with. But I was following orders, and I can prove it. Recycle is no more an exact science than remote boring. You get a security crew in here, let them stain the floor and walls, they'll lift blood trace—they'll find skin flakes, maybe even hair. Those wall hits . . . they'll tell you a lot." Crossing the room, Peste ran his hand over one of the broken sections of the wall, saying, "They'll find skin and blood trace underneath shot flecks. They'll be able to tell people were killed here. And they'll be able to determine something else: They'll see that the shot being used wasn't bearing shot. The pattern of cuts in the wall will show we were using flechette rounds."

Despite his years of experience, Hawkes showed a trace of reaction. Staring into Peste's eyes, he said, "Flechettes were banned on Earth forty years ago."

"That's right, Ambassador. Too horrible a weapon—cutting bodies apart. Banned on Earth, and never to be used on Mars. But when you've got the right patrons making sure you get what you need . . ."

Hawkes took a single step, stopping at exactly the right distance from Peste. Reaching out, he backhanded the prisoner once—twice. His knuckles smarting, he said,

"Now you listen to me, you smug son of a bitch. You're awfully cocky for someone who's in it as deep as you are. Helping us find the answers we need is all that's keeping you alive—and it may not do that much longer."

"Oh, certainly, Mr. Ambassador. Whatever you say. I'll just move to the back corner and strike a humble pose. You let me know when you're ready to dazzle us again with your legendary talents."

Hawkes turned his back on the prisoner, walking back to Waters and the Resolute members. He pulled them off to one side to discuss what they had found while the marines watched Peste. All the while, however, the ambassador was distracted by a nagging voice in the back of his mind—one suggesting that the prisoner knew something they did not . . . but that he should have been able to figure out.

When they finally left the Deep Below and returned to the Above, he discovered the one thing he had forgotten.

31

They could hear the sounds of disaster long before they could actually see what was happening. Not in the old tunnels, of course, but in the elevator coming up from the Deep Below. When they were still a third of the way down the shaft, the noise of the bloody turmoil above them began to reach their ears.

It did not take them long to understand what it was they were hearing.

"You knew." Hawkes turned on their prisoner. Slamming him up against the wall, the ambassador hissed, "You weren't warning us that riots were a possibility . . . you knew they were coming. You knew *when*!"

Peste stared down at Hawkes's hands on his coveralls and smiled thinly. "You can only kill me once, Ambassador. And then you lose whatever it is I have in my head."

"Another omission like this one," snarled Hawkes, pulling the prisoner away from the elevator wall, "and I may not care."

The ambassador stared into Peste's unblinking eyes for a moment, then flung him backward again, bouncing the man off the elevator wall. The car slid to a stop, and its thick double doors slid apart. As the outer door pulled back, the noise from beyond was suddenly amplified. Waters, the closest to the front, quickly moved out of the car, only to stop after several paces.

"Oh, my God . . ."

The Red Planet manager could not believe his eyes. There was smoke pouring through the air and fire in a half dozen different doorways. The elevator had opened at Recycle, the lowest, least populated level in the Above, normally a quiet, fairly empty place. Normally. What they found on the bottom concourse was a raging battle, but a battle without sides.

There was no telling who was fighting who—or why. When the riot had first started, it might have been labor against management, workers against security—but that had most likely passed quickly. There was no telling who believed in which cause—no uniforms, boundaries, or marks to tell true friends from enemies.

So it had turned into a melee, a nightmare of random violence where men and women simply battered each other, ran from each other, and killed each other for no better reason than that someone had declared it time to do so.

How? wondered Waters. What could have done such a thing? Turned his workers, his friends and neighbors—his world—into such a madhouse? Surely, he thought, hoped, and prayed, the people of Mars were not so easily turned into maniacs.

Stumbling another few steps forward, wondering what Peste and those who controlled him could possibly have done to bring such madness down upon all he knew, the manager suddenly balled his hands into fists and screamed, "Stop it!" Suddenly snapping out of his shock, he moved toward the maddened crowd before him. Grabbing two thrashing, bleeding people, he tried to pull them away from each other, demanding, "Stop it! For God's sake— what's wrong with you all? Can't you see that this is what they want?"

Hawkes sent one of the marines forward across the bloodstained, heavily littered pavement to grab Waters and pull him back before he got himself hurt. While he did, Jarolic grabbed Peste. Dragging the man's face up close to him, he snarled, "Your people started this, didn't they?"

"Good guess."

"And they're long gone, aren't they?" While Peste just smiled, the environmentalist continued, saying, "Stir it up and then run." Jarolic pulled back and then sent his fist several inches into the prisoner's abdomen. Leaving him against the wall, he turned away and shouted to Hawkes, "Mr. Ambassador, we've got to contain this somehow, before it's too late."

A plastic brick shattered near their crowd—a signal that they had been noticed. The female marine dragged Peste to his feet while her partner pulled Waters back toward the rest of the group. As Hawkes neared Jarolic, the environmentalist said, "None of this is the doing of the Resolute. All our leaders are right here. This is Peste's work."

"And good work it is," said Hawkes with a low voice. Reaching out to grab Waters by the shoulder, he asked the manager, "Sam, is there a public-address system that reaches all of the Above?"

When Waters assured him there was, the ambassador turned to the others and snapped off a round of orders. To the marines, he assigned the task of getting their prisoner back to his cell and keeping him alive. He instructed the Resolute members to get to their people and to spread the word to stop fighting and to get inside and stay there.

After that, he grabbed Jarolic and Waters, telling them, "All right . . . let's get to that voice box."

While the others moved off in other directions, Waters directed the ambassador and Jarolic back into the elevator. As they waited for the doors to reopen, gunfire broke out somewhere in the distance. One of the bullets struck the wall just yards from the trio.

When the doors suddenly began to open, Jarolic pushed Hawkes in first, pulled Waters in behind him. Something bounced off the doors as they closed, but none of the three had any idea what it was. Waters indexed the level they wanted. Then all three slumped back against different walls as they waited for the car to make the long climb ahead.

As they stood in silence, Hawkes thought about all the different riots he had witnessed in his time. Streets running red with blood; women and children screaming in the darkness; neighbors killing neighbors, stoning members of their own families, burning their own homes . . .

Just like here, the cynical side of his brain whispered to him. Just like now.

Breaking the silence in the elevator, Jarolic asked,

"You can see what they've done, can't you? You know what they're doing? This is all going to be used as an excuse."

"I know," agreed Hawkes. "I wouldn't be surprised if there are troopships already pushing off from the Moon."

"Troops?" sputtered Waters in disbelief. "You don't . . . heh, then again, sure you do. Sure you do." Looking at the level monitor, he said, "Next level. We'll have a good mile to go to get to the broadcast center."

"No telling what we'll find," said Jarolic, referring to the noise level coming from outside the car. Turning his neck first one way, then the other, he worked on the kinks he could feel in his back as he said, "We may have a real fight on our hands."

"We're human beings," said Hawkes, flashing the younger man an optimistic grin. "Every day fate lets us wake up again we have another real fight on our hands."

"You will grant that some days can be worse than others," asked Waters, some of his tension passing. "Won't you?" The elevator clicked quietly to a halt.

And then they were back in the midst of things. The new level was even smokier than Recycle had been. Waters theorized that someone might have sabotaged the air filtration system. Other systems seemed to have gone bad as well. The floor was wet, some unidentifiable liquid washing across the tiled concrete in sheets.

There were electrical hisses in the background, sounding danger-ously like live wires exposed to the open atmosphere.

Stopping in his tracks, Jarolic said, "Someone's got to check on the life-support systems—make certain they're actually running. Maybe there're people working on it now and I can give them a hand. Maybe there's . . . no one. Talking's more your jobs. You two go for the broadcast—I'll do what I do best." And then, before either Hawkes or Waters could say anything, the younger man was gone, headed in the opposite direction toward the main control section.

Moving on toward their own objective, they had not gone fifty yards when a swarm of angry, screaming people rounded a corner, coming straight for them. The ambassador hesitated a moment, but Waters moved forward, heading straight into the crowd.

"Stop," he shouted, his voice entreating friends rather than com-manding lackeys. "Please—for all our sakes. For the sake of Mars—please, stop!"

The crowd slowed its pace. This was something new. Since the riot had started, people had either run from them or attacked. No one had bothered to talk. Before they could act, Waters continued, "We've got to pull together. We've got to turn this around. If we don't, we're all going to die. All of us—our families, our children. We've got to stop, or we're all going to . . . die!"

The mob moved on toward Waters and Hawkes. They were bruised and bloody and angry. Their clothes were covered with the smell of smoke and their faces streaked with soot and tears. Many of them were carrying knives or makeshift clubs. Standing his ground before them, though, with Hawkes behind him, Waters put up his hands, begging, "Listen to me, please. Please . . . think. Think! Who are you fighting? No matter who you are, what you think you're fighting for—you're wrong. We were tricked. We've all been tricked!"

The ambassador studied the approaching crowd. The leaders seemed to be hearing Waters, moving slower, their anger diminishing as their attention began to focus on what Waters was saying. Here stood Waters, who was so ready to explain the intricate uses of sponge/mush fibers, who was so proud of his home garden and his hors d'oeuvres, bravely speaking out over the noise all around him.

"Someone out there wants us to fail—they want us to live in the dirt forever—never seeing the sun, never breathing fresh air, never seeing a lake . . . never knowing anything at all but work. Working to fill their pockets with plenty of bank, working to stuff their mouths with food we'll never taste, working until we drop, until we die, until our children and our grandchildren and our great-grandchildren die behind us."

The crowd stood, restless but listening. Hawkes knew that they had to be tired by that point; he and Waters had stumbled across this group when they were ready either to quit or to turn the march into a mindless rampage. He knew they were a powder keg, he only hoped Waters knew how to defuse them.

"And," the manager shouted, his voice harsh, his eyes dark and strained, "when we do finally die, do we get to leave this world in peace? No! After they're done working us to death, our bones aren't even buried. We're Recycled. *Recycled!* As if that were a fit way to spend eternity."

Waters paused to catch his breath. Every eye in the crowd was on him as they waited for him to speak again. As he began to realize that dozens of armed people had been stopped by his voice, he had time to be very afraid.

But before his fears could take complete hold of him, he felt his lungs fill and his pulse quicken. Pushing all his doubts aside, he shouted, "Well, no more. *No more!* We're not going to let them distill us down into the water they wash their feet with. We are not their dogs, their slaves, or their fools . . . not anymore. We're Martians! *Martians!* This is our world, not theirs . . . not any-body's but ours. And today we take it back!"

The crowd broke into cheers. This was no polite applause, but screaming, whooping, crying joy that thundered through the halls and corridors with an energy that increased with every new person it touched.

The crowd fell in with Waters, ready to obey his every word. As he led them to the broadcast center, Hawkes simply fell in step beside him, knowing there was nothing he needed to do. He had always known that he was only a mediator . . . that his job was not to wield power but to help others to understand how to use their own.

For the first time since landing on Mars—since he had left his ranch—he felt that things might turn out all right. Of course, his cynical side reminded him, it was also quite possible that within a few weeks everyone around him—himself included—might be dead.

Well, as long as we die fighting for what we believe in, that's all right, too.

With that, the ambassador gave up debating the future. He had finally stopped hating Mars. For Hawkes, it no longer mattered what the fourth planet lacked. Suddenly, it had something the Earth had lost a long time ago.

It had hope.

32

"All right, we know we don't have a whole lot of time, so let's get things in order."

Hawkes stood in front of the Martian General Assembly. It had been two days since Samuel Waters had dispersed the crowd in the hall to spread the word, and then gone on the broadcast network to make the same impassioned plea to all of the colony. It had taken that long to restore enough order to be able to have a meeting.

Jarolic had been correct about possible sabotage—more correct than he had thought. Peste's accomplices had released Deselysurgamide, a psychotropic hysteriant, into the air-recycling system. After it was certain to have reached all levels they had shut the system down, as well as overflowing the fresh water and sewage systems.

"We've learned a lot in the last two days. Now we need to review it and get down to what we're going to do about it."

Because they had been down in the Deep Below, Hawkes and the others had not been affected by the hysteriant. Jarolic had found it reasonably easy to get the air, water, and sewage systems running again. The saboteurs had not wrecked any of the necessary equipment—even they knew that if the systems had not been brought back up within a few days, everyone on the planet would have died. The people giving them their orders wanted a subdued colony, not a graveyard.

"We know that the violence Mars recently lived through was not the fault of her people. Outsiders drugged the entire colony, then incited the riots. During the madness the colony sustained a horrible amount of damage. Luckily, however, reports show that most of it was superficial in nature."

"The grandolds built Mars to last," came a cry from the assembly. Hawkes chuckled along with the rest before answering, "Well, then, let's take advantage of that."

Then the ambassador got down to the issues of the meeting. He started them small, getting easily finished business out of the way first so that everyone could enjoy a sense of having accomplished something by the time they broke for lunch.

First, the life-support managers reported on the status of the air and water systems. Next, Reclamation and Recycle reported on the cleanup efforts. They were followed by the colony medical staff, who gave what figures they had on the deaths and injuries that had occurred during the riots. They followed that with a report on what they had done to halt the spread of contagious diseases that might be caused by the sewage backups and water shortages.

Lunch was served in the assembly hall, for twenty minutes only. Having given them what he hoped was enough of a sense of accomplishment to get them charged up, and enough of a break to brace themselves for what came next, Hawkes called the afternoon session to order.

The head of security, a stocky, big-shouldered man named Norman Scully, took the podium at the ambassador's direction. He did not appear very happy. When the assembly heard his report, they were not very happy, either.

The forces Scully had available had been reduced by half. Nearly 190 of his people had been murdered during the riots, along with 30 of the *Bulldog's* marine contingent—including the pair assigned to guard Peste. Almost 160 security people were missing—no trace of them to be found anywhere in the Above or the Deep Below. The explanation for it all, given what Hawkes and Jarolic had learned on the outside, seemed simple to Scully.

"We believe that security was the department most heavily infiltrated by the outsiders. Apparently the Earth League has been sending people here for years in anticipation of what they did to us the other day."

"But, Norm," shouted out one of the assembly, "you said you searched the entire colony for this Peste son of a bitch and that he and all the rest of these buzz are missing. What do you mean, missing? Where the hell did they go?"

"Outside."

The single word threw the entire assembly into an uproar that took Hawkes a solid half minute to gavel into submission. Once he had restored order, he gave the floor back to Scully, who said, "The ambassador was set upon twice by people on the outside. It ain't hard to figure out they've got a base out there somewhere."

Cries of "How?" and "Where?" filled the room. After order had been restored, Scully answered them.

"We've checked the old, outer domes, but didn't find any trace of anyone using them. Likewise with the greenhouses, the vats, the factories . . . wherever the outsiders ran to, it wasn't anyplace we know." The security chief paused, then dropped his bombshell.

"There's little doubt that when the colony was first built, some other structure was put together in secret. Most likely it is below the surface. I've got people searching for it now, but it doesn't seem likely we'll be able to find anything for a few days."

The assembly went into an uproar again. Hawkes gaveled them into submission once more, thanked the security chief for his update, and promised that any pertinent facts discovered would be brought to the floor immediately. Then he turned things over to Waters so he could tell his fellow Martians what he had learned about the shipping, pricing, and profits on sponge/mush—both the figures the colony had been given over the years and what the real numbers might be.

As the manager began his speech, the ambassador accompanied Scully to the rear of the stage. Once they were far enough from everyone to talk privately, Hawkes said, "Good job. I liked that touch of bitterness in your voice when you said you didn't have any idea where our runaways could be hiding."

"Have to be careful," answered the big-shouldered man. "These people know me. Had to make it look real."

Hawkes and Scully knew exactly where their enemies were. In the opening days of Red Planet, Inc., an emergency shelter had been constructed to protect the workers in case of a systems failure. It had been closed down and forgotten years earlier—forgotten by everyone except a few old-timers like Scully.

"I agree with you that the League probably put most of its spies in my backyard," said the security chief in a low growl. "But that doesn't mean that they're the only ones. That bein' the case, it wouldn't make much sense to announce to some of them that I'm planning a raid on their brother snakes."

Hawkes had some misgivings about the plan. Even with the reinforcements from the marine contingent, Scully barely had a hundred people fit for combat. After making duty assignments for the minimum colony posts that would have to be monitored, he had only sixty-three troopers to take on his raid of the enemy stronghold—and that included the volunteers he had agreed to take from among the Resolute.

At first it had been argued that perhaps there was no need to go after the renegades, that the colony had more important things to worry about. Hawkes and Scully had pretended to agree, then gone ahead with their plans. Both men felt that having an uncontrolled force roaming Mars—with unknown amounts of supplies and munitions—was a threat too great to risk. They would have enough to worry about when the troopships arrived without having to look over their shoulders for Peste and his fellow traitors.

Traitors? To whom? he wondered. To Mars?

The ambassador turned the notion over in his mind. He had come to Mars searching for the people responsible for his own troubles—the ones who had attacked his ranch and killed his friends. He had hated the thought of Mars his entire life because of his father's tragic death.

Now, he thought to himself, you're acting like a Martian yourself.

As his eyes met Scully's, the ambassador calculated the odds against the older man. Their most conservative guesses had put their foes' strength at three times their own. Adding to that the fact that he would be laying siege to a strongly defended position, one manned by troops armed with weapons far more deadly than his own, the ambassador could but marvel at his courage.

Noting the look in Hawkes's eye, the old security man said, "Hey, don't worry, we'll get these bastards."

"I have no doubt," Hawkes lied.

"I appreciate the concern," Scully said, "but I'll get through this—all of it. I've been outnumbered and outgunned before. But I'm here. They ain't. End of story."

"I wasn't so much thinking of you, Scully," answered Hawkes. "You'll do what you have to. All of us will. We don't have much choice. I was just thinking about the troopships that launched from Earth two days ago."

The security man gave Hawkes a wink. "So was I." Patting the ambassador on the back, he said, "Buck up, sonny. You do your job, I'll do mine. We'll get this mess fixed up."

He turned and left the room, off to begin the preparations for his assault.

Turning back toward the assembly, Hawkes motioned to one of Waters's aides. The woman came over to him quickly. "Yes, sir. What can I do for you?"

"Tell Mr. Waters that I'm turning the rest of this afternoon's proceedings over to him."

"Yes, sir," responded the young woman. "Can I tell him what you'll be doing in case he needs to know?"

"My job," the ambassador answered. Then he turned and headed for the same door Scully had gone through, thinking, And, let's pray I start doing it right.

33

"**M**r. Ambassador," came Martel's voice over the com, "your call is ready."

"Think this will work?" asked Hawkes.

"We won't know until we try," she told him.

"All right," said the ambassador, indexing to open his vid circuit. "In that case, here goes nothing."

Forty-five minutes after the outbreak on Mars had begun, troops had been sent to the Skyhook. Their mission was approved, and appropriations were found. A force of more than a hundred thousand, prepared for urban combat, had been gathered, armed, and sent on its way . . . all in forty-five minutes. Hawkes knew there was no way such a thing was possible. No way at all.

Which means, he thought, carefully keeping his smile etched across his face, that some son of a bitch has been planning this for weeks. Maybe months.

"Benton," came Mick Carri's thick baritone. "What's up?"

"From what I hear," said Hawkes, forcing a tremor into his voice, "a lot of very heavily armed men . . . heading for Lunar

City . . . on their way here. Should I pretend to be politely amazed or just shocked?"

"Polite amazement will do," answered the senator. "No need to strain yourself."

"No need to send any troops, either," countered Hawkes. "We've got everything under control. Apparently you didn't have much faith that we could, but we have."

"No faith in you?" Carri put on a wounded face. "We've got all the faith in the world in you."

"Oh, I see," answered Hawkes. "You *do* have faith in us. You just happened to have a hundred thousand armed warriors standing by, all packed and ready to ship out for Mars . . . just in case we couldn't handle things."

"Okay, you want blunt, Ben, I'll be blunt. Yes. Yes, we've been getting troops ready for some time now. What did you expect? Pirate attacks, assassination attempts . . . and now, let's face it, you've got a situation on your hands."

"We do not have a situation."

"Of course you do, Ben. And it's one that's deteriorated to the point of a murderous uprising. I'm sorry if I've wounded your pride, but when things get this out of hand, steps have to be taken."

"I'm the territorial governor, Mick," sputtered Hawkes. Looking tense and worried, he glanced about the room as if searching for something, then added weakly, "I'm telling you we don't want those troops on our soil."

Carri made a noise halfway between a laugh and a bark. Then he rose out of his chair, thundering at the camera, "And I'm the head of the senate of the United States of America, Mr. Governor. And I'm telling you that the Earth League has requested we intervene in this matter, and with half the world's resources at stake, I'm inclined to follow through. Now, you make that sound any way you want. It's not going to change."

Hawkes's screen went blank, with only the words TRANSMISSION

ENDED flashing in its center. With a smile, the ambassador thought, Well, that should keep him feeling smug for a while. Now, on to a way out of this mess.

Indexing the console in front of him, Hawkes called Martel back in the broadcast center, asking if their second call—the one they actually wanted—had connected. When he was told his party was waiting, he thanked the operator and then indexed open the new vid circuit.

"This better be important to take an old man away from his golf game."

"Val," said Hawkes, "had any fun lately?"

"Yeah," answered Hensen, "I was having a good time playing golf until I was told I had to get to a vid because the governor of Mars was holding for me."

"Rank has its privileges."

Hawkes's old commander settled into an easy chair. "I've been following what I can of what's going on up there. You know they sent two troopships out. Word is they've got orders to impose martial law. Hints are being dropped that you're the root problem—that if the world goes hungry it'll be your fault."

"Knew about the ships—guessed the rest—but thanks for the warning. Good to know I still have a few friends left."

Hensen rolled his eyes in an exaggerated gesture, then said, "I tried to get through to you a few days back when things tore open, but they've got all transmissions to Mars blocked."

"We know."

"So, how'd you get through?"

"One of the smart young kids here figured out that Washington would take a call from us, and that while I kept them busy, she could splice off a beam to you and then maintain it when the initial connection was broken."

"Smart young woman, eh?" Hensen smiled. "Anyone I know?"

"I don't know if you'd recognize her in a wheelchair, but yes. You know her."

"Wheelchair?" The old man started violently.

Before he could say anything else, though, Hawkes added, "Yes, but she'll be all right. It's been a little rough up here. Doctors didn't think she'd be up and around for weeks. But, well . . . you know Dina."

"I certainly do. I hated to cut her orders that took her away from here . . . but I had a feeling you might need someone to watch the back of that hot head of yours." Hawkes almost blushed.

"Yes, well . . . I wanted to say thanks for that. She's pulled her weight and half of mine a few times so far."

"I'm still a step ahead of you, young Mr. Ambassador—always will be. But you didn't go to all this trouble to let me tell you that. What do you need?"

"Tell me, you think you could put together a consortium on short notice and buy a little stock for me?"

Hensen stared at the screen. He had been caught off guard for once and it showed clearly on his face.

"Oh, and just what do you have up your sleeve this time? Sure . . . okay, I'll bite. What stock?"

"Red Planet, Inc."

"R.P.I.?" Hensen's face dropped. As he tried to get his composure back, he asked, "Are you crazy? The stuff is worthless. Worse than worthless."

"Then it ought to be cheap enough that you could get a whole bunch of it—right?"

"I guess, I mean . . . why, Ben? Why in the . . . *why?*"

"Val . . . I've got an awfully risky proposition for you." Hawkes gave the words a moment to sink in, then started again. "But if it pans out . . . well, let me just ask, how'd you like to be the richest, most powerful man in the solar system?"

"Huh?" The ambassador's former commander pushed his lips into a thoughtful mold. Then, after a quiet moment, he looked up into his screen and said, "I always thought being the handsomest, smartest man in the solar system would be enough for me. But I don't know, a man gets older . . . his goals change."

A large smile crossing his face, Hensen asked, "Okay, wise guy, just what in hell are you up to this time?"

Hawkes smiled back, and then he told him.

34

A number of hours later, Norman Scully led his troops out across the coldly desolate Martian landscape. All of them were wearing the oversized work suits of space miners, ship hull workers, or deep tunnel diggers. The renegades had taken nearly all the lighter, more form-fitting style of pressure suits when they had bolted, leaving the bulky, slower-moving units behind. The old security man had taken the fact in stride, telling all his people to dress in as many extra layers of heat-reflecting clothing as they could stuff inside the suits.

"You ain't gonna have the power to waste on heat," he had lied, keeping his reasons to himself.

The sun had set long before. Just at twilight, Carl Jarolic had exited from the emergency air lock at the ruined dome in advance of Scully and his forces. Scully figured that Jarolic had the best chance of picking up the tracks he had spotted days earlier and locating the old emergency shelter.

Scully had a fair idea of where it should have been located. The problem was that it had not been sunk in a lava bubble like the rest of the colony. The main reason the spare bunker had been built was as a hedge against Murphy's Law. It was a "run-to" thrown up just in case the process of transforming the lava tunnels into living quarters turned out to have some unforeseen danger connected to it.

The shelter had been built in the style of the older Lunar City, dug out the old-fashioned way with the excavated soil dumped on top to serve as additional shielding from the various radiations from space. When the lava tunnels had proved perfectly safe, the cramped emergency shelter had eventually fallen into disrepair. Like the old bomb shelters considered so vital a hundred years earlier on the Earth, over time it had largely been forgotten.

There was Scully's problem: how to find one mound of dirt on the Martian surface that looked different from the rest of the terrain. Especially after decades of Martian winds playing over it. And after they found the mound, they would have to find the entrance, which Scully knew could be anywhere.

Jarolic's faint traces of footprints seemed Scully's best chance. As he and his people assembled on the surface, the security chief opened a com channel to Jarolic, mentally crossing his fingers. "Carl," he whispered into his helmet mike, "you out there?"

"I'm here," sounded the terse, static-muffled response in Scully's helmet's receiver. "Look north, northwest."

The security man turned his head in the direction given. He spotted a figure off toward the horizon after a few moments, both its arms waving animatedly. Calling back, he confirmed, "Got ya."

"Then follow me home."

Working mostly with hand signals, Scully got his people moving off toward the distant outline of Jarolic's pressure suit. Radio chatter was too easily detected and the old security man knew they needed every advantage they could get. He started his troops out, marching them out in single file, aiming them toward the retreating figure in the distance. As he joined the rank midway, he thought, This is gonna be a tough one, no matter what happens. Don't want to be expectin' the worst, but still, best to be strung out if they catch on to us.

Scully reached behind him, drumming his fingers against the heavy pack he had insisted on carrying. His excuse had been that Mars's lesser gravity made it easier to manage. The truth was that he did not want to entrust the responsibility of its contents to anyone else. His hand returning to his side, he thought, This mess may not go the way we want it to, but no matter what happens . . . we'll have at least a couple of surprises for the bastards.

Curling one side of his mouth into a sour grin, the old man kept moving across the broken Martian plain. The supplemental hydraulics in his pressure suit kept the heavy life-support unit going. He looked down to see his feet, but could not. The string of troopers in front of him were raising a sea of dust that had risen halfway to Scully's calf.

Watching the swirling dust billow further with each step, the old man thought to himself, Yeah, a couple of surprises. A couple.

Off along the horizon, quite some distance past the pressure-suited form the troopers were following, a lone figure sat patiently atop a dark bluff. He had been waiting for some sign of Jarolic's suit for several hours. When finally he caught a glimpse of it, a sigh of relief passed his lips.

Standing up, he stretched from side to side. Peste's second-in-command stared down at the slow-moving form of Jarolic's pressure suit—knowing it did not contain Carl Jarolic. The environmentalist had been captured much earlier. In the emergency shelter, the renegades had beaten him, drugged him, done everything they could to force him to surrender the details of Scully's plan.

He never talked. He screamed, he begged, in the depths of the madness brought on by his pain he even tried reason. But in the end, he told them nothing. He merely died, cursing their greed . . . the first true hero of the revolution.

And sadly, it was all in vain. The head of the renegade forces already had decided that Jarolic had to be a scout for some following war party. He simply sent one of his people out in the environmentalist's suit, counting on limited communications and the static sound of the older equipment to keep the switch from being detected.

And, thought the renegade, mightily pleased with himself, looks like it worked.

The Earth League plant thought of the years he had spent on Mars, playing the role of security man, riding herd on the Resolute. Like Peste, he had worked for half a decade to foment the troubles now ripping Red Planet apart. He knew that when the troopships arrived, harsh martial law would be imposed on the colony. He knew that he would no doubt be well rewarded for his part.

A smile spreading across his face as he watched the first of Scully's men marching into his death trap, he thought sometimes things really do work out for the best.

Then he took a step forward and gave a silent hand signal to his snipers positioned throughout the valley. Up and down the high-ridged cul-de-sac, men and women began checking their weapons. The long, strung-out line of troopers approaching their position was only a few minutes away.

The man forced himself not to laugh, not daring to risk being detected by Scully and his people.

No sense in blowing it now, he thought. Not now that it's all over . . . except for the slaughter, of course.

Silently, the renegade raised his weapon. Soon he would fire the first shot. And then it would be all over.

"**W**ell, you're home."

"Thank you, kind sir."

Hawkes opened the door to Martel's room, then pushed her wheelchair inside. Closing the door again, he moved her over to her bed, and then helped her climb onto it and slide under the sheet and blanket.

The young woman was exhausted. She was grateful to the doctors for not preventing her from returning to her duties. She knew she was not strong enough to do much, but the ambassador had praised what she had been able to do, and that was enough for her. Like Martel, the doctors knew what kind of tight squeeze the colony was in. If the governor was willing to take the responsibility for allowing her out of bed early, they were more than willing to sign off on her case. With the riots only a few days behind them, they still had enough patients to worry about.

Hawkes moved the wheelchair close enough to the bed for his aide to grab hold of it if she needed it for any reason after he was gone. Then, moving forward, he rested his hands on the edge of the bed and asked, "Comfortable?"

"As comfortable as I'm going to get, I suppose."

"Good." Hawkes flashed her a smile, then said, "I wanted to thank you again for coming up with a way to get that message through to Val. You may have helped our situation more than you can imagine."

"But you're still not going to tell me how, are you?"

"No," he admitted. "I've got to play this one close to the vest. The government's gone bad. What they've done here, the way they've used these people . . . anyone who stands against them is going to be in deep if things go wrong."

Martel moved her left hand toward his right, letting her fingers cover his. Squeezing them gently, she whispered, "You take very good care of me, you know that?" Almost blushing, Hawkes smiled gently, holding himself back. Scores of answers flashed through his head, but he brushed them aside for later, choosing simply to squeeze her hand back.

"Go to sleep," he said.

The ambassador looked at her for another moment, and had just turned to leave when a knock came at the door. He put his hand to the access panel and indexed the proper section, only to have the door come crashing in on him.

The force of the blow sent him staggering back toward the connecting wall. As he caught his balance, a figure rushed into the room, slammed the door closed, and then turned toward the ambassador. Pointing a large, heavy needler at Hawkes, Peste sneered as he said,

"My dear Mr. Ambassador . . . did you really think we *all* went outside?"

35

A single flare flashed up from atop the butte at the end of the cul-de-sac. It lit the entire valley floor, instantly blinding the troopers below—and it was the signal for Peste's forces to open fire. Instantly the rest of the renegades started blasting away at the troopers in the valley below them.

Seven pressure suits exploded in the first barrage. Five men and two women were dead before they had a chance to fire a shot, before they knew the war had even started. Desperately the troopers scattered for the sparse cover the valley floor had to offer. Shedding their packs, grabbing their weapons, they returned fire as best they could.

Their first return barrage was a waste of ammunition. All the shots they managed to fire went wild—too high, too low, everywhere but at their target. Their foes were so well placed, so certain of their trap, that the pitiful salvo coming up at them could not make most of them even flinch.

Completely undeterred, the renegades continued their attack. Five more of the troopers went down in the next volley. Mortal wounds were not required; any break in the suit seal would be enough to let external pressure do the rest.

Cries of agony could be heard through the interlinked helmet coms. Each new set of screams was brief, followed by a thin hiss and then a wet explosion. It had been less than a minute since the renegade flare had lit the valley. Forty-eight seconds, and eighteen of Scully's people were dead.

Listening to the slaughter all around him, the old security man growled, "Enough of this shit."

Digging into the heavy pack he had insisted on carrying, he pulled out the vac-unit he had struggled to bring with him. Three more of his people died as he got it placed in the thick dust of the valley. Another as he indexed its power source. Another as he indexed it into operation.

The draw unit hummed into life, sucking pounds of dust in through its intake. With no hose or container at the other end of its feed, it simply threw the dust into the air. In seconds it filled the base of the valley with a masking cloud of dust twenty feet deep.

Looking down into the growing billow, Peste's second-in-command chuckled to himself. Shaking his head sadly, almost with pity, he cued his mike, then ordered, "Somebody down there thinks this is the nineteenth century, people. Time to teach them a little different." Clicking a small switch on his helmet's visor, the commander finished his death sentence. "Switch to heat scan, everyone. Sight targets and fire at will. Let's get this over with."

"And just in case I have to say it . . . nobody scream."

Peste took a step forward toward Hawkes. He held his wicked-looking needler steady, keeping it pointed at the ambassador's face. Hawkes stared into the man's eyes, plumbing the depths of the hatred showing within them, trying to find anything he could reason with.

"Come, come, Ambassador, no speeches in mind? Nothing noble or uplifting or clever just hanging off the end of your brilliant tongue? Something high sounding that will force me to renounce my evil ways?"

"I must admit," answered Hawkes, his voice steady, almost dis-
interested, "nothing's coming to mind."

Keep it casual, his mind whispered. This guy wants to see us
sweat. The longer we blow him off, the longer we live. The longer
Dina lives.

"I'm almost disappointed," said Peste. "I stayed behind just for
the simple pleasure of being the one that killed you. Not so much
because I wanted to be the one that pulled the trigger . . . although I admit that is part of it, but more because I've always
wondered how people like you die."

When Hawkes made no reply, Peste said, "Oh, it's all right. Go
ahead, flatter yourself a little. You know what I meant. A hero. How
often do people get to see heroes die? We read about it, we watch
ridiculously silly vid presentations—put together by people without
the slightest notion of what heroism is all about—but *real* heroes,
actual people with *convictions* . . ."

The renegade stopped talking then. Taking two steps backward,
away from Hawkes, he pulled his weapon up, pointing it toward the
ceiling, but still to the ready. Martel dragged herself to the edge of
her bed. Peste noted her movements from the corner of his eye—
studied the desperation, the deep, fearful concern etched into her
face—then dismissed her. Turning his full attention back to the
ambassador, he said, "By rights, I suppose I just should have shot
you both down in the hallway. But I waited for you to enter, and
then made my grand little entrance. Do you know why?"

"To see how a hero dies?" asked Hawkes with a glib tone. Then,
before Peste could respond, he shifted gears, adding, "Or maybe
just to see if you had the nerve to kill one. Face-to-face, that is."

The renegade cocked his head to the side. Smiling as the ambassador warmed to the game, he remained silent, giving Hawkes the
floor.

"You want to know why you didn't just shoot us in the back?
That's easy. You wanted to show what a big man you were by at
least looking your unarmed victim in the eye before you murdered
him. Then, of course, I'm the only one you want dead." Turning to

point at Martel, he said, "Kill her, and there's no one to tell anyone who killed me. No one to get your name into the history books."

Hawkes took a step toward the connecting wall. Peste took a compensating step, turning his back on the woman in the bed to be able to keep his line of sight sharply on the ambassador. He started to order Hawkes not to try for the door, but the ambassador ran over his words.

"As for killing me, you haven't pulled the trigger yet because even a worthless bucket of sewage like you can't feel much like a big man gunning down someone as old as me. It's your sense of the ridiculous. Half my age and hiding behind a gun."

Hawkes took a breath, drawing out the pause as long as he dared, then added, "Of course, maybe you have a right to be scared. The last time you only had a knife and I almost handed you your head."

Peste's sneer turned sour at the memory. He started bringing the needler down, fully intending to shoot Hawkes and be done with it. But he was distracted by a sudden noise behind him. Half turning, he saw Martel push her wheelchair across the room toward him. For an instant his attention was split in two directions, paralyzing his ability to act.

Hawkes leaped. The needler fired. Martel screamed.

36

"We can't sight them!"

Variations on the same panicked sentence were repeated a dozen times over. Peste's second-in-command scanned the dust cloud himself, trying to spot any heat activity within it. Standing up to peer into the valley, he could not understand what was happening.

"Where are they?" he muttered. Moving his helmet back and forth, he tried desperately to spot the fierce red glow their heat generators should have been throwing off. All he could see were tiny ghost shadows of energy residue—barely visible trace patterns—nothing he could target. "Where the hell are they?"

The man knew the cold energy for the hydraulics—the radio sets, all the other smaller suit functions—would not give out anything their weapons could lock on to.

But the heat-pac generators. You can always spot those. So where are they? *Where are they?*

The thought was the second-in-command's last as a blast from below tore through his helmet, slicing off the top of his head. His pressure suit staggered, wobbling back and forth on the edge of the butte. Finally it toppled, falling over into the canyon. The man inside was dead before it had started to move.

On the cul-de-sac's floor, Scully and his troops were making up for their bad start, taking the battle to the renegades. The old security man had been right. He had feared they would not be able to take their enemies by surprise. When he had told everyone to dress as heavily as possible, he had had their heat-pacs in mind. He remembered the complaints his people had made then. Helping one of his lieutenants sight the mortar he had had brought down from the *Bulldog*'s stores, he thought, Nobody complaining now, I see.

Then, with the small mobile cannon stabilized and ready, he signaled the order to launch. The mortar's internal tracker zeroed in on the largest concentration of heat forms outside its program-set perimeter and then fired. Seconds later, a half dozen of the renegades were hurtling down, jarred loose by the cannon's first blast. Three lay dead where the shell had gone off.

The mortar launched again. Then again. In a matter of moments, scores of the enemy had fallen. Random shots rang down from the hills, but they found nothing inside the growing dust cloud. The renegades could not even target muzzle flashes through the ever-thickening billow.

"Keep after 'em," bellowed Scully into his helmet mike. "Sight and shoot. We've got them on the run. Pick 'em off, kill 'em all."

Through the dust, the old security man took careful aim at the warm, red outline of a figure desperately crawling down the side of the canyon wall. He coolly squeezed off his round, watching it flash straight toward the red glow. The figure froze, bounced, then dropped straight down and out of sight.

"Good," spat Scully, the word a curse hurled at all his foes. Then, scanning about for his next target, he shouted to his troops encouragingly, "They started this little game . . . now let's show 'em how to play it!"

In the cold silence of the dark Martian canyon, the opening battle of the solar system's first interplanetary war continued. The weapons were new, the techniques different. But in the end the motivations for the struggle were the same ones as always . . . as old as time, and just as pointless to the dead.

Hawkes felt the sting of the few needles that had connected with his side, ripping his clothes, his skin, muscle. He slammed into Peste with all the force he could muster. He had not tried to grab the man's weapon from his hand, or to strike a blow. His attack had been one of strict projectile force, aiming to bowl the man over.

It worked. Peste went down hard. His weapon hand struck the edge of the bed frame. The needler was jarred from his grasp, sent bouncing off toward the opposite wall.

Hawkes did not try to break their fall. He landed on Peste as hard as he could, driving his elbow into the man's stomach. They collided with the floor roughly, the shock of contact pounding through them both.

"You fuck," gasped Peste, struggling for breath. "I'll kill you."

Hawkes clambered to his knees. Putting everything he had into one punch, he made a clawed fist and launched it toward the renegade's throat. As his stiff fingers slammed into the man's Adam's apple, he felt something break underneath.

Peste exploded into a raging mill of arms and legs. Hawkes was thrown off balance, falling to one side. He landed badly on his shoulder, bouncing the back of his head off the floor. Struggling to his feet, Peste turned and kicked Hawkes in the stomach, then did it again.

As the ambassador howled in pain, the renegade closed in, aiming a splintering kick at the ambassador's ribs. The blow knocked all the wind from Hawkes and left him gagging on the floor.

Peste staggered back, gasping for air himself. He would kill the ambassador and then make his escape. Even with most of the security people in the colony gone, he knew there was no sense in taking any more chances.

You're dead, old man, he thought. I'm not wasting another minute on you. I'm just getting my gun, filling you full of tiny holes, and then getting back to carving out my throne.

Peste turned in the direction he knew his needler had fallen. When he did, he found Martel kneeling weakly at the edge of her bed, his weapon in her hands.

As if reading his mind, she asked, "Looking for this?"

And then she fired. The recoil knocked her over her bed and onto the floor on the other side. Her shot went wild, barely connecting with Peste. The volley of needles aimed at his chest went high and wide, tearing away the right side of his face. Blood exploded outward from the side of his head, splattering across the far wall and drenching the floor.

The renegade howled in agonizing pain. Whirling around, half-blind, he tried to focus what was left of his vision. His only thoughts were of finding the woman, finding his weapon, and killing everyone in the room.

Only one thing stood in his way.

Back on his feet, Hawkes tackled Peste, forcing him into the door. The metal panel buckled as the two men fell heavily against it, and the lock snapped. The pair fell out into the hall, landing side by side.

Making it to his feet first, the ambassador locked his hands into one large fist, and then slammed it against the still-solid side of Peste's face.

"Die, you son of a bitch!"

Hawkes knocked the renegade's head first one way and then the other. His hands covered in blood, breath coming in labored gasps, he continued to strike and scream, scream and strike, until long after Peste had lost consciousness.

Until long after he had died.

37

Hawkes mounted the stage, headed for the polished wooden podium at its center. He had written and rewritten his speech twenty times on the way back from Mars. For a while he had been comfortable with it, able to leave it alone and worry about other things. Now that it was finally time to give it, though, he was suddenly not certain it covered all the ground it needed to.

You don't have that much to say, he reminded himself. Besides, it's a little too late to change it now.

Stepping behind the podium, he looked out over the audience as he arranged his papers. He had come to address a joint session of the U.S. Congress, a session with a great number of powerful players. Nowhere before him did he see a friendly face.

Well, then, you didn't expect any, did you?

Just to prove his cynical side wrong, he turned to the left. There he saw Dina Martel, almost fully recovered, standing with Ed Keller. Martel had risked coming because, as she had put it, "I have things to do on Earth, I want to, and you're only my boss, Mr. Ambassador Benton Hawkes, not my keeper."

"It could be dangerous," he had warned her.

"Could be dangerous?" she repeated. Giving him a witheringly droll look, she asked, "And what in our lives isn't?"

Both of them had laughed. Their trip to Mars had indeed been dangerous. It had indeed been a number of other things as well, many of which the two had not even begun to figure out.

Hawkes turned back to his audience. He could see that quite a number of his enemies were present. Mick Carri had a prominent seat, as did Herbert Marrow of the Earth League, and a number of Clean Mountain Enterprise executives. Tapping his papers until they came together evenly, the ambassador took a final look out over the crowd, and then, with a gesture calling for silence, he began his speech.

"Ladies, gentlemen, I thank you all for coming. My intention is not to draw out these proceedings. I will try to make my points clearly and quickly. If there are any questions, I will endeavor to answer them to the best of my ability."

Hawkes glanced up, throwing his eye over the audience. He had several faces he wanted to be watching when he hit certain portions of his speech. Their reactions to what he had to say were going to be very important.

Memorize their seats now, he told himself. I doubt anyone's going to be getting up for popcorn once you get rolling.

"First off, I will address the matter of communications silence between Mars and Earth for the past month. This began at your end, with an executive order forced through by Senator Carri. This order called for a filter blanket to be placed between these two worlds to keep Martian messages from reaching the Earth. Since this is the way Earth felt, the Martian government decided that the sovereign mother planet must be right in all things, and complied, setting up a reciprocal blanket at our end."

Hawkes paused for a second, then conspicuously directed his attention to Carri as he asked, "I trust they did a good job? No messages got through, did they, Mick?"

A number of people in attendance chuckled. Not amused, the senator rose to ask, "You said that was the decision of the Martian government. What Martian government?"

"Sit down, Mick," answered the ambassador dismissively. "Q and A is later." As the senator sat down, red faced and steaming, Hawkes continued, saying, "As to the troops sent to Mars illegally . . ."

An uproar thundered through the great hall. Carri, bouncing back up out of his seat, bellowed over the other voices. "*Illegally?!* What are you talking about? What is all this?"

"And isn't that just what I'm doing here—trying to tell you just that?" Peering over his nose, Hawkes said, "It is illegal to send troops to invade an independent country without a formal declaration. It is illegal to make war on a peaceful people without just cause."

"You've gone mad, Hawkes," counted Carri. "You never traveled in space before, and now you've got loose oxygen in your brain. You're not well."

"And you are out of order, Senator. But in the interests of establishing friendly diplomatic relations, I will try to explain, if the interruptions can be kept to a minimum." Hawkes took a breath, then continued, "Two days before your troops arrived and established orbit, the newly elected Martian government passed the following resolutions . . ."

Again, pandemonium broke out. Getting order restored once more, the ambassador told the assembly, "Maybe I'd better just menu the facts for you people. Mars is no longer your plaything. No one in this congregation has any further power over the future of Mars."

"The hell we don't," roared Herb Marrow. "The goddamned hell we don't. The Earth League owns Red Planet, Inc., lock, stock, and barrel."

"Mr. Marrow," answered Hawkes, his voice dry and challenging, "aside from the fact that the new government could simply nationalize your equipment, buildings, et cetera, let's get down to the facts. You may not be aware of this, but the Earth League no longer has controlling interest in Red Planet. Over the past few weeks, that has been bought up and consigned to the new government for concessions that are to be granted later."

A sinister joy filling his voice, the ambassador went on, telling Marrow, "You and the rest of your cronies are out of a job, sir. Your powers of office have been curtailed. If you managed to hang on to a bit of stock, then you might still be some sort of minority stockholder. You can voice any grievances you want at the annual stockholders' meetings. They'll be held once every four months in Greentop."

"And where the hell is that?"

"It's a new gigantic-scale park being created by a talented man named Pebelion. You would know it as the old number ten dome . . . on Mars."

Another uproar ensued. Knowing it was time to hit the assembly with everything he had, Hawkes pulled a packet of vid chips from his coat pocket. Holding them up for everyone to see, he announced,

"I think the moment has come for me to let everyone know just what has happened. Please pay attention. Much like Israel so long ago, Mars has bought its freedom, drawn up a constitution, voted on it, ratified it, held elections, created itself a separate government. Although you tried to stack the deck against her, she played the game by your rules . . . and she's won."

The assembly finally went silent. For a month there had been no word of any kind from Mars. Not from Red Planet management, not from the troopships—nothing. The food barges had continued to arrive, but they were robot-piloted drift ships that brought no messages of any kind.

Now Hawkes had arrived out of the blue and was confirming far too much of what some in the assembly had already been suspecting. Hanging on his every word, they listened while he continued.

"When your troops discovered the actual situation on Mars, they surrendered."

"What?" roared Carri again.

"Yes. In fact, most of them do not have any intention of returning. I have their resignations on vid. They have applied for Martian citizenship and begun to draw their pay as security people working for Red Planet, Inc."

Targeting Marrow with his eyes, Hawkes said, "Considering that most of the murderers you sent to Mars to kill anyone who didn't follow your party line are now dead, the planet did need a new army. But don't worry, Herb . . . I only said 'most.' There are a few on their way back."

As the Earth League head squirmed in his seat, Hawkes added, "You might want to go confer with your lawyers, Herb. Although I beat your handpicked assassin Peste to death myself—the *fourth* time he tried to kill me—it seems he was afraid you might try to double-cross him. He kept a complete set of records on his activities." Morrow got up out of his seat and began heading for the aisle.

"He names you quite prominently." As the Earth League leader moved for the back door, the ambassador raised his voice, and said, "He was even considerate enough to get firm-vid of you ordering my death." As Morrow disappeared out through the door, others began to leave the room as well. Having known it would start sooner or later, Hawkes ignored the small exodus, addressing those remaining.

"Let me try to give you who have remained something to work with. As you know, food and supplies have continued to be shipped to Earth. The Martian government has assured me this will not stop. Earth bank units are fairly useless to Mars, but there are things they want, and they are willing to trade for them."

"Trade?" came a lone voice. "Trade for what?"

"Seeds. Animals. Plants. More advanced robotics. Ice. And a few more frivolities—entertainment. Art. It's a long list. Don't worry about it now." His hands gripping the podium, Hawkes looked out over the crowd, then said,

"Believe me when I say that Mars doesn't want to see mass

starvation, it doesn't want to see riots. It doesn't want war. Greedy, soulless men here on Earth have already visited riots and war on Mars. No one there wants to see any more of it . . . or cause any of it."

The ambassador took a deep breath. He held it for what seemed a long moment. Closing his eyes a split second, he spent what seemed to be a lifetime in the moment of darkness, then came back to the world once more, telling it, "What happens next is up to Earth. If her leaders can accept the simple fact that the people of Mars are human beings and not cattle to be herded and slaughtered for their pleasure . . . if they can accept that they are going to have to ask from now on, instead of demand, then we will all know peace."

"But if not," he said, letting his tone go dark and grim, "then Earth will know suffering like it never has in all its history. Any— *any*—act of aggression against Mars, including interfering with me or my people, *from this moment forward,* will be considered a dec- laration of war. If this happens, all food and materials barges will be stopped—destroyed, if necessary. This is no idle threat. Mars is a self-sufficient planet. It is not a comfortable life, but it is not a life dependant on Earth for anything. Earth depends on Mars. Try and shackle her again, and it will mean the end of life as you know it here."

A flurry of noise and activity followed. A hundred questions were hurled toward the ambassador. Choosing those few he would an- swer, he told them, "I shall leave the vid-pac I showed you earlier with the sergeant-at-arms. How he disposes of it, what you do with it, is up to you. This will make clear what the Earth League has been doing over the last half century. It will show you the crimes that this body—and every other major governing body on this world—are guilty of. How this is handled is up to you."

Another breath, and then—his arms shaking, his forehead bead- ing with perspiration, but his soul clear and calm—he went on, saying, "Mars does not care what you do to these people. For them, sweet freedom is enough. They have paid for it in toil, they have paid for it in sweat. Its price has been met in courage and in blood and with an honor sorely lacking here . . . and it shall not be taken away."

At that point, Hawkes motioned to the sergeant-at-arms to come to the podium. Handing him the vid-pac, he turned back to the assembly and announced, "I shall be returning to the Martian embassy, where I will stay for the next two weeks. Then I shall be returning to Mars."

"Embassy?" came a confused cry. "Where is there a Martian embassy? And why would you be returning to Mars?"

Wearily, the ambassador picked up his papers, then said, "The embassy is in Wyoming, in the most beautiful part of the Absaroka mountain range. I'm sure Mick Carri can tell you where it is."

Refolding his papers, Hawkes returned them to his inner jacket pocket, telling the crowd at the same time, "As to why I'll be returning off-world . . . well, ever since the elections . . . I suppose that's where I belong."

And then the first prime minister of Mars turned and left the stage. He walked slowly but straight backed, knowing that no matter how much this felt like an ending, it was really all just beginning.

EPILOGUE

"So," asked Martel, "what do you think of the news?"

Sitting down on the side porch, accepting a cup of coffee from Cook, Hawkes asked, "With all the news in the world right now, you wouldn't want to give an old man a clue, would you?"

"Mick Carri's little series of speeches?" When the prime minister merely rolled his eyes, she said, "He's making a big push to grab the presidential nomination. He gets it, it'll make it awfully hard to pin any crimes on him."

"Pinnin' crimes on a senator's like rubbin' fat on a hog," said Cook as she headed back into the kitchen. "What would be the point?"

Martel narrowed her eyes, giving the old woman a playfully evil look. Hawkes merely smiled. Sitting back in his chair, he took a long sip from his cup, then said, "I don't care what happens to him—what happens here—anymore. I really don't. Now that the ranch is Martian property, Clean Mountain can't touch it. If Carri tries to annex it, it's a declaration of war. He got into bed with CME and the Earth League just to get at me. The way things have been turned around on all of them, they've got a lot bigger problems on their hands than revenge for the moment."

"Does that mean you don't think things will end in war?"

Hawkes took a long time to answer. "I wish I had a good answer for you, but really . . . I don't know. I hope not. I hope the race can get past its usual, first solution for once." Hawkes tilted his head to one side. "I hope."

" 'Hope,' " quoted Martel, " 'of all ills that men endure/ The only cheap and universal cure.' "

"Abraham Crowley," answered the prime minister. Countering her cynical reference, he responded, " 'Everything that is done in the world is done by hope.' "

"Martin Luther?" she guessed. He nodded, impressed. "I'd expect a churchman to put a good spin on the idea," she said. "Give me Ben Franklin any day."

" 'He that lives on hope will die fasting'?" When she nodded, he told her, "Shame on you. You're young. I'm the one that's supposed to be the old, embittered cynic. Can't you come up with one positive thought on the subject?"

"Oh, maybe," she said, standing up out of her chair. Stepping off the porch, trying hard to hide a devilish grin, she said, "Let me take a walk and think about it."

Hawkes watched her leave, wondering what she was up to. Knowing he would find out sooner or later, he decided to simply sit back quietly and try to enjoy his home while he was still there.

Emptying his head, leaving intrigue and war and all thoughts of the past few months behind, he turned his attention outward, enjoying the feel of the wind against his face. His mind filled with sensory images instead of facts and words—the smell of his fields, his trees, the feel of the wood of his porch under his boots, of the arm of his chair under his fingers, the simple sounds of his animals in the distant pasture, of the sun-grown life ripening all around him.

Closing his eyes, he brought his cup up to his nostrils. Inhaling deeply, he remembered how he had missed the smell of South American coffee. Yes, he thought, they had coffee on Mars. But it was hydroponically grown coffee. All of it from the same source. All of it tasting exactly the same.

"Small price," he whispered.

"What's a small price?" came Martel's voice from behind him.

Without turning, he told her, "Nothing, really. I was just thinking that there are a lot of things that I am going to miss when we return to Mars."

Without commenting, Martel simply recited,

> " 'Hope' is the thing without feathers
> That perches in the soul—
> And sings the tune without words
> And never stops—at all."

When Hawkes turned around toward her, not having even a guess as to where she had gotten the bit of verse, she said, "Emily Dickinson," and then handed him a large, obviously heavy cardboard box, saying, "Here. You shouldn't have to miss everything when you go back."

The prime minister took the box from her hands, raising one eyebrow as it shook in his hands. He rested it on the floor in front of him and was reaching to open its lid when it suddenly burst open of its own accord, forced upward by its occupant. As Hawkes pulled back, an awkward, big-pawed puppy pushed its way up and over the edge, stumbling into the surprised man's arms.

Pulling the puppy up into his lap, he tried to talk, but found his mouth would not work—his throat could not form any words. The puppy pushed its way up his chest, flopping against him, licking his face.

And deep inside the prime minister, something dark crumpled. The dog continued to clamber over him until it reached the point where its eyes met Hawkes's. The two souls searched each other for a long, open moment, and then, a flow of tears broke from the man's eyes, large, free-falling streams that splashed down across his cheeks and old leather vest.

The puppy pushed forward, licking at the running salt. Crushing the joyous dog to him, he stroked it and whispered to it and sobbed bitterly, finally weeping for all those fallen and gone.

Martel stepped away softly, leaving man and pup alone.

No matter what was going to happen, she thought, no matter what comes next, he deserves this.

Rounding the far corner of the ranch house, she looked up into the daytime sky, not able to see Mars at all. Then she whispered, "Hope, Benton? 'Hope is the universal liar.'"

And then she walked off toward the forest to take her last breath of pine.